ADVANCE PRAISE FOR
WHAT COMES ECH...

"This is Leo McKay Jr. at his best: furio... ered by profound empathy. No writer ca... ...cters more. On one level, this is a hard contemporary story about the toxic mix of technology and violence in today's high schools, but at another, deeper level, it is also a hymn to the healing power of art. Listen to *What Comes Echoing Back*. It's one of those tender, beautiful songs that you already know, but need to hear again and again."
ALEXANDER MACLEOD

"Leo McKay Jr. writes contemporary novels that read like classics pulled off the shelf of favourites. I'm in awe, simultaneously heartbroken and uplifted with a quiet sort of courage. He really is the bard of the underdog. McKay is a brilliant storyteller. *What Comes Echoing Back* is compelling, captivating, and expertly crafted, a novel heralding the return of an essential voice in Canadian literature."
CHRISTY-ANN CONLIN

"Leo McKay, as ever, writes with depth and tender insight. This story of two young people caught up in a violent online vortex is timely, heartbreaking and completely inspiring."
LYNN COADY

PRAISE FOR *TWENTY-SIX*

"Swift, honest, unsentimental storytelling and characters, both real and imagined, vivid enough to rise above their hard, often tragic lives. [*Twenty-Six*] hits you like the kick of a miner's drill."
MACLEAN'S

WHAT COMES ECHOING BACK

Vagrant Press is an imprint of
Nimbus Publishing Limited
3660 Strawberry Hill St, Halifax, NS, B3K 5A9
(902) 455-4286 nimbus.ca

Printed and bound in Canada

Editor: Stephanie Domet
Editor for the press: Whitney Moran
Cover design: Ben Brush
Typesetting: Rudi Tusek
NB1583

Excerpt from "True Patriot Love" used with the permission of Joel Plaskett, Songs for the Gang Inc.

Library and Archives Canada Cataloguing in Publication
Title: What comes echoing back / Leo McKay Jr.
Names: McKay, Leo, Jr., 1964- author.
Identifiers: Canadiana (print) 20220469903 | Canadiana (ebook) 20220469911 | ISBN 9781774711668 (softcover) | ISBN 9781774711675 (EPUB)
Subjects: LCGFT: Novels.
Classification: LCC PS8575.K28747 W43 2023 | DDC C813/.54—dc23

Nimbus Publishing acknowledges the financial support for its publishing activities from the Government of Canada, the Canada Council for the Arts, and from the Province of Nova Scotia. We are pleased to work in partnership with the Province of Nova Scotia to develop and promote our creative industries for the benefit of all Nova Scotians.

WHAT COMES ECHOING BACK

LEO MCKAY JR.

Vagrant
PRESS

I

MAY

The double buzz of his phone, muffled by the weight of his discarded pants, vibrated against the wood floor. He'd been in a deep sleep, and when he opened his eyes, the first light of morning was coming up beyond the curtains of the window opposite. The window itself seemed to be in the wrong place at first, like a portal in a dream. Where was he, even? This was a room he'd only been in this once.

As he shifted beneath the sheets, he felt the long-forgotten stresses and relief of having had sex, but the details were still trying to reassemble themselves in his mind. The phone buzzed incessantly. Behind him, there was soft snoring, and before he turned around to look, he remembered Lynne, remembered the night before. The long drive to Sydney. The hug at the door. All the things that had happened after that hug.

"Hello? Hello?" he spoke into the cold glass of the phone. The thing remained silent and still a moment, then buzzed angrily again against the side of his face. There had been a notification on the screen, but his eyes were not focusing yet.

"Uncle Ray? Uncle Ray?" The voice came at last. The person on the other end was upset. Shouting, more or less.

"It's Ray," Ray said.

"Ray?" came Lynne's soft, half asleep voice from the bed behind him.

"Uncle Ray! Something bad has happened. Oh my God! Ray! Something very, very bad. I know it's first thing. I waited until six to call. I need help, Uncle Ray. It's Patty. Something terrible has happened to her. I don't know who else I can count on."

"I'll be there as soon as I can."

Ray hung up and pulled his feet from beneath the bed covers. He sat on the edge of the mattress a moment, scrubbed his face with his palms.

"What is it, Ray?" Lynne said. She came to his side and sat as he was sitting, both feet on the floor.

"Family. Family thing." Ray himself did not fully understand. He took in the stark white intimacy of Lynne's bare toes. He smelled the scent of her shampoo, her skincare products, her stale morning breath. They'd known each other a little in high school, but that was a long, long time ago. And they'd shared a lot recently through months of Facebook Messenger contact. But last night had been the first time they'd actually seen each other in decades.

"What family, Ray? Is everyone okay?"

"I don't think so," Ray said. "I don't think everyone's okay. I don't think anyone's dead. But it sounds bad. I'm going to have to drive to the Valley. Right away."

"The Valley? The Annapolis Valley?"

Ray nodded and stood up, naked in daylight in front of a woman for the first time in years. "I'm sorry. This is a terrible thing to do to you. Rush off first thing in the morning like some irresponsible..."

"Nonsense," Lynne said. "You've got..."

"It's my niece. And her daughter. It sounds bad. They don't have anyone else."

2

"Let me get you breakfast and coffee," Lynne said. She stood up and turned to face him. She put her arms around him and drew his body to her own. "Let me send you off with coffee and breakfast. It's a long drive."

"I'd like that," Ray said. "I can't drive to the Valley on an empty stomach. But I have to get out the door fast."

"Let's move fast, then," Lynne said. She pulled a robe off a hook on the back of her bedroom door and made her way quickly to the kitchen, pulling the robe around her.

2

FOUR MONTHS LATER: SEPTEMBER

His name was Robot. With the visor down across the fiery ball of the sun, the view before him was a dark block of car ceiling, a light stripe of sun, a dark bar of visor, the scrolling blue-black tarmac of the highway, the dust-covered dashboard. Out the passenger window, the gravel shoulder, the rising and falling levels of the ditch, the approaching and receding trees. Farm fields and swamps. Layers of cloud and sky, the closer parts moving across those farther away.

So much open space. Mile after mile of highway with the green of summer still in the grass and trees.

It was a ninety-minute drive, and Melhart tried to engage him in conversation as she drove, but he felt himself tightening up in anticipation of getting home. He gave her a few one-word replies at first, but found he could not loosen his voice to say more.

He'd already said plenty to Melhart today, or at least in front of her. She had been at the final meeting before his release. He'd spent a year getting ready for this day, and Melhart had checked in on him a lot in that time. She'd been part of the team of professional people, including his worker at the youth criminal detention centre, and several teachers, who'd helped him put a plan together. A reintegration plan. A plan for how to go back to his old life.

It was called a plan, but now that he'd been released, he realized it was not really a plan at all. It was just a three-item list. A list of three things for him to focus on when he was free again. Playing music. Teaching music. Going to school.

There had been an okay electric guitar at the Springtown Youth Detention Centre. A Samick strat he'd found at the back of a storage room. It had played well enough after he'd cleaned it up, put a new set of Slinkys on it, and frigged around with the intonation. So he'd kept his chops up over the last year. Improved them, really.

Any guitar he'd played for any length of time was bound to feel like a friend, and it had been hard that morning to put the strat down for the last time. But his mind was focused on his own guitar, the Les Paul in his bedroom that he had not seen in a year. He looked down at his hands as the countryside near Hubtown flashed past the car windows and pictured the guitar there, the pickups gleaming.

They entered the town from a highway exit Robot had rarely used, drove through the little industrial area on the outskirts, between the highway and the residential downtown neighbourhood where he lived. Even with the windows in the car wound the whole way up, several distinct industrial smells were discernible, one at a time, as the car passed through them: the raw sour scent of the feed silos high in the back of his sinuses, motor oil and petrochemicals from some factory-looking building behind a fence, then finally the strongest and worst smell of all, the burnt and rotting smell of boiled animals from the rendering plant.

"I haven't been to Hubtown in a while," Tracey Melhart said. "But the smell is certainly bringing back some memories." She allowed herself a little chuckle at the town's expense, then looked wryly across the front seat at Robot. She was a broad-faced lady with a big smile that he found calming.

"Hubtown," said Robot. "Come for the stink, stay for the stink."

So much was flooding into him as the car entered his neighbourhood and rolled quietly down the few blocks to Lemon Street: flashes of faces, echoes of voices.

As they got near the spot where Travis Cody Mancomb died, Robot closed his eyes. He was going to have to walk past here every day on the way to school, but he could not face it right now.

Melhart parked the car parallel to the curb on Lemon Street and applied the parking brake against the steep grade of the hill. Robot opened his eyes, took in a breath through his nose, and let it out slowly, so that he could feel the air passing through the back of his throat. He looked at the boxy three-storey house where his mother rented a flat. Where he'd lived before they sent him away for murder. For manslaughter. A rush of fear flooded through him and he struggled to keep his breath even, to hide his fear from Tracey Melhart.

"Let me come in with you," Melhart said. She made a move to open the driver's door.

Robot shook his head so slightly he realized Melhart may not have caught it, then did it again. "Thanks for everything," he said. "This is going to work or not work based on what I do myself."

Melhart placed a hand on his shoulder. "It'll work," she said. But her tone revealed that this was what she hoped to be true, not what she believed.

He reached into the back seat and picked up the boxy brown and gold sports bag that contained everything from his year of serving time. A few pairs of socks, some boxer briefs, three pairs of jeans, T-shirts, hoodie. His winter coat was folded up at the bottom. A book called *Man's Search for Meaning* which he'd read twice and that his teacher said he could have. His shitty old iPod Nano was zipped into a side pocket. The eight gigs of music on there was everything he'd listened to for a year.

"You have my cell number," Melhart said. There was no way she did not see fear in his eyes. "You have an appointment for next week, with a counsellor. Our office will contact you with details. But you can call me any time before that. Call ten minutes from now if you think you have to. If you want to. I'll be driving, but I'll pull over and pick up."

"Thanks," Robot said. He nudged the car door closed and turned to face the rest of his life.

Whatever shittiness he'd had to cope with at Springtown, the building itself was pretty okay. The interior was sterile and institutional. But sterile was clean. His mom's shitty rental flat, on a bad block of Lemon Street, was dingy and in poor repair. The large, seventies-style wooden siding looked disproportionate on this hundred-year-old building: a newer, misplaced retrofit that had long gone old. There were uneven spots where shingles had come loose and hung crookedly. In many places, the white paint had chalked off down to the bare woodgrain. And the landscape-width dimensions of the windows did not suit the exterior walls that had once had portrait-dimension windows in them.

There was a cracked and heaved concrete walkway, choking on nettles and dandelion greens at every gap. The lawn was a couple of postage stamps on either side of the walkway, asprout with ugly, broad-leafed weeds that shaded an underlayer of unheeded-looking soil, light brown in colour and hard-packed smooth to shininess in the places it showed between the scraggly plants. A bone-thin, drug-addled woman in a floral dress and cardigan sat on a lop-sided folding camp chair beside the large concrete slab that served as a front step and landing. Her knees were together, her feet were apart, her head dropped almost to the level of the knees, her straw-like brown-blond hair cascaded down in a curtain from the top of her neck.

At the sound of Tracey Melhart's car pulling away, the woman sat up and leaned against the backrest of her chair. Her cheeks were hollow, her face sunken in over missing teeth. She winced hard, and with her eyes closed, felt around her torso and legs until she came up with a soiled-looking green and gold water bottle with a squirt-style lid. With her head back and her eyes still closed, she squirted liquid into her mouth. Her whole body convulsed twice, as though she would vomit. Then her head flopped forward again. This time she continued to fold forward until her forehead came to rest on her knees.

Robot was sure he'd never seen this woman before. But he had enough experience with people in advanced stages of addiction to know that this might be an unrecognizable version of someone who used to be familiar to him.

This is how people go missing, he thought. Thinking of his own situation now, and not that of the woman near the door. This is how people disappear. Their support worker or parole officer, or whoever, drops them off at a door like this, they take a quick glance at the life they're returning to, then they run the hell in the other direction.

9

He stood frozen in place at the curb, both his hands in fists. He turned a slow 360 degrees and took in his old neighbourhood, the lower end of Lemon Street. The many homes in various colours and states of repair. The steep hill that led to the top of the street and a whole other neighbourhood, one of newer, nicer, owner-lived-in houses. The deep green of the big park was visible in a fringe of treeline over the roofs. The apartment building across the street, the one everyone in town called The Old Hotel, was rickety and ratchet, with makeshift additions and four kinds of siding. A big piece of wooden clapboarding hung from an eave, rotten at the hanging end, coming to a ragged, soft-looking point. He wondered who was living there now. Matt Sutcliffe, who worked with him at Jordan's Music, had had a one-room studio apartment there last year. On the third floor. There was a tiny balcony on the park side, with just enough room for two small kitchen chairs on it. Maybe he could stay there instead of his mother's house. Maybe he could steal a blanket off a clothesline somewhere and spend a few nights sleeping rough in the park. He'd done that drunk and without the benefit of planning a few times before. But that had always been in the high days of summer. And even then he'd woken up at dawn, soaked with icy dew-water, shivering, his muscles so contracted with cold he'd found himself wondering whether someone had kicked the shit out of him in the night.

The woman in the folding chair had slumped back into her seat when Robot turned to face the front door of his mother's building. She was so motionless he wondered if she might have died just then. She was someone else's responsibility if she had. He had his own problems.

The front door of the building opened into a grubby little alcove. There was a grey, short-napped carpet on the floor, worn to frayed yarn and dirty plywood in several places. The smell filled his head like a mouthful of dirt. There were three doors in the alcove, like a parable about choice. The walls were misapplied plaster, cracked and unrepaired, painted a gloss white that had long since faded dull grey. The door of his mother's flat was on the left. Four panels and a brass knob. It was unlocked and, because she would have known this was his release day, the place had been cleared of liquor bottles. None in the front room, the side hall, or the kitchen. But Robot could tell that things were bad. The place was desperately empty.

The smell of alcohol was layered, several smells on top of each other. The top layers were the apartment's smells, the layers of newer and older booze that built up in a place where an alcoholic lived. Congealed puddles of spilled rum on the floor. Stray millilitres from the bottoms of empties cast aside without their tops. The smell that rose from a kitchen sink when so much booze had been carelessly slopped down it. But the underlying layer was the smell of partially metabolized liquor as it oozed from the body of a living drunk. When a person had repeatedly soaked herself with alcohol, year after year until the cleansing organs in the gut got tired, the stuff just came out through the skin, converted slightly to an oily musk.

The apartment was relatively clean. The floors had been swept. The kitchen had been mopped. But it was spare. It contained less than half of what it had a year ago. In the living room, the TV was gone. The stereo he had saved up for and bought himself: gone. The turntable, the cassette deck, the CD player with the jack for an aux cord. The cabinet on which the stereo had sat was still against the wall, a fading imprint of dust still visible where the components and the speakers had been. The vinyl records were gone, too. And the CDs. He had not had many of either. He had never been a collector. But he knew there was no point looking for them. They'd been in crates beside the window. She'd Kijijied it all. Panic rose in his chest. He dropped his bag on the floor and swivelled in multiple directions as though about to begin a frantic search. But he stopped himself. The couch was gone. But the matching loveseat remained. He needed to brace himself for the worst. He plopped into the loveseat and with a few hard twisting shoves of his feet, he turned it to face the bedrooms. Two matching doors. Behind the one on his left, his mother lay asleep. Or rather, drunk asleep. The sour smell of her living decay was everywhere. The door on his right led to his own room. He did not care what else was missing from that room. Not his bed. Not his clothing. If the guitar was gone, he did not know what he might do. He'd already killed someone, though he had not meant to. What would he do if the guitar was gone? He was too old for Springtown now. It would be adult prison.

Through his mother's bedroom door he heard her deep drunken breaths. The sound sawed its way into his mind.

That instrument was everything to him.

He stood up from the loveseat. He closed his eyes and put out his hand for the doorknob as he stepped blindly forward. The door swung back on its hinges with an empty creak.

He opened his eyes on stark, dark squares: walls, floor. A mattress. He crossed to the window that looked out on the lane and the neighbour lady's driveway. Her sons were playing ball hockey against the backdrop of the garage door. He could see them through the slats of the venetian blind. He'd made enough movement to catch their attention. They looked over at him and their eyes widened with shock and excitement. He raised a hand to wave, but the two boys looked at each other in surprise and ran around to their back door. Through the closed up window, he heard "(something something) out of jail!" as they fled.

With the room lit, he turned and sat on the edge of what was left of his bed: a mattress only, where once there had been a steel frame, box spring, and headboard.

He'd left the guitar in its hardshell case in the corner opposite the window; beside it had been the Peavey tube amp, the closest he could afford to a Fender. For the last twelve months he'd pictured the two items sitting there, awaiting his return. Like a photo in his mind, they were the last things he'd looked at before leaving to serve his sentence at the end of last summer.

He knew he did not have to search further. The guitar and amp were gone. Sold on Kijiji. His mother had sold their good laptop for a bottle several years back. Once it was gone, she accessed the internet from the library. Robot had to secretly adopt an old Acer with one broken hinge from a guy who taught mandolin at Jordan's Music, where he himself taught guitar. He'd slid it between his bed and the wall when it wasn't in use, to keep his mother from selling it. Now even that was gone.

He lay back on his bed. He wanted to smash out the window and throw the bed through it. He wanted to kick his bedroom door until it broke. He wanted to find whatever alcohol she had hidden, and he wanted to go into her room and drown her in it, force it down her throat until she was dead.

A sudden thought came to him and he leapt from the mattress. The hundred dollars! He'd almost forgotten. Just before going to Springtown, he'd sold his pedals: a Boss distortion, a Boss tuner, and a Dunlop wah. He'd listed them as an inseparable unit on Kijiji and sold them for a hundred and fifty dollars, a complete steal of a price that he knew he could get someone to agree to quickly. Fifty dollars he'd brought with him to Springtown, cash in his pocket. The other hundred he'd put in an envelope and hidden on the shelf above the closet in his room. With nothing left in the room he could stand on, he rushed to the kitchen and brought back a chair. He ran a hand across the front of the shelf, but there was nothing there. Once he climbed onto the chair, he saw the envelope immediately, thumb-tacked to the drywall on the left side of the closet above the shelf.

He pulled the envelope loose, ripped off the end, and counted out five twenties from inside it before slipping them into the front pocket of his jeans. Hiding that hundred dollars was one of the smartest things he'd ever done. He'd thought a full year ahead and made a plan, something he had not even remembered having done when his anger management teacher at Springtown asked him to make a list of things he felt proud of.

That hundred dollars would not buy him back his Les Paul. It would not put a down payment on a similar guitar. It was not even enough money to feel like an incentive to save more money to go with it. But it was one good thing.

He lay back on the mattress, his right hand over the

place at the front of his pants where the money was. The silence of the apartment rose up around him. And into that silence seeped the grotesque sound of his mother's drunken breath. It rose up and faded off in waves. The Les Paul was gone. The amp was gone. He should have been playing right now, cranking the volume on the amp until the sound forced his drunken mother awake and the neighbours came pounding at the door.

He was trying to muster the same compassion that he would have liked others to extend to him—something else he'd learned in anger management. In the room in which every missing object was a direct and knowing act of betrayal, it was so easy to see his mother only as she appeared to him: irresponsible, uncaring, selfish, pathetic, out of control. But how must she see herself? How did it feel to be her and to be doing this to herself and to her own son?

She had been by his side for every minute of his hearing. And she'd been sober for it, as far as he could tell. She'd testified on his behalf before sentencing, and had wept ferociously when his own lawyer asked her to assess what kind of mother she had been.

It took a few minutes of lying on the mattress, a mix of complex emotions flooding through him, before Robot could summon the courage to go into his mother's bedroom. He stood at the door with his hand on the doorknob for an extra second or two, and when he finally opened it, there was a fetid smell of unwashed bedding, stale vomit, and alcohol sweat. He'd washed out the largest water tumbler he could find in the kitchen, dropped a couple of uneven ice cubes into it from the poorly-balanced tray in the freezer. He managed to find a shrivelled lemon wedge in the fridge and it had yielded a few drops of juice after he'd rinsed it under the tap.

He knew what it was like to be cared for. His mother had taught him that when he was little, before alcohol had made her goodness so hard to see. And he entered her bedroom now the same way she had once entered his. He tiptoed his way to the bedside, a mattress on the floor, like his own. The smells in the room were strong enough that he did not think he could tolerate them long. He left the door behind him open and wound the window all the way out. Within seconds the air in the room had replenished itself. In the half-light that came through the closed venetian blind, his mother's face was bony and grey. Her hair was a shock of grey and black wires, dipped at the ends in chestnut brown where her home colouring kit had all but grown out.

The closer he got to her face, the more she smelled of tooth decay. She stirred and moaned as he sat on the edge of the mattress. Her lips moved to speak before her eyes were fully open, but her mouth was so dry, nothing came out but a couple of pasty glicks.

"Here, Ma. Sit up. I brought you some water with lemon in it." He held her under her bony arm as she came up onto her elbows. She put both hands out for the water, but Robot did not dare let go the glass. He doubted she had the strength to hold it. The bitter lemon sent a shiver through her that seemed to wake her significantly, and she came straight up now with her back against the wall, put out both hands again for the glass, and when he passed it to her, she downed it at a gulp. Her eyes rolled back into her head and she took in a deep, satisfied breath.

"Robert?" He took the glass from her and she put her

hands to his cheeks and held his face to examine it. Her fingers were thin as twigs and all of her rings were gone: engagement ring, wedding band, even the little silver ring with her first initial that her grandmother had given her as a child.

"Robert! You're home!"

"It's my release day, Ma."

"I tried to clean the place up. Did that social worker come inside?"

"I turned eighteen. They're like Dracula now, Ma. They can't come in unless we invite them."

Suddenly his mother came to fully and sat straight up. "You didn't go into your room yet, did you, Robert?"

"Well, I did, Ma."

She covered her face with her hands. And though she clamped her jaw and tightened her lips against it, she began to sob, quietly at first, but in short order she was bawling. "I'm sorry, Robert. I know how important the guitar was to you. We'll get it back. We'll get you a new one. We'll get you a better one." His mother slumped sideways on the bed and sobbed hard for several minutes until she fell back to sleep.

He patted her sinewy back between the shoulder blades and pulled the blanket back up to her shoulders. He clenched his fists hard, squeezed his eyes shut, and walked deliberately but unsteadily out of his mother's bedroom as a rush of bodily rage went through him.

He was out beyond the reaches of self-control, but another moment and the crazy thoughts and impulses would pass. When he got back to the living room with the closed door between himself and his mother, the rage evaporated more quickly. This was only what he'd expected to find when he got home. He plopped onto the loveseat and stared at the dust-layered stand where the stereo had been.

In the middle of a dust-free square, there was a chip of plastic, a bit bigger than a toonie and shaped like a map of South America. He recognized it as a fragment of the turn-table's dust cover. When he leaned forward and picked it up, there was something underneath.

3

SEPTEMBER

Her name was Sam. She sat in her uncle Ray's kitchen, waiting for the trauma worker to take her to her first day at her new school. She looked down into her lap, at one hand clenched over the other, where, at the centre of the inside hand, lay Morganne's little sketchbook. The one Morganne's parents had given her after Becky died. After Becky killed herself. After Morganne basically disappeared from her life. After all the shit had come down on three of them and only two of them had made it out alive.

You could see so much of Morganne in her artwork. Even in the tiny doodles in this little sketchbook. And Sam did not dare open the pages now, that would be too much. But she squeezed the little book until she felt the corner at the centre of her palm would break the skin. She brought the book to her lips as though in prayer.

"We got this," she whispered into its black cover. On the back of the hand that squeezed the sketchbook, right at the base of the thumb, there was the oval scar of her own teethmarks, where she'd bitten herself in agony and grief. And inside that oval, a stick-and-poke tattoo done by Morganne's cousin MacKenzie from the Running Brook First Nation. The tattoo was a miniature version of one of Morganne's doodles. A girl with spirals for eyes and a triangular swirl for a dress. The girl was leaning over to smell a flower half her size. "We got this," Sam told the girl in the tattoo.

"Finish that up, now, Patricia," Uncle Ray was saying. He had his back turned to her, fussing over something on the stove. Uncle Ray was not going to call her Sam. She had reckoned with that from the start. He knew her as Patricia. It was her original name, after all, though her mom had always called her Patty or Pattycakes, and to the kids at school she'd always been Trisha, until the very end, when people had turned ugly on her and they'd given her ugly names to make themselves feel better about the fact that they were such shitty people themselves.

Uncle Ray was not exactly her uncle. He was her mom's uncle, her mom's father's younger brother. Uncle Ray meant no harm by using a name she herself no longer favoured. And even if he did, she would not have felt comfortable arguing about it, at least not at this early stage. Uncle Ray's kitchen was still unfamiliar to her. She'd been living in his house for less than a week. He'd said to think of the place as her home, and she did, except...maybe not completely.

She'd managed to eat almost half of her omelet today, the most she'd ever done. But Uncle Ray was not pleased.

Ray had unmovable ideas about things. For one, he was convinced that breakfast meant bacon and eggs and orange juice and coffee. Every day since she'd been with him, he'd made her something called a bacon weave omelet, an enormous contraption that included, but was not limited to, many slices of bacon (she'd never been able to get an accurate count) woven into a single, human-hand-sized mini-blanket. Uncle Ray, up and about long before she got out of bed, had always already eaten, so if he himself ever ate a bacon-weave omelet, Sam had never witnessed the feat.

Ray had a girlfriend, a hookup, whatever old people called it, named Lynne, a super-chill lady from Cape Breton who Sam had met in the Valley during the terrible summer, and had seen again since coming to Uncle Ray's. And Sam was sure she heard Lynne, in her quiet and understated way, say the word "bomb-let" once with a smirk on her face that Sam thought she immediately understood.

The sound of popping gravel under tires broke the mild tension on the issue of finishing breakfast. Uncle Ray launched himself to his feet and nosed a quick glance out at the driveway before lurching to the back door.

"We were starting to think you weren't coming," he said, stepping to the side of the doorway.

The trauma worker's name was Maureen. She held out her left forearm, where a large black and grey Timex sports watch, a man's watch that did not look at all out of place on her strong, thick-wristed arm, was strapped in place by a black resin band.

"I said I'd be here at 8:15. It is now 8:12. A.M. Atlantic Daylight Time." She announced the exact time without looking at her watch, but held out her wrist a moment longer in case Ray wanted to double-check.

Maureen's job was over a two-hour drive away, back in the Valley, where Sam used to live. Coming to Hubtown today, coming all this way to help Sam get settled into her new school, was not something Maureen was required to do. In fact, several other professional people on Sam's case—doctors, nurses—made sure Sam understood that

Maureen was going out of her way to help Sam like this, as if Sam could not figure that out on her own.

Since they'd met, Maureen had refrained from commenting on Sam's appearance. Even at first, when Sam was still in the hospital, swollen and bruised from the assault. Maureen had gently taken her hand, looked her directly in the eyes, and held her hand a long time in both of hers.

So when Maureen looked Sam up and down in Ray's sunlit kitchen on the morning of her first day in a whole new school, a whole new life, Sam understood she meant it when she said kindly but still somehow matter-of-factly: "Gosh, don't you look sweet!"

Despite Maureen's sincerity, Sam was not at all confident that she looked sweet, and in fact sweet was not ever going to be a look she was going for. But Maureen was only being kind. And if anything would have caused Maureen to respond the way she did, it would have been raw contrast. Maureen had seen her almost dead, and here she was alive.

As she and Maureen drove toward her new school, the streets that had been so empty just days before now seemed alarmingly filled with high-school-aged kids. They kicked along on skateboards, stood waiting for green lights at intersections. They crossed crosswalks, walked down sidewalks, and sat in cars with their friends and family, windows rolled down, snippets of conversation audible through the open windows of Maureen's car. People looked happy and light, glowing with a first day of school shine.

Maureen parked against the brick wall of the main building and led the way from the car to the door near the student services office. Sam had her bookbag over her shoulder and held onto the straps as though getting ready for a parachute jump. Maureen was carrying Sam's guitar, but she was not used to the bulk of the case, and it bounced off her leg with every step, sounding a *clop* that Sam cringed at each time, certain it was drawing attention.

This school was almost ten times the size of her old school. The number of people just in this corner of the parking lot seemed impossible. In the midst of the noisy pack of humanity that encircled the building she felt her heart begin to race. She scanned the mass of faces, looking for someone familiar. They were like masks. The emotions they expressed seemed impossible. Impossible to read. Impossible to understand. Then all at once they turned angry and bitter. Jeering disrespectfully. The day suddenly became overwhelmingly bright. She closed her eyes to keep from going blind and everything came to a standstill. A coldness dropped through her body and there was silence.

"Sam." It was Maureen's quiet, reassuring voice in her ear. She could feel the woman's gentle arm around her shoulders. "Sam," she said. "We're at your new school. Take a moment to come back and when you're ready, open your eyes. You're going to be fine. You're safe here."

When she opened her eyes, she and Maureen were at the entrance to the building. They'd made it across the parking lot before she had frozen. With the brick and glass entrance of the new school before her, Sam turned slowly in a standing circle to see who had witnessed her losing it. There were kids at a distance, presumably off school property, smoking cigarettes, blowing clouds of vape smoke, grabbing hats off each other's heads. Six girls nearby were gathered around another girl's phone, thumbing through pictures. One girl giggled harshly and a jolt of panic ran down Sam's spine like a drop of ice water.

"Oh my gosh! He's so cute!" said another girl. "And you look stunning in that dress!"

"That was the day of my cousin's wedding," the girl with the phone said.

—

THE BUILDING WAS OLD, AND EVEN THOUGH IT WAS WELL KEPT up—the floors and walls not only clean, but relatively recently tiled and painted—the hallways were narrow and cut off almost completely from natural light.

A vice principal, a lady even larger and sturdier in appearance than Maureen, met them halfway across the front foyer. She said her name, but Sam immediately forgot. She took them on a quick tour through several hallways to show Sam where the two classes on her morning schedule would be.

Down a hallway and around a corner from the student services office there was a quiet room with two couches and a big, soft-looking armchair. "Any time you feel over-whelmed. Any time your anxiety gets bad enough that you don't think you can make it through class. You come down here and just sit. There might be one other person in here. There might not be. But this is a quiet space. It's meant to be peaceful and comfortable and non-threatening."

The furniture in the chill-out room was upholstered in dark brown fake leather. The walls were grey and institutional, but soothing prints were hung there. Watercoloury. Abstract. Just two prints, on opposite walls. On another wall there was a framed sign that said *Respect People*. Plain black letters on white paper behind glass.

Maureen told the vice principal that Sam might sometimes communicate by writing things down instead of speaking. And the vice principal had not batted an eye.

"We can accommodate multiple strategies," the lady had said, as though half the students in the school wrote their thoughts on a notepad instead of speaking out loud. "I can make a note of that in PowerSchool and send an email to teachers making sure they read that note. We call that a First Day Notice." By this time, they were in the vice principal's office, and she swivelled sideways in her chair and said, "I'll do that right now." She began clicking away at her keyboard.

On the desk in front of the vice principal were framed portraits of two young adults: a man and a woman. Their broad faces and square hairlines at the top of their foreheads made clear that they were the vice principal's children. There were two certificates in frames on the wall behind her. Between them, off-centre in a much smaller frame, were the words *It is what it is* printed in black, like the *Respect People* sign in the room with the fake leather furniture.

"Now," the woman stopped typing and turned back to Sam and Maureen, "tell me what your teachers need to know..." There was a pause while the woman selected her words. "...about...trauma."

Sam felt her body tighten. She was tired of talking about what had happened to her. Tired of saying the same things over and over again. Tired of what her body went through, the cold shock that squeezed the air out of her lungs.

Maureen put a hand on Sam's forearm, waited a calming moment, and said: "It's okay. We don't have to talk about anything right now."

"Say: 'Has recently experienced trauma,'" Maureen told the vice principal. She scribbled something on the back of one of her business cards. "Provide this link. It explains what teachers need to know about students who have had trauma."

When it was just about time for her first class to begin, Sam looked at the clock above the door of the vice principal's office, where the threshold gave onto a corner of the front foyer.

"I don't want to be late for my first class."

"You don't want to be late for your first class."

Sam and Maureen spoke at the same time.

"Jinx," Maureen said, and laughed a slightly uncharacteristic laugh. Sam did not understand what Maureen meant by exclaiming *jinx*, but she took comfort from Maureen's laugh. A small tremor of hope took up fluttering residence in her chest.

———

SAM WAS GOING TO HOLD OFF VISITING THAT COMFORTABLE little room, the one with the plush brown furniture, as long as she could. She did not want to miss class time. Getting behind in school work was only going to worsen her anxiety. And despite the encouragement of the vice principal, she decided not to write down words to communicate unless the alternative was pretty much death. That would only draw attention to her. It would make her a freak in the eyes of the other students. She did not feel the need for any social contact whatsoever. She did not want to make new friends, but making herself stand out as the girl who spoke by writing notes would make her a target. And however minor a target she might be for scribbling in a notepad, she did not need any such attention.

Anything she did that attracted curiosity, as a new face in the school, as someone people were wondering about, might lead to online snooping, people creeping social media to figure out who she was. She had deleted her Facebook, Instagram, Twitter, and Snapchat. She'd even gone back and deleted all the old accounts she had not used in a long time: Tumblr, ask.fm. She'd got rid of it all. But she knew that pictures of her were still in circulation. You could protest and notify social media sites when they popped up. And you could mostly count on them being taken down. But people still had them on their phones or their hard drives. Though the terrible pics were grainy and blurred, you could tell it was her in them. Her and Morganne and Becky. She looked different now, in full light, in real life, her hair cropped short. But still. She existed online, or some hateful version of her did. She'd already had to get Facebook to delete abusive accounts in her name. Three times.

This school was only a few hundred kilometres from her old school. How long before the people here figured out who she was, what she was, how low she was? How deserving of hatred and scorn? She'd never wanted another cellphone in her life, but her mother had insisted. She'd bought her a Samsung Galaxy and paid for a Telus plan with unlimited texting that she could also make a few calls a month on. Her mom and Uncle Ray were the only two people who ever texted. She kept it on silent mode, zipped into a side pocket of her floral bookbag, and even though it was turned off, she could almost feel it vibrating through the floral fabric.

Her best friend Morganne's mom had been given the number, too, though Sam had yet to hear from Morganne since moving. She planned to check the phone every day after school. She could see the shape of it, its rounded corners, through the fabric of the bag. It was like some horrible succubus that had latched onto her. She felt like hitting it with a stick and killing it.

Uncle Ray told her this school would be more anonymous than her old one. And it only took her until lunch on the first day to realize exactly what that meant. The school was so big that most of the teachers did not know most of the students' names on the first day. And because this school went from grade ten to grade twelve, a third of all students, all the grade tens, were as new to the building as she was.

She'd sat in class with her eyes lowered, steeling herself for the negative attention she thought was inevitable. A sneering face. A sarcastic comment made under the breath. But so far none had come. She felt herself lowering her emotional guard a little.

She kept Morganne's sketchbook in the front pocket of her jeans. The pocket was small, but so was the book. When she sat down, a corner of the book sometimes dug painfully into the flesh at the top of her thigh.

Now that Becky was gone, taken from the face of the earth, and now that Morganne was gone from Sam's life, the little sketchbook felt like a benevolent horcrux to her. A piece of some collective soul she'd shared with her two closest friends. When she placed a hand over its hard little rectangle, she could look down and see the tattoo at the heel of her thumb, the lopsided girl and the flower that was almost as big as the girl.

———

ON THE LAST PERIOD OF THE DAY, SAM WALKED INTO MUSIC CLASS nervous and disoriented. The class was down a dark hallway and around a corner, right at the heart of the building, far from a window and from any natural light. She was carrying a big, awkward guitar case, which she had not yet figured out how to do comfortably. The size and hulking press of the guitar against her body as she carried it, the audible *clop* it made when her arm got tired and she had to set it on the floor, or when she strayed too close to a wall or a door casing, these violated her wish to be smaller, quieter, less conspicuous.

And the music classroom was not really a classroom like the others. There were chairs, but no desks. It was not immediately obvious, upon entering, what a student of Instrumental Strings was supposed to do. The class ahead of hers, it seemed, was much more advanced. Students were scampering about the room as Sam's class came in, folding up impossibly difficult-looking sheet music. They were putting away instruments Sam thought she knew to name—a trumpet, a trombone, a saxophone—along with some others she was not sure of.

The main pieces of furniture were the chairs the previous class had been sitting in, each of which had a black music stand with the name of the school stencilled in white.

One of the kids from the previous class was wiping down a trumpet and putting it in its case. He was directly in front of the chair Sam had chosen as the one she would sit in if she could gather the courage to sit.

The trumpet player had a long, triangular face, and a ball of frizzed-out light brown hair that grew slightly back and away from where gravity suggested it might naturally go. He wore a black T-shirt with the words *Shut Up* hand-painted across the front in white.

The room was well lit, despite the lack of windows. The floor was covered by a dull, slate-coloured carpet that was probably the source of the musty smell. At the lowest point of the classroom, against the wall, there was an old-school blackboard, five separate panels, each trimmed with gouged, pen-scarred wood. Two of the panels had permanently-drawn music lines, some of which were chalked over with what looked like mini-lessons on one musical point or another. There was a yellow chalk arrow that pointed at a circled section that had been dotted with musical notes. At the far end of the arrow, the words *You need to know this!* *This* was underlined three times.

The man at the front of the room, with his back turned, scribbling away in yellow chalk at the centre panel of the blackboard, was young for a teacher. He wore black pants, a black belt, and a charcoal short-sleeved button-up shirt. His shoes too were black, polished, long and narrow and sort of funky-looking without making too bold of a statement.

Mr. J. Foley, said the chalk message the teacher was writing on the board. *Please take a seat, quietly take your instrument from its case. Place a music stand in front of you. Place your notebook or binder on the music stand. Please do not play or sound notes from your instrument until invited to do so. (This includes tuning!)*

Students were still settling in and getting out their instruments when the bell rang. Mr. Foley went over to his desk, sat down at the clunky-looking desktop computer there, and started taking attendance.

Sam felt her anxiety level rising as the teacher made his way through the list. Would he call her *Sam* or *Patricia*? The vice principal had said they would put her preferred name in the computer and that teachers would know to call her that. Even though no one had made a mistake yet, Sam was tired at the end of a full day. And the mere thought of being called the wrong name had her close to tears.

Her hands felt light and jittery. How would she ever steady them on the guitar's strings? Tension was building in her chest, strangling her voice further. The urge to spring to her feet and run almost overtook her. She knew, in the back of her mind, that she could use slow, deep breaths to calm herself, but she was high up and exposed in her seat at the back of the class.

She put her left hand flat against the centre of her chest and felt the heart there, racing against her ribs. Before Mr. Foley got to her name, there was a quick double-knock at the classroom door.

A brief expression passed across Mr. Foley's face: unchecked annoyance.

There was a long, narrow window in the top half of the classroom door. An impassive male face looked in from the hallway.

Immediately a stir went through the room. *Robot*, she thought she heard people say. Mr. Foley hesitated at his desk, computer mouse still in hand as he took attendance. But when he climbed up the few tiers from the front to the back of the classroom and stepped into the hall to talk to the student who had come late, the voices of student exclamations got louder, clearer. "Holy fuck," a kid two rows in front of her said. He was leaning over close to the ear of the guy beside him, but making no apparent attempt to hush his voice. The teacher was in the hallway now, talking to the late student, snippets of their conversation coming through the open door.

"This is not your class," the teacher said.

"Yes it is," the kid said.

"Instrumental Strings is introductory. You're way beyond this."

"Does that mean you're letting me into Music 12? It was full when I registered."

The teacher shook his head. "There's a hard cap at thirty-two."

"I don't know what that means."

"It means Music 12 is full."

"Well. Check your list. I'm in this class."

"He's out of jail? Already?" the other kid in front of her said.

"Check this," the first kid dug out his cellphone, and in a few seconds he was using his thumb to scroll down a list of videos.

"Turn the sound off," the second guy said.

Sam squeezed her eyes shut. If the attention of almost everyone in the class had not already been on the door, she might have made a run for it.

In a burst of restless energy, she stood up quickly. When she opened her eyes, she could see a couple of people had turned toward her sudden movement. But most of the class's attention was still on the door. There was motion on the phone screen that the two guys in front of her were watching.

"Fuck!" the first guy said. "Look at that! One punch. Down! Fuck!"

"I've seen this a hundred times," the second guy said.

"Fucking Gink," said the first guy. "Down. Dead. One punch. I didn't even know you could kill a guy with one punch."

"People are mortal," the second guy said. "Sometimes you don't even need a reason. Boom! The guy dies. Was it the poutine he was eating? Was it genetic?"

The video was on a loop. Just a few seconds long. Sam could see the repeated motion, but the image was not clear. And she would not allow her attention to rest on the screen. Someone was getting killed in the video. Someone these assholes knew. Over and over and over. And they were watching it. For what reason? Fun?

This was a fucking nightmare. This was a test. Sam looked quietly about the room, sat back down, and closed her eyes again.

"What is this?" she heard the teacher ask the guy at the door.

"It's a ukulele," the guy called Robot said.

"This is a guitar class," the teacher said.

She heard Robot sigh in frustration. "Really? You're going to do this?" Robot said. "On the first day? This class is called Instrumental Strings."

"The course description says *must have own instrument*."

"This is my instrument."

"A ukulele is not a serious instrument. It's a toy."

"I used to think the same thing. Look. Just let me in. I'm

sorry I'm late. I promise I won't be late again. This ukulele is pretty legit. Give it a try. I bet you'll agree."

Sam's heart slowed down as the commotion eased. The teacher had finally relented and let Robot into the room. The only free seat near the door was right next to her. And so he'd settled in there. So close she could smell the soap he'd used in the shower that morning. And he'd killed someone, apparently. And been in jail for it. And there was a video of the death. And apparently a lot of people had seen it.

As the teacher continued with attendance, he did not even pause when he got to Sam's name. She had her eyes closed in anticipation. *Sam.* At the sound of the right name, most of what had been locked tightly in her chest seemed to loosen. She took a deep, slow breath and opened her eyes. Robot's real name was Robert, apparently. The teacher made a deal out of saying *tardy* after he called the name.

With her cousin's acoustic guitar pressed tightly to her ribs, Sam looked over to Robert. She let her gaze slide up, beginning at her own shoe, from his bookbag, to the ukulele in his lap, to the three-quarters profile she got of his face from this angle. He was a big guy. She got that, even though he was seated. His upper arm was enormous in the sleeve of his T-shirt. His forearm wide and beefy and freckled. His jawline square, his cheekbones square above it. Those who knew how to tune their instruments had been given permission to do so. Robert's eyes were intensely focused on the tuning pegs of the ukulele.

Sam hugged the body of her guitar to her, both arms around the instrument's waist. She rested a cheek on the side of the body, against a part of the guitar that, according to a labelled diagram on a chart near the chalkboard, was called the upper bout. A complicated mix of emotions went through her. Fear. Worry. Anger at the kids in front of her for not giving Robert one minute back to school before they played some shitty video he obviously had no control over.

Mostly what she felt, with a twinge of guilt for feeling it, was relief. Whatever else Robert was, whoever else he was, whatever he'd done, she understood that he was a distraction. He was a huge gravitational mass of personal and social agony. There was no way she'd catch anyone's attention right now. Not with this killer in the same music class, this killer whose crime was apparently shareable, something anyone could watch. She'd never stand out to anyone here. Not as freakish or new or interesting in any way.

There was a cool, soothing smoothness to the side of the guitar that pressed into her left cheek. The soft sounds of the strings on Robert's ukulele as he tuned it were soothing as well.

Just then Robert put his instrument down and turned toward her. He said something that, with her mind partially drifted off and one ear pressed against the guitar, she did not hear.

She sat up straight and looked at him. In the practiced manner of someone used to communicating through facial expression alone, she raised her eyebrows at him to say *What? Pardon?*

"I can tune that thing for you, if you want." He was not smiling. But his voice was calm and, if not friendly, at least not hostile. He reached out a hand.

She hesitated a second, then passed him the guitar.

4

FOUR MONTHS EARLIER: MAY

The cookware set was Lagostina. Hand-hammered copper. Top of the line. Even on sale the price topped a thousand dollars. The box was bigger than a large microwave oven. It had two pre-punched handgrips, factory perforated, one on each side, to make it carriable.

Eleanor was hiding in a rack of reduced shirts: old-school black and red check with a black quilted liner. Her right cheek was against a soft, silky liner, her left against the scratchy fibres of the 30 percent wool outer shirt. She knew the guy was going to steal the cookware set as soon as he picked it up. There was a blindered way people looked at what they were about to steal, completely the opposite of how thieves were depicted in TV shows. No looking guiltily over each shoulder, just a brisk approach, a matter-of-fact planting of the feet.

The man bent from the waist, like the bad example in an occupational safety video. He straightened up more slowly than he expected to, Eleanor noticed. His hands gripped the box, he started to lift, then as the full weight of the cookware connected with his extended arms, his rise slowed noticeably. He'd decided to steal something based on the dollar value without asking himself how heavy it was going to be.

The shirt rack Eleanor was hiding in was circular, with a small space in the centre just large enough for her to retreat

into for a minute to contact her manager. One of the car-
dinal rules of being a floor walker was not to take your eyes
off the shoplifter while you were still in pursuit. They stuff
a package of batteries under their shirt in aisle 94, but if
they've gotten cold feet between there and the door and you
missed them dumping the package in the paint aisle, that is
a major embarrassment and a waste of several people's time.

But there was no way for this guy to dump that massive
cookware set without her noticing. So she retreated into the
shirt rack and retrieved the palm-sized VHF radio from the
cargo pocket on the thigh of her pants. "Following a male
suspect. He's headed for the Garden Centre doors," she said
into the black plastic grille of the radio.

A moment later, her phone buzzed against the side of
her leg. She rolled her eyes in frustration. "Please answer
using radio," she said into the VHF. Again more buzzing.
"What is the point of making me carry this stupid radio and
insisting that I use it to contact you if you're not going to
use it to reply to me?"

In frustration, she reached into a different pocket and
pulled out her phone. Three texts in a row from her manager:

Can you describe him?

*I can't find the radio. It's here in my office. I can hear it,
but I can't see it.*

Garden Centre is not open till June.

Jesus, Eleanor thought. I know when the Garden Centre
opens. But now that she was limited to thumbing texts,
she was going to have to keep her communication to its
essentials.

Pls send someone to help. Send Brian. Or Tyler. Pls.

She poked her head out through the top of the shirt rack

and looked down the sale aisle toward the Garden Centre doors. An older lady in a striped shirt was pulling a massive shelving unit, still in its box, from a top shelf. She had big, black-rimmed glasses, a white, floppy bucket hat. Her wiry grey hair ran straight down the sides of her face, the length and texture of the business end of a corn broom.

The lady was standing on the edge of a bottom shelf, gripping the box of shelving at the corners, which were wider apart than her shoulders, and she was partially swinging from the box she was struggling to budge, as though it were a piece of gym equipment. With her feet barely reaching the outer edge of the steel shelf beneath her, she swung her hips inward, then back. Each back swing inched the giant box above her farther out over her head. Two or three more successful pushes and pulls and the pressboard TV stand and entertainment centre, the size of a one-man kayak from Sporting Goods and, with the weight of a large man, was going to flatten this lady into the polished tiles of the sale aisle, between a tower of three-ply toilet paper and a pegboard display of pocket tools.

"Ma'am! Ma'am!" Eleanor ran down the sale aisle, getting within earshot of the dangling lady just as the box she was hanging from began to reach the point at which it would teeter over.

"Ma'am, please! An associate will get that for you!" The woman's toes lost their purchase on the shelf she'd been standing on, and at the sound of Eleanor's voice, she turned her head as far as it would turn in Eleanor's direction, her right cheek hard against the upper part of her arm as she clung, hanging off the edge of the package she was so anxious to dislodge.

"Please let go of the box, ma'am," Eleanor said. She could feel the emotion building in her voice. "Tyler! Brian!"

A look of anger and fear crossed the old lady's face. "God damn it!" the lady shouted. Eleanor did not have the height to catch the box before it came down. She caught the woman around the waist, hugged her hard, her face pressed into the back of the woman's ribcage, and lifted.

"Let go, ma'am! Please let go!" The old lady smelled of baby powder and nicotine.

"I need a new TV stand," the lady was saying.

"We'll get that for you. *Tyler!*" Tyler was a sweet-faced high school boy, a year older than Eleanor's daughter, Patricia.

"Oh my god," she heard Tyler say. But with her face pressed hard into the wide stripes of the woman's shirt, she could not see him.

"Tyler will get that down for you, ma'am," Eleanor said. She could hear Tyler laughing from over her shoulder. "Tyler. FFS, tell her you'll get it for her." None of the younger people she worked with actually said *FFS*. It was texting shorthand. But they all knew what it meant. And she'd found it a useful intensifier on more than one occasion.

"Let me get that, ma'am," Tyler said at last. Eleanor watched as Tyler gently pried the lady's fingers from the box. The full weight of the woman's body fell into Eleanor's grip, and she could feel something let go in her lower back as she set the lady gently on the floor. There was a twinge just above her waist, about a hand's length from her right butt cheek. The pain jabbed into her lower back, then flashed down the leg to her ankle in repeated pulses.

She was bent over, her hands on the epicentre of pain, as the old lady turned angrily on her and Tyler.

"Yar yar yar," the woman seemed to be saying. Eleanor did not have time to contemplate whether the incomprehensibility of the woman's words was a result of her own pain or the woman's agitation. When she turned to Tyler, he had a hand on the upright of a shelf and was leaning back, laughing out loud, pointing at something behind her. "The same box is on the two lower shelves," he managed to say between guffaws.

"Look. I don't have time for this," Eleanor said. "I'm following..." She raised her eyebrows significantly. "Somebody."

She left Tyler to look after the old lady, but her progress toward where she'd last seen the cookware thief was severely impeded by the pain that was now shooting from her lower back, through her right butt cheek, and down the back of her leg almost to the ankle.

Her phone must have buzzed as she was dealing with the dangling grey-haired lady. When she flicked to her texting app, there were several messages from the manager, the last of which was *What's going on?*

She shuffled to the end of the store. On a hunch, she turned left at the locked Garden Centre doors, and began a counter-clockwise route around the store's periphery. She was bent over and shuffling, and counter to the proven method of floor walking, which began and ended with being as close to invisible as possible, she noticed that her wounded, shuffling gait was drawing the attention of customers as she dragged her throbbing right leg behind her.

She caught up to the guy with the box of cookware as he passed in front of the Customer Service desk.

I'm at Customer Service. Send Brian here now!

Where's Tyler? I sent Tyler.

Jesus! Tyler's busy. Brian, pls.

The guy did three laps of the store with the heavy box against the tops of his legs, his arms hung the whole way down at his sides. His face locked dead straight forward, never seeming to look left or right. And Eleanor followed him the whole way round each time, the pain in her back and down her leg worse and worse until by the end, her right leg felt all but paralyzed from the hip down. The only feeling she had below the knee was a painful explosion of pins and needles every time her foot made contact with the floor.

By the third time past the customer service desk, there was not an employee in the store who was unaware of the cookware thief. When he hooked right at last and exited the main doors, all four cashiers on duty got up on their tiptoes to watch him walk out.

"Excuse me, sir. Excuse me, sir," Eleanor called from behind him. He quickened his pace slightly, but otherwise showed no sign that he'd heard her at all. "Sir. You have not paid for that item. Stop, sir! Stop!" There was a concrete walkway that ran the length of the store, and Eleanor was halfway down that when she stopped. She had to lean over, her hand on her right thigh to support her throbbing back and leg.

Both Tyler and Brian were behind her by now. "Here," she said. She passed Tyler the VHF radio. "Follow that guy. Do not let him out of your sight. Keep telling him to stop. Do not try to stop him."

"What the hell," Tyler said.

Brian was only a few years older than Tyler. Already graduated from high school. He'd worked out west a couple of years, then came back to Nova Scotia for some sort of corrections course at the NSCC. He had shaggy brown hair and a frustrated scowl on his face. "I fucking love working at Canadian Tire," he said sarcastically. Eleanor managed to thumb *Cookware thief did not stop at door. Call police. Tyler and Brian are following him* into her phone and sent that off to Steve, the manager. She'd made her way back almost to the main doors when Steve came through them. He waggled the yellow and black VHF radio at her. "Hey! I found the radio," he said. He had a big grin on his face. He did not give one shit that she'd just ruined her back for the sake of a pea-brained old lady and an overpriced cookware set.

"I found the radio!" he said into the radio. When he released the *call* button, Tyler's voice came back: "What?"

Eleanor put out her hand for the radio and Steve passed it over. "Did you call the police?" she asked Steve.

"Police?" Fuck.

"Where are you now?" she said into the radio. Tyler, Brian, and the thief had walked the whole length of the store and were out of her sight.

"Can you please just call the cops?" she said to Steve.

He put up both of his hands. "Okay! Okay!" He looked over his shoulder into the store. "I'd better use the store's phone. I'm out of minutes."

"We're out behind the store," came Tyler's voice over the radio.

"There's nothing back there. Where's he going?" Eleanor said.

"He's headed through the field."

"He won't get far. The river's back there."

There was a long moment of quiet, during which it occurred to Eleanor that she had not had a text from Patricia in several hours. She leaned back against the concrete store-front of the Canadian Tire building and rested her shoulders against the wall. She stretched both legs from her butt cheeks to the backs of her ankles. After being indoors for her whole shift, the late light of May reinvigorated her brain. She took in a deep breath and opened her texting app. The last text she'd had from her daughter was at the end of the school day.

Getting on the bus to Morganne's.

Hey, Pattycakes, Eleanor texted. *Just checking in. Still at Morganne's?*

"He's in the river," came Tyler's voice over the VHF.

"What!" she yelled back.

"He's in the river. He's walking into the river. There he goes. He's swimming. He's swimming across the river."

"With that fucking cookware set?"

"No. No cookware. No box. Just him. Swimming. He's a pretty good swimmer, too. Overhand stroke."

"Where's the Lagostina?"

"The what?"

"The Lagostina. The cookware. The box."

"No sign of it. We can't see it anywhere."

By the time the police were pulling up in front of the main doors with the thief in the back seat of the cruiser, forty-five minutes had elapsed since Eleanor yelled for Steve to call them. The store was closed. Steve had told both Brian and Tyler they could go home. The police had the swimmer handcuffed in the backseat and they just needed Eleanor to ID him. She'd been sitting at the empty Customer Service counter, the pain shooting down her leg had dulled to a tender stiffness, and she was texting Patricia every five minutes with no text back.

When Eleanor was a girl, the town had had its own police force. But the town had shrunken. Policing had gotten expensive. Almost a decade ago, town council had voted to contract the job to the RCMP. The guy who came through the main entrance of the store for her was someone she knew pretty well. Corporal Vernon was his name, though she was not certain if that was his first or last name. He was about thirty. Slim waist. He looked like he might be jacked beneath his bulletproof vest, his holster, and the bulky cop shirt.

The cops were laughing and calling the guy they'd arrested The Triathlete. He'd swum to the opposite bank of the river, then collapsed from exhaustion and exposure. He was still lying face up in the reeds when the police arrived.

Eleanor limped out to the Mounties' car and poked her head through the driver's side back door, opposite to where the thief was sitting.

The thief did not turn in her direction, and Eleanor wondered if the guy had some kind of condition. Autism, maybe. Why else would he not look at her now? His clothing was ragged and soaked. His hair was matted against the side of his face. The river water must have been freezing this time of year, and he was hunched over his handcuffed wrists, shivering. His teeth chattering audibly.

"He needs a blanket," Eleanor said.

"It's him?" asked Corporal Vernon. She nodded.

Steve was back at the entrance to the store. "Any sign of that cookware set?"

Vernon shook his head. "He doesn't want to talk about that, apparently. That or anything else." He pointed at the black bulb of the camera over the doorway. "But you've got him on tape, right? Leaving the store with it?"

Steve nodded. "I have not checked. But it'll be there."

"I'll need that first thing in the morning," Vernon said. "Put it on a whatever. A thumb stick."

"Wait a minute," Eleanor said. She went back into the store, which was fully lit, but empty. She looked back over her shoulder at the glass of the front entrance, which looked like polished black marble now that darkness had fully fallen. She shuffled as fast as her sore leg would allow and found the rack of quilted shirts she'd been hiding in earlier. She pulled a 2XL off its hanger and went back outside.

"What are you doing with that?" Steve said. He and the two police officers were standing back against the concrete storefront. Eleanor walked straight past without replying.

The back door of the cop car was still open. She crawled across the nylon fabric of the seat and draped the shirt over the shoulders of the thief, who wiggled to nestle his shoulders into the shirt, but still did not look at her. He smelled like river water and mouldy tomato sauce.

"Who's paying for that shirt?" Steve was saying as she crossed back into the store, but she did not feel like talking to him.

———

BY THE TIME ELEANOR GOT HOME, IT HAD BEEN HOURS SINCE she'd heard from Patricia. She was not in a panic. Not yet. But the only thing that kept her from being in a panic was her own inner voice telling her again and again not to.

The light over the front door came on automatically in the dark, but it was the only light on in the rundown mini home, and she could tell at a glance that the house was empty.

She keyed open the front door and despite herself, shouted hopefully: "Patty! Pattycakes!" But it was only her own voice she heard, thin and desperate in the empty rooms.

She checked the caller ID on the landline in the kitchen: nothing. She opened the beat-up laptop in her bedroom and logged into her Gmail account, as though Patricia were going to email her from somewhere.

She opened her Facebook, looked at Patricia's profile, then made a post on her own account:

Has anyone seen Patricia? Please contact me immediately.

A slow trickle of responses to the Facebook post began to come in. Exclamations of dismay. Sincere expressions of concern. Fake expressions of concern that anyone could see were nothing more than nosey attempts to get more information. Her phone began to light up with text messages from people who had seen the post.

Let me know if I can help.

Keep me posted, girl.

I hope everything is okay over there.

The only one she replied to was from her son, Simon, in Alberta. *WTF. Where is Trisha?*

I have a terrible feeling, she texted back. And within a minute, Simon called on the landline.

"Mom. I can tell you're upset. But this is irresponsible. It's irresponsible to post what you did, then tell me nothing but that you have a terrible feeling."

"Simon, I don't know what to do. I was at work. I came home. She's not here. I have not heard from her in hours."

"Where do you think she might be?"

"I thought she was at Morganne's house. But I have no number for Morganne. I have no number for her parents."

"You have to go over there. Get in the car and drive over to the house."

The dark had set in hard by the time Eleanor got into her car and drove to Morganne's house. She had taken an extra-strength Advil, and that, plus her growing feeling that something terrible had happened, had completely eliminated the pain in her lower back and leg.

The sky was cold black. No stars. No moon. Some neighbourhoods, the few with street lamps that lit them up, illuminated a grey halo of cloud above them.

If she passed a car coming in the opposite direction, it did not register in her memory. It was almost midnight and people were cocooned in their homes. Cars in yards. Curtains closed. Each house made a dim little bubble of illumined earth about it. The car radio was tuned to that pop station from Halifax that Patricia was obsessed with. The signal was coming from so far away that it was mostly static and white noise. As soon as Eleanor registered its presence, which took more than half the twenty-minute drive, she shut it off with a push of a button.

Morganne's house was completely dark. Eleanor pulled the car over to the curb. Even in the dark, even from a car parked at the curb, Eleanor could see that Morganne's house was for people with a level of income that she herself would never attain. There were raised, cedar-mulched garden beds shaped in curved lines by a landscape designer, in which grew thick, healthy evergreen shrubs. The front door, the windows, the siding were all up to date in style and in tip-top repair. Eleanor had registered all these details before, when dropping Patricia off or picking her up from Morganne's house. But the stark contrast between the dumpy, rundown mini home she could barely afford and the house where all afternoon and most the evening she'd just assumed Trisha to be, that contrast was so sharp there was just no way not to register it. Along with everything else she felt as she sat there in her rundown car, the fear, the panic even, the helplessness in the face of the looming white unknown, she also felt self-conscious, a lower-class person out of place in an upper-class neighbourhood.

Her phone buzzed against the plastic in the change holder where she'd placed it.

Well? It was Simon texting her.

I'm here, she replied. *Morganne's house. Nothing. No sign of her.*

Did you knock on the door?

She looked at the time in the corner of the phone's screen. It was now well after midnight.

Knock on the door.

It's late. It's after midnight.

This is more important than how late it is. Knock.

I did.

No you did not.

There was almost a half tank of gas when she pulled away from the curb at the front of Morganne's house. And she used it to cruise slowly and aimlessly through street after residential street. More and more houses were dark as she drove, several of them turning dark before her eyes as the last person awake inside it flipped off the light and went to bed.

Simon was three time zones away and getting ready for an overnight shift. As Eleanor drove, her phone stopped buzzing with Simon's texts, and she was left alone in the muffled interior of the car. Homes and cars and neighbour-hoods drifted past on the outside. Cutouts. They felt as unreal to her as props in a puppet theatre.

It was almost 3:00 A.M. when she turned the corner onto her own street. The Mountie car was sitting in her drive-way, the lights mercifully turned off so its presence was not alerting the entire neighbourhood. Eleanor parked on the street. The two cops were silhouettes in the front seat as she approached. Only the driver got out. It was Corporal Vernon, nearing the end of a shift that had begun with chasing down the swimming cookware thief out behind Canadian Tire.

"Eleanor," he said. And the buttons and badges and metal and plastic fasteners across his chest caught what ambient light there was in the dark driveway. They glittered against his dark shirt, blurring, becoming larger and less distinct, light reaching out across darkness to light.

5

SEPTEMBER

Robot leaned forward in his seat to get a closer look at the South America–shaped plastic chip on the empty stereo stand. When he picked it up, there was a rounded triangle beneath it: a Jordan's Music guitar pick. White nylon. *Jordan's Music Hubtown* in black lettering. Through the closed door of his mother's bedroom, he could hear the sound of her drunken snoring. Jordan Jordan had been good to him while he'd worked there—because Robot had been good for Jordan's business; his guitar chops were well-known and kids wanted to take lessons from good players. Once he'd been convicted of a crime, especially a violent crime, he became a liability. What parent would pay to have their kid sit in a room alone with a known killer?

But everything good in Robot's life had come from music. Music was two of the three items on the reintegration plan he'd worked on while still in youth detention. And when he got home and discovered his mother had sold his Les Paul, his mind went floundering for anything good to cling to.

It was well past mid-afternoon when he left the apartment. September was the month when this shitty neighbourhood looked its best. The green of summer was still high in the trees. The grass still green and growing. As he walked the decrepit concrete of old sidewalks in the direction of downtown, leaves and late-blooming flowers distracted from the sagging houses whose front steps needed replacement, whose window panes were cracked, the frames rotten, the clapboard peeling, the roofing shingles dripping into the crooked eavestroughs.

There was almost nowhere Robot could go without passing the little park where it had happened. It was just a short distance from his house. He paused for a moment on the sidewalk, in a place where he could see the patch of grass where, after Gink had gone down, he himself had stopped running and lain down, where he'd looked up at the sky and waited for what he'd done to catch up to him.

—

ROBOT REACHED JORDAN'S MUSIC BEFORE CONSCIOUSLY registering that that's where he'd been headed. He stood on the sidewalk a moment, his back to the parking metres and cars, and looked at the store's old-timey facade: the forest green and chrome. The display windows designed for some long-gone business in a previous century. The posters taped to the glass that advertised upcoming musical events in Hubtown. There was a display of hand drums on the left side of the entryway. Djembes, cajóns, a pair of congas on a stand. In the right side window, two small PA systems at two different price points, the rack of used guitars against the slate grey wall behind them.

Robot was not at all surprised when Jordan Jordan met him less than a step inside the door and stared him down.

There was a god-awful buzzer that sounded every time the door opened at Jordan's Music. Jordan Jordan's father, the shop's original owner, had rigged it up himself way back in the sixties. Two strips of metal, one at the tip of a wired brace attached to the top of the door, the other on a bigger brace attached to the door frame. Depending on the weather, sometimes sparks were visible jumping through the air between the two strips. And on top of the terrible sound of the buzzer, which came from a box mounted on the far wall of Jordan Jordan's office, there was a disconcerting electric crackle that came from the metal strips when they made contact.

"Hi, Jordan," Robot said. They were so close it was awkward. He could not step forward, but he could not close the door in order to step back a pace. The buzzer was complaining from Jordan's office. And the crackling of the electrical contact just above his head sent a chill down his spine. There were two or three customers in the place. Robot could see two employees over Jordan's shoulder: Bria DeMont, a fiddle teacher who sometimes worked the sales floor, and his friend Matt Sutcliffe, a twenty-five-year-old sales clerk who also did a bit of repair work on the stringed instruments. Neither Matt nor Bria dared look Robot in the eye while their boss was confronting him, but Robot saw them exchanging wide-eyed looks across the shop floor.

"Can I help you?" Jordan said. He was a narrow-shouldered man with a soft, widening waistline. His physical presence was not at all intimidating to someone as tall and solid as Robot. He had small, intense eyes, a forehead etched from east to west with thick worry wrinkles. And his puff of short, brown, curly hair was noticeably thinning on top.

Robot inched closer and Jordan instinctively backed up, but only an inch or so. Robot let the door go behind him and the shop immediately went quiet.

"Just. Ah." He might as well say what he was there for. "Wondering about starting up some lessons, if there's any interest."

"There is no interest," Jordan snapped. He inched in Robot's direction. As Robot turned to exit, Matt came sidling past a rack of cables to intervene. Matt was the guy who'd first brought him to Jordan's and told Jordan Jordan to check out his chops.

"Jordan," Matt said, "Robot's on the way out. Let me talk to him a minute."

Jordan Jordan's face clouded over with a new and darker curtain of anger, directed at Matt this time.

"Seriously," Matt said. "We're in the doorway."

Jordan's face lightened slightly.

"I got this," Matt said.

Jordan looked at Matt, scowled a cartoonish scowl at Robot, then backed up a few steps until he stood in front of the sales counter, his arms folded and immobile across his chest.

"You're out, man," Matt said. It was not clear whether he was talking about being out of jail or out of favour with Jordan Jordan.

"Ya," Robot replied. He was flushed with humiliation.

"There's no way Jordan..."

"I should have known," Robot said.

"I can put the word out for you," Matt said. "If you're looking for private students."

"Fuck that," Robot said.

"Seriously, man. You're the best."

"I got nothing right now. I got no studio to teach in. I don't even have an instrument."

54

"I wondered about that. Pretty sure I saw your LP on Kijiji a few months ago. That must have been your mom who did that, right? That must fucking suck."

"Any idea who bought it?"

Matt shook his head. "You could put up another ad. Looking for who bought it."

"I don't have the money for it now, anyway. You still living on Lemon Street? Over at The Old Hotel?"

Matt chuckled. "I'm living here now."

"No way."

Matt pointed at the ceiling. "You know the rooms behind the teaching studio? Jordan converted them to an apartment."

"So...he's signing your paycheque and then you're signing it right back to him for rent?"

"Rent's reasonable."

"Your landlord isn't."

"The apartment is brand new. New bathroom. New drywall. He even put in new windows. It's all freshly painted. This is the first apartment I've ever had that wasn't a dump."

There was a long silence that turned awkward as they realized there was no more point in Robot standing there.

As Robot turned toward the door, he noticed a rack of tiny instruments behind Matt. Like mini-guitars, some of them. It took Robot a moment to register: ukuleles.

"What are these?" Robot said, his curiosity piqued. Matt shot a quick look back at Jordan, who appeared to have chilled out about the situation and slunk back into his office. "Ukuleles," Matt said.

"Ya. I can see they're ukuleles. But *ukuleles*? And there's, like, a thousand of them."

Matt was a real musician, someone with a true love and excitement about all things musical, and he could not suppress an enthusiastic grin as he said: "It's crazy! They're flying out the door."

"Ukuleles?"

Matt shrugged.

The ukuleles on the rack looked like real instruments, not the plasticky toy ukuleles which were the only ukes Robot had ever seen before. These had real wood in them. And the frets and nut and tuning machines looked like the hardware used on real instruments.

"Come back some time it's quieter," Matt said. He raised his eyebrows and flipped his gaze in the direction of Jordan Jordan's office.

Out on the sidewalk in front of Jordan's Music, Robot stood for several stunned moments and felt complicated emotions surge through him. Anger. Guilt. Embarrassment. Fear. Had Jordan Jordan heard that he had been released from Springtown? Had he been standing by all day, steps from the door, waiting to block his entry? It was probably just a coincidence. Jordan had probably just happened to be standing near the door and noticed Robot on the other side of it.

Only a year ago he'd been Jordan's golden boy. His face had once been at the centre of the instructor board. If there was ever a photo for the newspaper, Jordan made sure Robot was in it. When some new gear came in: the flame top Schechters two years back, a new Boss Loop Station, Jordan liked to put a two- or three-minute demo video on the store's YouTube channel, and it was always Jordan in the foreground talking about the new gear. A brief history of the company that made the item, a few specs for the tech heads. Robot would be winding away at low volume in the background, the rack of hanging electrics behind him. In every video there came a moment where Jordan would step aside and say: "Here's the man they call the Robot, he'll show you what this rig can do."

Anyone who had ever stuck with the practice of a musical instrument beyond the fumbling first few hours could tell from Robot's demo videos that what they were seeing and hearing was not about a piece of gear they could buy. Musicianship, dedication, hours and years of practice: real musicians knew what that sounded like. All the same, Robot's demo videos had "moved a lot of product" in Jordan's words. People knew that money was not going to buy them Robot's skill with the Boss DD-3 delay unit. But if you were sixteen years old, sitting at home looking at the paycheque McDonald's had just deposited in your account on one Firefox tab, and on the other you were listening to the epic sounds of the Robot winding out like Hendrix, Van Halen, Yngwie Malmsteen, and Eric Clapton rolled into one, you might know what your hundred and twenty dollars could not buy. But it was plain and clear what it could.

———

THE PUBLIC LIBRARY WAS ONLY A FEW BLOCKS FROM JORDAN'S Music. It was a beautiful September day, a clear sky with a light breeze. The maples in this part of town were several hundred years old and towered above the two- and three-storey buildings. Their leaves shimmered golden green in the sun. None of the rank industrial smells of the town was present, and there was no trace of fall yet in the air, just the ripe scent of full-on summer. He caught a couple of wide-eyed and frightened looks on the sidewalk along the way. Several people craned their heads around quickly in cars that rode past. Three cars in a row full of teenagers went by just as he was arriving at the wide lawn in front of the library. There was a commotion at the sight of him. Someone shouted *murderer!* out the open window of a vehicle that had already gone a half-block past.

On the landing inside the main library door, he stopped and pretended to look at the tack board. There were posters for punk and metal shows, local indie band flyers with pastel artwork. Robot closed his eyes and gathered himself together. He felt like running for shelter, he felt like bursting out through the library doors and pelting home. But there was no shelter at home. He'd only have to deal with his mother there.

In the little square of old-school desktop computers between the magazines and the main entrance, it would only take a moment to log on to the internet, but he sat motionless in front of the screen for some time before he did so.

The internet had gone toxic on him before he'd been sent to Springtown. There was a video of his one-punch fight with Travis Cody Mancomb. There were comments about the video. There were videos about the comments, videos about the video, and videos about the videos about the comments.

When he finally clicked on the Jordan's Music YouTube channel, it was just as he'd expected: all of his videos had been deleted. In the year since his sentencing, only five new videos had been put up on the Jordan's Music channel, all of them two minutes in length, all of them featuring Jordan Jordan only. It was all acoustic guitar, all Jordan alone, by himself in front of his ancient video camera on a tripod in the centre of the guitar room floor. All the videos were the same: Jordan Jordan holding up a newly arrived guitar. Describing its tonewoods and cosmetic features, explaining some of the characteristics of its sound and playability. Then Jordan would play it himself for a half-minute or so. He played the same hokey sixties-style fingerpicking patterns that were already out of date when he was learning them twenty years ago. But he played them well and smoothly and his face took on the same juvenile aspect it always did when Jordan Jordan played guitar: smug self-confidence.

Robot sat back from the library computer monitor and let his gaze drift past the racks of newspapers and magazines to the light of the windows on the other side of the reading room. He felt ill and emptied out. He had worked at other jobs before his conviction. He was not even going to try to get those jobs back. He'd been nobody special there. And he had not expected to pick right up where he left off at Jordan's. He did not expect Jordan Jordan to feature his name and photo at the centre of the instructor board again, as it had been. He'd even expected to be taken down from the YouTube channel. These were all business decisions. But he was a good musician and a good music teacher. And he'd hoped that some of his former students would come back. He valued and respected music. Revered it, even. He hoped his students knew who he was. He'd made a grievous error. But music went beyond that. It was something awesome and powerful, something that put people in touch with what was best in themselves and in the universe.

And the truth was, he liked teaching music just as much as he liked playing. Sure, there was a lot of bullshit. There were kids who didn't practice; they were taking lessons to please their parents. There were cancellations. Even the ones who called too late and still had to pay were a pain. You had to be there and be prepared, regardless. It was a letdown when they didn't turn up.

But there was no better feeling than when a kid came in excited about some song or some riff. They had a chart they'd downloaded off the internet, or a half-baked tab sheet somebody who did not know what they were doing had posted. And they wanted him to help them play. They needed him. Half the time it was a simple trick: a double-stop bend, or a riff that required hammer-ons. But there was no better feeling than helping someone connect with and reach a musical goal. He liked breaking complex songs down into teachable components. Zeroing in on what chord changes would be most challenging. He liked entering into what he called *projects* with students. Difficult skills or challenging tunes that were going to require work.

The teaching at Jordan's took place upstairs. They could have let him in the back way. They didn't even have to advertise his name. It could be all word of mouth. There were so many things Jordan Jordan could have done aside from cutting him off like that.

As he was about to click away from the Jordan's Music YouTube page, he noticed a new link. There was a cartoonish icon of what might have been a guitar but obviously was meant to be a ukulele on the tab. And a box around the image said *Keep on Ukin*. He clicked through to the single video listed there.

The video began with Jordan Jordan front and centre, but he was not in the Jordan's Music guitar room. The National Association of Music Merchants logo was behind him. At his side was a rack of ukuleles identical to the one Robot had seen not an hour before. "This is Jordan Jordan from Jordan's Music. And today we're coming at you from NAMM, all the way down in Anaheim, California. This year at NAMM, everyone is talking ukulele. You heard that right. Ukulele. This right here," he put his hand on the ukulele rack, "is a display we know is going to be a big hit at Jordan's Music. Kaha Ukuleles from over in Eugene, Oregon. I was just talking to Jean Klempmann. She's the Kaha representative here at NAMM. And Jean is doing the order up right now. You can't see her over there on the other side of the camera. She's doing up our order for a Kaha display just like this. Coming to Jordan's Music soon. Kaha ukes are a good choice for beginners, and the entry-level instrument features real tonewoods and solid intonation, allowing beginners to grow into that great ukulele sound."

The camera moved in past Jordan to centre on the rack of ukuleles. There must have been a dozen or more instruments. There was an abrupt edit back to Jordan Jordan in the foreground. "Jean Klempmann just introduced me to her friend, ukulele virtuoso Ukulele Rick Hobart." The camera panned out and swivelled slightly to the right until there were two men in the shot.

Ukulele virtuoso, Robot thought. He snickered out loud in the library, then checked over his shoulders to make sure no one had heard. Leave it to Jordan Jordan. Robot had had the volume low at this point, the sound coming through the built-in speakers of the library desktop. But this Rick

Hobart had caught his attention, so he pulled his iPod out of his pocket, disconnected the earbuds, and plugged into the front of the computer. He adjusted the volume up now that only he could hear it.

"Now, Rick. The Kaha is not your regular instrument, is that right?" Jordan was saying.

"That's right, Jordan. I have several handmade ukuleles from some of the top ukulele luthiers in the world. And I don't like dwelling too long on money. We ukulele players tend to get misty-eyed and cranky if we think about money too much..."

Jordan Jordan laughed out loud and looked up at the camera.

"But I think it's safe to say that this Kaha in my hand here," Ukelele Rick held up a model that looked like solid mahogany, "this sweet little thing here is a fraction of what my high-end ukes cost."

"And how do they play?"

"Well," Ukulele Rick looked meditatively downward a moment and paused, "these little Kahas are an excellent choice for a beginner or intermediate player."

"Could you...ah..." Jordan motioned at Ukulele Rick's hands, where they clutched the ukulele in question.

Ukulele Rick took on a suddenly polished aspect. His words became the practiced patter of an experienced show-man. "I'm going to play a little tune here I wrote a while back. It's a sort of bluegrass instrumental number I call 'Cabbages for Balls.'"

"Cabbages...for...balls," Jordan repeated with uncertainty. He looked awkwardly at the camera.

"Now. There's a whole story that goes along with the

title. But...ah..." Ukulele Rick pointed at the video camera. "How much tape you got in that thing?"

Jordan stuck his head back into the shot and smiled at the camera. "Maybe you should just..."

"Maybe I should just shut up and do what I came here for."

The camera zoomed in closer. Jordan Jordan had disappeared from the shot. Ukulele Rick's eyes blinked hypnotically, and his knee moved tentatively with the tapping of his foot as he pulled the right tempo out of the air.

What followed was a musical experience that Robot was completely unprepared for. The first three minutes of "Cabbages for Balls" was a blast of sophisticated, urbanized, jazz-aware bluegrass that was bursting with raw energy and virtuosic bravado. Then at the three-minute mark, just when Robot thought Ukulele Rick had played himself out, there came an almost impossible tempo increase. The whole tune repeated at double the speed.

The low-tech camera did not do a good job of keeping up with Ukulele Rick's fingerwork. All the same, Robot could tell by the fingerings of some of the scales he flew through that he had to be using a guitar-like tuning. At least the three highest strings had to be tuned to intervals similar to guitar.

This was like nothing he had ever seen. The chord changes in the piece were slightly modified bluegrass changes. And the way Ukulele Rick's phrases sidled away from and then rubbed back up against the one and the five note was so clever and funny. It was set up to sound like straight-ahead bluegrass, but there were slick, dissonant notes thrown in here and there that said: *Look at me, I'm going to write a tune that you're going to think is a bluegrass tune, but guess what notes I'm going to throw in! Guess where I'm going to resolve this phrase! Guess what chord I'm going to throw in now!* This guy was doing the impossible. He was playing a tune that paid straight up homage to a whole genre of music while at the same time quietly giving the whole thing the finger. And he was doing it on a sixty-dollar shitbox of a ukulele.

Robot stood up from the library computer in such a state of elation that he almost forgot to log out. He stepped back, then forward again. The earbuds reached the end of their tether and popped out of his ears.

Once logged out, he turned and hurried for the library door. Outside, he moved faster. At first, he ran in the direction of his mother's house. Halfway there he did a one-eighty on the sidewalk, and ran back the other way.

He passed the library in a blur and came to a stop a few blocks later, on the sidewalk outside Jordan's Music. He rested a hand on the wood frame of the display window until he caught his breath. He could see the back of the ukulele rack, could make out the differences between some lighter and darker tonewoods on the backs and on the necks of some instruments.

Through the glass in the doorway, he could see that Jordan Jordan was out back, in his office. Bria was at the far end of the store, handing a woman a pamphlet Robot recognized as the Yamaha Keyboard model comparison sheet. Matt was behind the counter, digging guitar strings out of cardboard packing boxes and fitting them carefully into the squares in the display case where each belonged. Robot stayed back on the sidewalk, mostly hidden by the wooden post at the edge of the display window. As Matt was bending down for another handful of D'Addarios, Robot pushed the door open just to the point before it would set off the electric buzzer it was attached to, and squeezed into the store. He slid behind the ukulele rack, hunched down to make himself smaller, and perused the instruments from the reverse end.

To a skilled eye like Robot's, the back of an instrument revealed almost as much as the front. He was not one hundred percent sure what sort of tonewood a ukulele luthier might use, but these instruments seemed constructed a lot like guitars. The one closest to him looked like maple back and sides. Some of these woods seemed like mahogany. For under a hundred dollars, he was sure the backs and sides had to be laminate, not solid wood. And as guitar makers were doing, he'd bet the ukulele company was putting solid wood in the top of the instrument, where almost all the sound was generated.

At the top of the rack, a dark-grained tonewood caught his eye. He grasped the headstock and yoinked the instrument over to where he stood. A tag dangled from the strap peg at the bottom. On one side of the cream-coloured cardstock, handwritten with an extra-fine-tipped Sharpie in the weirdly angled writing Robot recognized as Jordan Jordan's, the price: $75. He could not help himself. He looked over his shoulder at the top rack of electric guitars. The tags twisted slowly in the currents of circulated air. The closest guitar to his Gibson LP Studio would be, he knew without looking at the tags, $750, $800. Minimum. Robot turned over the card that hung from the ukulele. It read: *Solid spruce top, rosewood back and sides*. Robot followed the grain lines in the spruce and saw how they continued over the lip of the wood at the soundhole: confirmation that this was indeed solid spruce.

The top had a nice glossy finish that would protect the wood in the long term from heavy strumming and picking and the dings any instrument got just from being played.

In his hands, the ukulele was feather-light. Compared to the feel of an electric or even an acoustic guitar, it was almost non-existent. He peeked through the instruments on the ukulele rack, where he could see that the room seemed to be empty at the moment. He flicked a fingernail against the spruce top, just below the bridge plate. It sounded a round, satisfying *pop*. He checked the open strings by plucking them gently, one at a time, with a corner of his thumb. The string closest to his face was of a lighter gauge than the one beside it. This would give the instrument a banjo-like sound. And there was very little sustain. But the thing was tuned very much like a guitar. What would have been the D string on the guitar was probably an A or a G on these short strings. He sharpened up the second string with the tuning peg and peeled back some of the sharpness in the first string.

With one finger on the second fret of that G or A string, he made a simple chord that would have been a big, ringing Em on guitar. The chord rang true, but died away almost immediately.

Using a thumb and forefinger to pluck, he tried a major scale, then a minor scale on open strings. Then did the same scales at the fifth fret. The intonation on this little thing was impeccable, and he was surprised. It was not so much poor tone that was the hallmark of a crappy instrument, but poor intonation. He plucked the open third string and listened to the sweet note quickly decay. He played an octave higher. The note decayed very fast, but sounded dead-on true to his ear. The notes above the twelfth fret were not true, but

66

they were close, and they were way the hell up the neck where you'd rarely play.

Overcome with enthusiasm, Robot forgot where he was, and that he was supposed to be hiding. He banged out the closest chords he could think of to "Seven Nation Army." And with his head down, looking at this mini music box in his hands, cute as a kazoo, he chuckled at the juxtaposition of the tune and the instrument. He picked out the first two bars of "Yankee Doodle," and feeling patriotic and hearing the humming, feedback-laced Big Sugar version in his head, he followed that up with a bit of "O Canada." When he got as far as the notes for *true patriot love*, he remembered the Joel Plaskett song and jangled out the chords, singing along in a low whisper: "Oh, my love, what have you done? Gone to the arms of another one..."

With his head still down, he became aware of a blue and white pair of Vans that walked into his field of vision. Shit. He'd totally forgotten himself. As he stood to his full height, an awkward four-note chord clanged out of the ukulele.

Matt's widened eyes passed from Robot to a space over Robot's shoulder.

"I thought I told you..." Jordan said when Robot turned around.

"I've got something for you, Jordan," Robot said. He thrust his hand into his front pocket and pulled out the five twenties, the polymer bills smooth and rubbery in his grip. Robot knew he could pretty well hypnotize Jordan with a handful of twenties. And his confidence gave him the nerve to say: "Are you going to kick me out before I buy this ukulele?"

He waited a long time in the silence that followed. The

angry look never left Jordan's face, but the man actually backed up a half step and Robot said: "I didn't think so." When Jordan stepped around behind the till to serve him, Robot said, "I'd rather Matt rang this through." Jordan straightened up. His face went blank. He looked at Matt and gave him a nod.

Matt came around behind the till and Robot put the ukulele on the counter. Jordan retreated in the direction of his office. His expression softened, but he stood in the doorway with his arms crossed.

Matt leaned in Robot's direction. "When I said come back when it's quieter, I meant..."

"Sorry, man," Robot said. "I know what you meant. I watched that Rick Hobart video."

"'Cabbages for Balls.'"

Robot shook his head. "Fuck. That guy..."

"I know," Matt said. "You can play these things. They're real. I always thought ukuleles were toys. Anyway...you picked the best instrument off the rack. I'm not surprised. You've got the ear." He reached under the counter and brought out a clear plastic bag with something black inside it. "Comes with a free gig bag," he said. He pointed at the case of guitar picks. "You get two complimentary picks with the purchase of a stringed instrument. I recommend you use what you're used to. But listen, now." Matt leaned in conspiratorially. "If you really want to learn to play this thing"—he raised his eyebrows significantly—"use your fingers," he glanced down at Robot's right hand, where the five twenties were still balled up unevenly.

"Try strumming with your index finger. Straight out. Like this." He showed Robot. "The sweet spot for strumming and picking is not the same as it is for guitar. Try where the neck joins the body."

Robot thought about that a moment. It might have taken him hours to break the guitar habit of strumming over the soundhole to figure that out on his own.

"Good tip," he said. "Thanks."

He chose two black Jim Dunlop picks, nylon. One millimetre thick. He plopped them on the counter and laid the twenties out beside them.

Matt had dug the ukulele's factory cardboard box out of the back room and was packing the instrument into it when Robot took the gig bag out of its plastic wrapper and unfolded it onto the counter. Two steel reinforcement bars were sewn into the back for support. The zippers were heavy-duty, military grade. The seams were all flawless and tight. The foam liner of the black ballistic nylon was lightweight and strong and covered with soft black microfiber.

"This gig bag is not a piece of shit," he said.

"No way, man," Matt said. "I've got this exact model myself and I've dragged that gig bag hell west and crooked. It holds up."

"Listen. Chuck the box. I'll take it out in the gig bag."

Matt placed the two picks in the front zippered pouch.

Robot looked uncomfortably around the room to make sure that what was about to happen was between him and Matt only.

"I did not mean to kill him," Robot said. "I did not mean to kill Gink. You know that, right?"

Matt lowered his gaze and appeared to be trembling slightly. "I hardly knew Gink. Nobody knew him, really. I guess he was a good guy," he said. "And so were you. So *are* you."

Robot slung the ukulele over his shoulder.

"I used to think life was music and music was life," Robot said. He backed away from the counter in preparation to head for the door. "But music is 99 percent practice, 1 percent performance."

Matt was silent for what seemed a long time.

"I told his mother I was sorry," Robot said. "I meant it."

—

AS ROBOT WALKED DOWN THE STREET WITH THE UKULELE IN ITS gig bag slung over his shoulder, a cold fear settled in his gut.

He'd had a chance to speak a year ago, at the end of his hearing. He'd pleaded guilty, so there was no need for an actual trial. And he'd used the opportunity to apologize to the family of Travis Cody Mancomb.

Mancomb's mother was thin and frail-looking. She appeared more frightened than angry as Robot spoke. She had an older son who lived out west and he stood beside her, his arm around her shoulders. That was everything Travis Cody Mancomb had for family. No father, no cousins. Nobody else to stand up for his memory in court.

As his release date had neared, Robot had wondered about contacting Mrs. Mancomb as part of his reintegration plan. He did not know what he wanted from contacting her. He pictured a moment less tensely public than what had happened in court.

He asked Tracey Melhart about the possibility of arranging a meeting or even a phone call. A few days later, Melhart reported that she'd been unable to make contact. A lawyer had told her he thought Mrs. Mancomb had moved out west.

He put the gig bag down on a rust-coloured picnic table

on the lawn in front of the library. The zipper made a satisfying sound as he peeled back the tab.

It took a moment to get the tuning set up right, but as soon as he did, he started a simple strum pattern, a 4/4 with a bit of a 2/4 feel to it. A reggae strum. As a percussive move, he dampened the strings with the four fingers of his left hand and let his right index sweep across the strings as he repositioned the damping fingers to a sweet spot all the way back at the nut. There was a crisp, responsive *chunk* to the strum now, and he settled into the rhythm. He kicked back and let the beat take over for itself. He closed his eyes and let his awareness move out to the trees nearby, at the edge of the library lawn. Birds he could not identify were stirring and grousing, giving each other shit. The wind came up and the quiet flutter of the leaves rose up over the birds a moment. Then the whooshing of cars as they passed on the street. He loosened up the damping of the strings and heard the edges of notes in them as they strained to begin singing. When he tightened up again, he felt the rhythm of the instrument's sound box against his ribs.

Without breaking the beat, his mind went searching for a chord he could play to this feel. He tried what would have been a Dm if he were playing guitar. But it was a bit tinny for the sound he wanted now. He fingered a chord of mostly open strings, what would have been an Em, then had a change of heart and added the note to make it major.

He played the major one chord for two beats, then switched to the minor two chord for two more. The most cliché reggae chord choices ever. But the quick turnaround of it, the satisfying little loop, sank calmingly through him.

He opened his eyes and remembered that he was in

front of the library. He kept playing and turned from the street, swung his feet to the other side of the picnic table so he faced the library door. There was a hint of slapback echo coming off the library wall and it gave him a warm feeling, as though he were playing with a partner.

He could do this, he thought. He could learn to play this thing and be proud of how he played it. Be satisfied even, maybe. He was not sure how this tiny instrument would fit in with a band or ensemble. But that was not in the cards now anyway. He'd played once, just before Gink's death, with the Jazz Kids, the best players in the school. And although he should have graduated in June, most of the Jazz Kids were a year younger. They'd just be starting their grade twelve year. Even back then he'd been foolish to think that musical relationship would last. Those Jazz Kids and he were just cut from different cloth. They were all polite middle-class kids whose lives were steered by their parents. And now he was a convicted killer.

He sat in front of the library for some time, lost in the music he was learning to make. He was thinking back to the Rick Hobart video, trying to reconstruct the licks of "Cabbages for Balls." The chord progression was simple. But he could not figure out the voicings Hobart had used.

"What the fuck is that? A mandolin?"

The smell of a bargain brand of cigarettes hit him before he looked up, and before his mind had fully registered who was talking to him, he was already packing the ukulele into the gig bag.

"Hey, hey, hey," the voice stayed in his ear as he walked quickly to the sidewalk. Scuffling footsteps followed. Fucking Lucas Shortt. The guy who thought it was cool to post a homicide on YouTube. Somehow, Robot now understood, Lucas Shortt had manipulated both him and Gink into a fight that neither of them had wanted. Shortt had not cared that the two people he'd been goading were actual people. They were like animals to him, trained monkeys he could make do what he wanted, like characters in a video game.

Lucas Shortt had insinuated himself and his mob of idiot followers into the lives of two people who did not want him in their lives. And now one of those people was dead. And the other one had been convicted of the killing. And what price had Lucas Shortt had to pay?

Robot did not know. He'd heard that Shortt and Suitjon, the camera guy, had both been suspended from school for the rest of the year. And that they had not gone back in September of last year, while Robot was in Springtown.

They'd been interviewed by police. Transcripts of those interviews appeared in Robot's own legal files. Had they been charged with anything? Had they ever stood trial? He did not know and he did not care. The biggest mistake of his life had resulted from his ever acknowledging they existed. He'd decided soon after his own arrest that he would not allow those fools any further room in his mind.

"So you're out," Shortt said. They'd reached the corner by the Scotiabank. The last thing Robot wanted was for Lucas Shortt to follow him to his house, so he turned to face him.

"Ya. I'm out," Robot said. "And I want to stay out. So get away from me." Shortt had a narrow face with big blue eyes. His hair was thick and wavy, and he had a couple of days' growth of stubble on his high cheeks. His cigarette was halfway smoked, but it seemed he'd given up on it and it burned away on its own in his hand.

"What's...what's that mean?" Shortt sneered.

"I'm staying the hell away from you," Robot said. "So you stay the hell away from me."

"You know it wasn't me, right? I mean, who put that video up. That was Suitjon. He had the account password. I never wanted that up there. I told him. I told him to break the camera. Put a nail through his iPhone. That's what I told him."

So many crazy emotions and thoughts were coursing through Robot's mind right now. Part of him was flashing back on the video that had been posted. Part of him was seeing from his own eyes as Gink went down. Part of him was crying in his room at Springtown, alone, under the covers of his bed, late at night when he hoped no one could hear.

"The whole thing was Suitjon's idea. The *whole* thing. The whole YouTube channel. The fight with Gink. Everything. I don't know why I let that bastard talk me into it."

Robot closed his eyes and tried hard to let Shortt's claim go without comment.

"You know what I think?" Shortt said. "I think you and I should go after the bastard, go after Suitjon. Seriously. I know where he lives."

The phrase *go after* went through Robot's body like a toothache on a sharpened stick. They were the exact words Shortt had used a year ago about Travis Cody Mancomb. *If I were you, I'd go after the bastard.*

He knew now that he had the power to kill a man. And he felt close to doing just that. With his heart gone crazy on him in his chest, he backed up against the stone front of the Scotiabank building, away from the big glass windows, conscious of staying out of sight. He hugged the ukulele to his chest loosely with both hands and closed his eyes.

"What are you doing?" Shortt said.

Robot heard Shortt's feet scuffing uncomfortably.

"Are you crazy?" Shortt said.

"Get away from me," Robot said. His eyes were still closed. The light of day fluttered against his lids. He whispered quietly enough that only Shortt could hear.

"What?" Shortt said, but Robot was certain Shortt had heard him.

"Get away from me. Get away from me," Robot whispered. He clamped his eyes tighter until the daylight beyond them was a yellow hint. "Get away from me. Get away from me. Get away from me. Get away from me." He said it until the sounds lost meaning, until several people must have passed in the street and wondered what the fuck. But he kept saying it until his mouth got dry and his jaw was tired and starting to clench up and become stiff.

When he opened his eyes, Lucas Shortt was gone.

6

FOUR MONTHS EARLIER: MAY

Trisha wants to remember this feeling. The warmth and the quiet contentment. She is propped at the end of Morganne's bed. Morganne has a weighted comforter, and even though the room is at a comfortable temperature, Trisha has it tucked around her body, its pressure like a reassuring hug. Across the room, Morganne is absorbed in drawing, black ink on the creamy paper of a sketchbook. From where Trisha is propped, half lying down, half sitting, she cannot see the image Morganne is working on. But she recognizes the deep tranquility of Morganne's posture. The slow sounds of Morganne's deep breaths as she sinks into her creative mode: Trisha gets her own vicarious tranquility from doing this. She loves and admires her friend's absorptive state. She envies Morganne's artistic side. She's always wanted to do something creative, like Morganne does. To draw or paint or play music or write poetry. But she can never seem to muster the focusing power. Her mind scatters off as soon as she tries to draw together its attentive faculties.

When Trisha gets away from Morganne, when she's back in her own dumpy room in her own dumpy house, over in the shitty neighbourhood she lives in, a mini-home park that doesn't even have a name (Morganne's house is in a subdivision called Hillcrest), it's easy for her to feel jealous or frustrated when she thinks about Morganne's ability to draw. But in the room with her friend, peace comes upon her when she watches Morganne this way. The line between their identities, hers and Morganne's, gets blurred. It feels as though it is she herself fussing over the lines on paper until they form a wobbly little collection of black squiggles on white.

Morganne mostly does not seem to mind Trisha's close attention as she draws. In the past, she's handed her a pen and a piece of paper and encouraged Trisha to try drawing for herself. And Trisha has tried to draw. Of course she has. But her fingers never seem in control of the pen. She lacks a sense of visual proportion. When she does a self-portrait, while looking at her IG profile pic, her nose always comes out too big. Her ears are too far down her head. Or else the portrait turns out fine, you can see a face in it, but it never looks like her.

Snugged beneath the weighted comforter, Trisha gets a glimpse of a square of sky through Morganne's bedroom window. A blue blurred grey-white with the thin markings of an overcast of cloud. The black branches of the maple trees like cracks in a broken plate. Small clusters of green finger out at the ends of branches, too far developed to be called buds, not yet the size and shape of leaves.

Three sleek blackbirds, two facing the window, one turned away, pivot their necks and scan Morganne's back-yard with the tiny black marbles of their eyes. At the foot of the bed, on the floor where Trisha cannot see her, is Morganne's cousin Becky. She was lying on her back with her cellphone a few centimetres from her face the last time Trisha had the energy to raise her head and look, swiping an index finger up and up and up as she scrolled through social media.

"Fuck around, Trisha," Morganne says suddenly. Her voice is slow and dreamy. *Fuck around* is Becky's saying. And Morganne is using it to make fun of Becky. It's the first part of a two-part admonishment: *Fuck around and you'll be laying around.* Everyone else says *Fuck around and find out,* but Becky is like that, like she's from somewhere else where they say and do everything different. Trisha can tell from Morganne's voice that she's sort of joking when she threatens her with that phrase. She's expressing mild annoyance that Trisha is watching her so closely. Morganne is capable, though, of saying *fuck around* in a way that makes it clear she means business. Becky, on the other hand, is the least intimidating person ever. She says *fuck around* and Morganne and Trisha just laugh.

"I wish I could draw like you can," Trisha says.

"I used to wish I could draw. Then I just started doing it," says Morganne. "And you know what? I couldn't draw. Not at first. But I kept trying."

Morganne leans over her desk, all her attention on the page in front of her as she speaks. On the spare, uncluttered surface of the desk are her two most important sketchbooks. The little one that fits into the front pocket of her backpack and that contains only her collection of funky female figures that Morganne herself calls *Girly Girls,* but that Trisha calls *The Beckys* because she says, and Morganne and Becky agree, that the drawings look a lot like Becky. The other, bigger book, contains more. More variety. Sillier doodles. Cartoon sketches of almost nude pics from Kim Kardashian's Instagram. Serious pen and ink portraits of her friends.

Drawings from the Instagram accounts of the cutest guys at their school. Reproductions of pictures from the accounts of Malluvain, Instagrim, and WatercolourBrother, three of her favourite Instagram artists. While she sketches away in one book or the other with her left hand, she's got her phone on the right. She looks intently at whatever she is sketching, focusing for long minutes. Her breaths more and more shallow and infrequent until she looks as though she might pass out. Then she sits up, looks at the image on her phone, scans the room, pulls in several big breaths in a row.

"Get off Tinder," Trisha says, mocking the obsessive way Morganne is regarding her phone right now. She laughs, rolls onto her side, scans the floor for one of Morganne's old stuffies, and throws it at her friend. A plush Dora the Explorer, the size of two of Trisha's own fists.

Morganne is a serious athlete with wicked reflexes. She toggles her neck to the right and the stuffed Dora misses her completely, bounces off the whiteboard on the wall above the desk.

"I'm not on Tinder! Fuck! What am I, that much of a loser?!" Morganne laughs and wags her head mockingly as she speaks. And she is not on Tinder. Trisha can see it clearly from where she is, see it right between her own waggly feet at the end of Morganne's bed.

But Becky is totally on Tinder. Both Morganne and Trisha know it. And Becky knows they know. She has not been trying to hide it. She's on the floor at the foot of Morganne's bed. She's got a big cushion under her that she brought in from the living room. And she's backed into a corner and mostly out of sight of Morganne or Trisha. She's got an ancient iPhone, the screen scrawled with cracks that chunk the images on it into uneven and unnameable shapes. A few of the smaller screen chunks have gone permanently black. Becky is holding the phone in both hands, with the screen a few inches from her face. She's got Tinder and Snapchat going. She's switching back and forth between the two. She's doing ironic duckface selfies to her friends on Snapchat, writing messages on the screen by typing with both thumbs. She sent Trisha one, from across the room, not even ten minutes ago. Her teeth were bared in that shot. Her eyes wide open and crazy looking. *Fuck this is boring* was the message she'd typed across it in the text box.

Trisha can tell when Becky is on Tinder. She'll laugh. She'll swipe one way, then the other. She'll say little phrases out loud, like, "yeah right" in response to what some guy says about himself. Or, in a deeper voice: "Hmm. He's cute."

Trisha loves it at Morganne's house. It's the only friend's house she ever gets invited to that is not ratchet. Not even a little bit. It's in a small, fancy subdivision outside of town. There are only four or five streets in the Hillcrest neighbourhood and only a couple of dozen houses. But the yards are all big and spacious with shrubs that have raised beds mulched with bark chips. The driveways in Hillcrest are paved. Every house has a two-car garage. Morganne's has garage doors with remote openers that work. Trisha has seen them in action herself, has stood in Morganne's living room, looked out the big front window, and watched Morganne's mom reach up to the visor to press the button, the big door rolling instantly back on its overhead runners.

Morganne has grown up with a strong connection to her Mi'kmaw heritage. She has a print on the wall beside her door that she calls "Mi'kmaw Butterfly," a whimsical, bow tie–shaped figure outlined in squiggly black, by an artist named Alan Syliboy. The colours are bright, cheerful yellows and reds. Beside the print is a small poster from a mawio'mi she went to down on the south shore last year at the start of the summer.

Morganne's dad is a lawyer. He works for the band council at Running Brook First Nation, about twenty kilometres from the town that Hillcrest borders. He grew up in Running Brook. And Morganne says he is the first member of the Running Brook community to graduate from law school.

Morganne's mom is white. And Trisha always gets the sense that it was the mom's idea for the family to move away from Running Brook, where they used to live. No one has ever said so in front of her, but it was the way everyone in the room went quiet that one time Trisha asked why they'd moved that made her think it was about the mom. The looks that went from Morganne to her dad and back. The mom did not raise her eyes to get a look from anyone.

Morganne never calls her mom white. When anyone asks about her family, she says, "My dad's a Mi'kmaw warrior lawyer and my mom's an Amazonian princess." When they were little, Trisha thought this was actually true, that Morganne's mom was an actual princess. She carried herself like one: tall and graceful and self-possessed. One day, just a year or so ago, Trisha Googled *Amazonian princess* and realized this could not be. There was no such thing as an Amazonian princess. But Morganne's mom is big. She is way over six feet tall and has wide shoulders and muscular arms. On a hot day the previous summer when Trisha and Morganne were sitting on Morganne's back deck, the mom walked by in a pair of short shorts. Morganne watched

Trisha checking out her mom's massive quads on the way by. "Mom never skips leg day," Morganne said when her mom got around the corner to the driveway. She was an athlete when she was young. She set a record for junior high girls shot put that, according to Morganne, no one has yet beaten. She went to college in the US on a basketball scholarship, and her job had something to do with girls in sports. Development of something or other. For the province.

Morganne is big like her mother. At sixteen, she is six feet tall. She throws javelin. She's a starter at front court for her volleyball teams: varsity and club. "Have you seen this girl's vertical?" Morganne's volleyball friends say about her. Trisha is not exactly sure she knows what that means, but she thinks it probably has to do with jumping. There's a university volleyball coach in New Brunswick who has already scouted her. He makes a point of seeing her play a couple of times through club season. He gave her a pamphlet on how to workout for volleyball over the summer. The pamphlet is stuck to the whiteboard over Morganne's desk with a blue plastic magnet the size of a loonie.

Becky is Morganne's cousin on her mother's side. She's a white girl, like Trisha, as far as Trisha can tell. She's been living at Morganne's house for the last year. Her family lives not far away. Moving to Morganne's house did not require changing schools. But nobody ever talks about why she moved in with Morganne. "My family has issues," Becky says now and then, especially after she gets a text from her mom. One time, when Becky's mom came to Morganne's house while Trisha was there, Becky left the basement TV room to meet her mom in the kitchen. Morganne and Trisha had stayed downstairs. They were halfway through a crazy tense episode of *Riverdale*. After Becky had left the room, they could hear her mom's voice from the kitchen upstairs. Morganne made a bottle of alcohol gesture with her thumb toward her mouth. But when Trisha said: "What? Really?" Morganne had shut right up and pretended she had not done the gesture at all.

Becky has her down days, days when she does not want to get out of bed and barely manages to drag herself through the school day in a slump. She has a dark, heather grey hoodie with the hood part all stretched out and she pulls that up over her head, pulls the sides of the hood forward and tightens up the drawstring so all anyone can see is a dark O where her face should be. Half the school thinks this is hilarious and the other half thinks it is annoying.

Some days she is loud and energetic and full of a scary, edgy sort of life force. And you never know which Becky you'll be getting from one day to the next. One day Trisha and Morganne will have to help Becky get her butt out of the chair in the cafeteria and down the hallway to her first class after lunch. The next day they will almost get into a fist fight with half a dozen people because Becky is running through the halls of school at lunch squirting every couple she sees making out with a big yellow squirt gun from the Dollar Store, Trisha and Morganne running behind her, laughing and trying half-heartedly to stop her.

And Becky will just up and leave school sometimes. In the middle of the day. Sometimes she posts about it beforehand in her group chat with Trisha and Morganne. *Getting out of this place rn.* And then they will not see her again for the rest of the day.

Sometimes she'll walk out in the middle of a class and not even say anything.

Most of the time Trisha has no idea where Becky goes when she peaces out like that, and she doubts Morganne does either. Trisha and Morganne might stay in the cafeteria a few extra minutes to get Morganne's cousin off to class or rush through the school to try to keep her out of trouble, but there is no way Morganne or Trisha are leaving the school building during the school day, no matter what Becky might be up to. That's not the kind of students they are.

Trisha understands that it's school that brings her and Morganne together, even though their backgrounds are so different.

She feels relaxed and happy at Morganne's house. The three girls can come here like this. Get off the school bus on a Friday when Morganne does not have a volleyball tournament. And they can watch something stupid on Netflix. Some low-budget movie with giant sea creatures in it that makes no sense. And they can take a bag of cherries from the fridge and Morganne can rinse the whole bag at the sink and bring them back to her room with a bowl to spit seeds in and a couple of napkins and Trisha can just tell that Morganne intends the three of them to eat the whole bag of cherries and Trisha knows Morganne has no idea that this is twelve dollars' worth of cherries or what twelve dollars' worth of cherries even means. Nobody back in the mini-home park is eating twelve dollars' worth of cherries in an afternoon just because they're bored.

There is a comforter on Morganne's bed that actually comforts, and the bed smells like Tide Plus Sport laundry detergent. And even though the bed and the comforter are soft and Trisha loves the floaty way she sinks into it, the shell of the comforter has a stiffness, a crispness to it that Trisha treasures against her skin. When she lies on Morganne's bed, she likes to slither a bit against that crispness, feel it brush against her cheek, her bare arms, her lower legs when she is in shorts.

She and Morganne are both in shorts today, and both wearing grey athletic boy's cut T-shirts. Becky was wearing the exact same combination when she came into the room. She'd changed into the shorts and top right after they'd got off the school bus. But she took one look at Trisha and Morganne and moaned, "Jesus, you guys. You can't wear what I'm wearing!"

Trisha laughed.

"We're not wearing what you're wearing," Morganne said. "You're wearing what we're wearing."

"You two are lesbian twins or something," Becky said. And Trisha laughed even more. But she felt nervous. She loved Morganne so much and did not want anything to come between them, to change their relationship at all. And if they were going to be mocked and called lesbians because of what they wore, that could mess everything up.

In the end, Becky had gone back to her room and changed into a pair of knockoff Lululemon pants and a white T-shirt.

Trisha hates the way her shorts hang loose on her hips and down over her thighs. She has hardly any chest at all, and even when she sits up straight, the ends of her boobs barely manage to poke out against her T-shirts. She envies the completeness of Morganne's body. Her hips round out the backside of her real Lulu shorts. Her thighs are strongly muscled and curve outward, pushing against the legs of the shorts, filling them out. Trisha's shorts hang away from her body. Last year, when thigh gaps were a thing, everybody she knew said they envied her thigh gap. *I'm jelly*, they commented on Instagram butt pics. *You are my thigh goals.* People she didn't even know. She'd get over a hundred likes. But she still hated her bony butt.

In the mirror, the cuffs of the shorts legs jut out square and boxy from her thighs. The shorts hang away from her flesh and shape her silhouette, turn her butt into a rectangle. Morganne's body shapes the shorts she wears. Her silhouette in shorts is the same as her shape without them.

Sometimes Trisha wonders if she might actually be a lesbian. It seems like she is obsessed with the bodies of other girls. Why is she even looking at Morganne's butt? When she thinks about why, it never seems as though she wants to touch her friend. Not in that way. She does not long to hold or caress Morganne. It seems mostly, at times like this when she's prone to get overcome with emotion, that she longs to *be* Morganne. She wants to have the long and shapely legs. She wants the killer vertical that is the envy of the volleyball team. She wants the two parents with professional jobs, the house in Hillcrest. The father who is a Mi'kmaw warrior lawyer. The mother who is an Amazonian princess.

The cherries are long since eaten. The fleshy pits lie damp and clinging to each other in a bleeding clump in a white bowl that Morganne has pushed back to the far right desk corner. Three napkins, marked with the juice from the girls' drenched lips, are squeezed into slowly loosening balls on top.

A bowl on the opposite corner of the desk contains a few dark crumbs that are the remainder of a cinnamon and honey facemask that Becky had made from instructions on some YouTube account she followed. She'd been stuffed into her little corner at the foot of the bed for a long time, quietly staring down into her phone. Then suddenly she got up and rushed out into the kitchen where they could hear her clanking around. When she came back, her face was covered with a thick layer of brown goop, two white circles around her eyes. She was carrying a bowl of the same mush she had on her face. A smell like fresh baking filled the room.

"What the hell, Becky," Morganne said. "Nice blackface. How are you enjoying your new racism?"

Trisha laughed.

"You guys. You totally have to try this," Becky said.

"Try racism?" Morganne said. "No thanks!"

"What is it?" Trisha asked.

"It's a cinnamon honey face mask. It's, like, calming. It's cleansing. It'll make you feel amazing."

"You don't seem all that calm," Trisha said.

"Or all that clean!" said Morganne.

"But I do feel amazing," Becky said.

"Is this from YouTube?" Trisha asked.

Becky nodded.

"Is this from the girl you're in love with? The girl who smokes weed and does yoga in the nude?"

Trisha could see that Becky was getting tired of Morganne's sarcasm. "I'll try it," she said, and Becky approached her with the bowl.

In the end, Morganne tried Becky's face mask, too. She even admitted that it felt amazing, just like Becky said.

———

MORGANNE HAS SETTLED IN DEEP TO A LONG, MEDITATIVE SES-
sion of sketching in her larger book. She has a printed photo
flat on the desk's surface before her. It's a shot she took
herself over a year ago. The rocks and water at Peggys Cove
in the background. The flowers of several blossoming weeds,
growing straight up from the rocks in the foreground. This is
one thing she likes to do: scroll through some old Instagram
pics of her own, screenshot the whole thing, Instagram logo,
frame, hearted "like" numbers and all. Plug the phone into
the photo print machine at Superstore and make an actual
paper copy of a photo for herself to sketch from.

Morganne looks calm and peaceful now, but Trisha
knows she is capable of using her creativity to stir up trouble,
too. She sometimes calls herself "Stalker Extraordinaire"
because she has an uncanny way of accessing other people's
phone passwords and even their social media login info.
Once she secretly got into Becky's phone and drew a careful
detailed sketch of a dick pic some creep had sent Becky on
Tinder, including the gross comment. She left it out where
Becky could find it, but it took days for Becky to realize
what it was.

That caused turmoil, a noisy, angry spat between
Morganne and Becky that went on for most of a week and
was an exception to the peacefulness that Trisha associated
with Morganne's artwork.

As she sketches, Morganne focuses on the photo, then on
the sketch. Back to the photo. Back to the page. And for most
of the late afternoon, Trisha has watched her, just as intently,
from the bed. They've all washed off their face masks by now,
but there are little cinnamon crumbs left over from it that
cling to Morganne's cheeks. And Trisha's eyes still burn a

little from the cinnamon. But watching Morganne perform these meditative actions, the act of watching becomes meditative. Morganne's breaths become slower, more deliberate. All the restlessness falls away from her as she clarifies the image she is working on.

Trisha's breaths, too, become slower and more deliberate. Her eyelids droop and she blinks lazily in an attempt to stay awake. She longs to do something creative, just like Morganne. She longs to do it so unselfconsciously, in a manner that seems as natural as breathing. She feels as though, if she lies close to Morganne when she's drawing, if she watches carefully and asks the right questions, maybe she can learn to express herself in some artistic way.

Becky is slumped over at the foot of the bed. She's sleeping and then she's awake. When she's asleep, she snores in a low, quiet growl that, if she picks up on it, Morganne will imitate as she draws.

Zert. Zert. Trisha's phone buzzes against her side. She digs it out from under her and sees the notification. Her mom has texted. *Hey Pattycakes. Just checking in. Still at Morganne's?* Duh. Where does her mom think she is? She told her she was going on the bus to Morganne's after school.

"Tell me what you're thinking when you're doing this," Trisha says to Morganne. She puts the phone back between her side and the mattress.

"When I'm imitating Becky?" Morganne says. She does not turn around. She does not pause in her actions of looking at the photo then turning her eye and her pen back to the page in her sketchbook.

Trisha does not want to honour silliness right now. She's asked a serious question, and she'll wait for a serious answer.

After a long pause, Morganne asks, "Doing what?"

"I want to know...what...what goes on in your head when you're sketching. When you're drawing. What are you thinking about?"

Morganne's left hand comes to a stop for a moment. She looks up from the page, but most of her gaze is turned away from Trisha. She's facing the other way. Her head tilts back and to the side. She looks up, high on the wall of her bedroom, almost to the ceiling. Her head pivots suddenly and she looks quietly at Trisha. Then she hunches back over the paper. Her left hand begins moving again before she speaks. She makes a couple of short marks with her pen, says: "I'm not sure. I'm not sure I'm thinking at all. Either drawing is not about thinking or else it's about a kind of thinking you do without words. It's like. When you look at something in everyday life. You just sort of partially see it. You see, like, the thing for what you need it for. *Oh, a cup! I know what that's for. I'm going to make tea in it.* So you don't really see the thing for what it is. You're not thinking about the thing. You're thinking about yourself. It's like. Drawing. When you draw the cup. You're not using it for anything. You're drawing it. It's like you're breaking down the barrier between yourself and the outside world."

Morganne turns all the way around in her chair. The steel and plastic in the chair make a straining, creaking noise as she does so. She looks at Trisha with a sort of shocked surprise. Her eyes are wider than usual. There is a lopsided smile starting to form in the lines around her mouth. A cinnamon face mask crumb falls from her chin to her shirt, but she does not notice it.

"Fuck," Trisha says. "That's deep. Seriously."

"I know!" Morganne says. Her voice is high-pitched with excitement. "I just blew my own mind over here!"

Trisha feels her ab muscles tightening up with laughter and she curls up around them and closes her eyes.

Becky starts awake when their laughter gets loud. "Fuck around, you guys," she shouts. But it's all groggy and slurred. And Morganne and Trisha just start laughing harder.

"Fuzza wuzza la la!" Morganne says in an exaggerated imitation of what Becky just said. She reaches for the stuffy Dora they'd been throwing earlier and catches the lip of the cherry pit bowl. Pits and napkins get launched in a spinning, disintegrating blob halfway across the room. A fragment of the blob plummets downward to where Becky is lying.

"Fuck! Around!" Becky protests. "What is this! It's all over me!"

"It's a totally cleansing face mask!" Morganne says. She and Trisha are laughing so hard now that Trisha almost feels like she's going to throw up.

"Aw! Fuck! Look at this mess, now!" Becky says. But she's so lazy and chilled out that she does not move.

Morganne throws the stuffy Dora at Trisha and Trisha can't get her hand up in time. It gets her full on the cheek. Morganne threw it with enough force that it sort of hurts. "Ow! Fuck off!" Trisha yells. "Dora's fingers just got me in the—"

"Swiper! No swiping!" Morganne yells and they both lose it again laughing. In their present context the words are complete nonsense, but it is something they both remember from watching Dora when they were little, so it seems hilarious.

"Fuck! That fucking Dora is a loud-mouthed bitch!" Trisha says. "Think about it! What a pain in the ass!" Morganne comes over to the bed to try to find Dora to throw again, but collapses with laughter. Her head bounces off the edge of the mattress on the way down. "Ow! Ow, my head!" she yells and she slumps to the floor, rolls away from the bed and clutches at her stomach as the laughter takes her.

When Morganne stops laughing she lies on her back in the centre of the bedroom floor. As far as Trisha can tell, Morganne has her eyes open and stares straight up at the ceiling, blinking.

Trisha is lying on Morganne's bed. She's on her stomach, her arms down against her sides. Her face is turned so she can see Morganne lying on the floor, her chest rising and falling with her breathing. She cannot see Becky, but she can hear her, breathing deeply at the foot of the bed, seemingly about to drift off again to sleep. Trisha can see the desk. The whiteboard. She can see both sketchbooks, square bumps on the top of the desk. She cannot see what's drawn there. She'd have to get up for that.

When she closes her eyes, she can smell the laundry detergent in the bedding. She can smell Morganne's shampoo. There is the smell of cinnamon from her own face. She notices some red blotches on the surface of the whiteboard above the desk. The cherries splashed up higher than she would have thought.

She falls asleep and in an instant starts awake. She hears Morganne breathing deeply. So deeply. So evenly. She must be sleeping, too. And then she drifts away.

They are all so happy, that afternoon at Morganne's house. Full of expensive cherries, relaxed from drawing, from Becky's cleansing face mask, and from watching a best friend draw. Worn out with laughter and with the peacefulness that comes from knowing you have friends.

7

TWELVE MONTHS EARLIER: MAY

I t is the trumpet player. The skinny kid with the wild hair. The one who has *Shut Up* across the front of every shirt he owns. He is the one who approaches Robot about jamming with the Jazz Kids. Robot is sure the invitation is based on a video he did for the Jordan's Music YouTube channel, a tricky Tal Farlow tune on which he played chords exclusively.

The day after that video goes up, Trumpet Boy stops Robot as they pass each other in the hall.

"Do you know how to play quietly?" Trumpet Boy says.

They are headed in opposite directions outside a Bio lab. Robot can smell formaldehyde drifting out the lab door. "A girl fainted over her fetal pig," someone in front of him says. And the reply from behind him: "LOL."

Robot does not understand at first that Trumpet Boy is speaking to him. He keeps walking.

Trumpet Boy follows him. "Do you know how to play quietly?" he says again. The break between classes is short, and the hallways are crammed with people pushing their way through in both directions.

"What?" Robot says when it registers he is being addressed.

"Do you know how to play quietly?" says Trumpet Boy. It is the third time he's uttered the phrase, but he has not varied his delivery at all. Same volume. Same deadpan tone.

"What is this?" Robot says. They are stopped at a T-intersection with a stairway to the side. Robot is set to go in one direction, Trumpet Boy in the other. People are swirling about them. "Are you talking about playing guitar?"

"Most guitar players do not know how to play quietly."

Robot rolls his eyes. "There are two volume controls. One on the guitar, one on the amp. You turn one or both of those down. Boom! You're playing quietly."

"Have you played this way?"

"With the volume down?"

Trumpet Boy nods.

"I've tried it a few times. I didn't really like it. I didn't see the point." Robot cracks a grin at Trumpet Boy that does not get returned.

"Could you do it consistently. Upon request. As required by context?"

Though nothing in Trumpet Boy's demeanour indicates he is joking, Robot laughs out loud. "What is this?" he says.

"Here," Trumpet Boy says. "Come to this address. Tonight at 7 P.M. Bring your guitar and a patch cord. We've got an amp you can use. We'll be in the garage. Use the side door."

Trumpet Boy hands Robot a piece of paper with an address on it. It is a perfect quarter of a sheet of loose-leaf, torn with great care along an impossibly straight edge: *56 Wren Crescent.*

When Robot looks up from the paper, Trumpet Boy is gone; he's slipped off down the hallway in whatever direction he was headed to begin with. Robot folds the paper twice and shoves it down into his left jeans pocket. Before Robot has a chance to puzzle over his encounter with Trumpet Boy, he hears a voice that goes through him like an arrow.

"I guess you don't mind people talking shit about you." A stale smell of bargain cigarettes.

Lucas Shortt has a head of thick, wavy black hair, just long enough on top to comb sideways, trimmed short over his ears. He's got a prominent jaw and a square mouth that, when he smiles his studied smile, reveals perfectly straight, white teeth.

Shortt's voice is smooth, with an edge of insistence. It gets into Robot's head like a wasp in a bottle, bumping angrily against the insides of his skull. Trying to ignore it is like trying to ignore a loaded pistol.

"I told you. I don't care about fucking Gink," Robot says. "Now get away from me."

And it's never only Shortt. He either comes seeking out Robot with an entourage already assembled, or else he attracts an instant grinning cadre whose faces reflect and encircle Shortt's as he speaks, like a clown face in a kaleidoscope. The closest face to Shortt's today is the sweaty, narrow face of the kid everyone calls Suitjon. His upper lip is dark with what he's doubtless hoped would be a moustache, but that is mostly just a fuzzy, darkened lip. His hair is brown and shaggy, but even though he cannot be more than seventeen years old, it is already thinning quite noticeably on top.

"Gink is shit-talking you, Robot," someone says. It is not Lucas Shortt. Robot is looking right at *him*. It does not appear to be Suitjon, either. Who are these assholes even?

Up comes Suitjon's camera. It's an old iPhone mounted to some sort of film-schooly rig. It's got a black handle that extends a fist-width below it. An external mic that juts up a short distance over the top of the phone. Suitjon is not supposed to be using it on school property. He's been

warned. Everyone knows that. Robot looks around and realizes suddenly where they've managed to surround him. He's
just past the T-intersection that goes down to the cafeteria.
There is a security camera blind spot right here.

"Is there a fight?" Robot hears a voice say. It's what
people think when they see Lucas Shortt and Suitjon with
his camera.

Fuck. Please don't let Gink be here, Robot thinks. His
pulse is throbbing in his head. The crowd, almost exclusively
boys, is jostling and restless. "Fight." He hears several
people saying the word in anticipation. "Are these the guys
from *Prank Fights?*" someone asks in the crowd. If there's
an answer, Robot does not hear it. On top of the fear and
anger, he's got another layer: shame. As he scans the crowd
for the face of Gink, the kid Lucas Shortt has been trying for
weeks to goad him into fighting, he knows his panic must
seem like fear to the kids watching him. It is fear.

Like a professional TV reporter, Lucas Shortt turns
quickly so his back is to Robot. "Make sure you get us both
in the shot," he says to Suitjon. "Here we are in the hallway,
and the tension building up between these two is rising. A
fight seems inevitable. Smash that subscribe button. You
do not want to miss this when it happens."

—

WHEN ROBOT GETS HOME FROM SCHOOL, HIS MOTHER IS FAR
gone drunk. She's in the kitchen with one of the gross men
who come over almost every day with a bottle.

This guy is bald, the skin on the top of his head an
unnatural white above the horseshoe of short brown hair

that rings it. He's wearing a dirty white T-shirt tucked into a pair of cheap-looking black dress pants. Whether the shirt and pants have ever fit him is unclear. His back is turned toward the living room when Robot comes in, and he is so skinny that he does not have a noticeable waistline or discernible buttocks beneath the bunched up folds of his clothing where the belt, high above his waist, cinches the fabric close to his skin. Robot does not want to think about what his mother is doing with these men, the shift-like rotation of them that turns up at their door. But as far as he knows, she's got very little money and the forties of gin or vodka or rum they show up with are not cheap.

Both of the people in the kitchen are deeply intoxicated and they do not even seem to have registered that Robot has come home. They face each other across the filthy table. His mother's head rests heavily against her own hand. Her elbow is held up by the table. The man was standing unsteadily when Robot came in. Wavering back and forth like a mirage. But he's made his way to a seat now, his arms crossed low on his chest, his back curved forward, resting against the chairback. They are talking to each other. Drunkenly. Angrily. Robot has trained himself to block out his mother's words when her voice descends that deeply into drunkenness.

He and his mother do not have their own Wi-Fi. That was one of the first things to go as his mother's drinking ramped up. But there is some neighbour, he's not even sure they're in the same building, whose unfortunate password choice, "password," has enabled Robot to access between two and three bars of Wi-Fi from just about anywhere in the apartment. He sits on his bed, with the door closed between himself and the drunks in the kitchen, and opens his shitty old Acer laptop. Because of the broken hinge, when he opens the screen, he has to keep one hand in place so the device does not slowly close on itself. There they are: three out of four Wi-Fi bands in the lower right corner of the screen.

The first thing he does is check the video he put up on the Jordan's Music page the day before. Three hundred and fifty views. Pretty good for barely twenty-four hours. Down at the thumbs-up icon, where likes are registered, there are only four, and when he checks: sure enough, one of them is from The Shut Up Shirts, Trumpet Boy's account. All the flashy fingerwork he's posted before—Van Halen licks; Thunderstruck intro; the massive, lightning-fast arpeggios he'd done while demonstrating a wah-delay combination—the Jazz Kids were apparently unimpressed by that. But the very first time he makes a chord-based post, that's what gets their attention.

He has to Google Maps the address. Wren Crescent is not in town, he's sure of that. He'd have heard of it.

Shit. Fifty-minute walk from Lemon Street. Carrying his guitar. It's across the tracks, across the river. Way over in what the map made look like a cluster of blossoms. Three circular central drives, each ringed with three or four petal-like crescents.

He closes the loose little bundle of the Acer and lies back on the bed. The more he thinks about his conversation with Trumpet Boy, the more the whole exchange angers him. The kid did not ask if he was interested in coming to jam. He just assumed he could snap his fingers and Robot would come running. Like a sucker. Even though none of these snobby Jazz Kids ever spoke to him. Even though... He sits up and silently gives the finger to the closed laptop. He holds his hand up like that for a good fifteen seconds, in futile and satisfying defiance.

He tries to imagine what it would feel like not to go. To let seven o'clock come rolling around and to be here still, holed up in this shitty room in this shitty apartment, two drunken adults on the other side of the wall, inching themselves closer by the minute to matching comas.

But it is unimaginable. Trumpet Boy knows there is no way he is going to pass up a chance to jam with the best players in the school.

He takes his phone out of his jeans pocket and thumbs it awake. His notifications have blown up. They roll down the screen in a frightening flash. *You have 126 new messages.*

Come out and play, motherfucker.

Gink says you're a pussy.

Gink is talking shit about you.

You better do something about Gink.

You are a chickenshit.

You are such a pathetic piece of shit.

Fuck. Who gave his fucking number to these assholes?

8

SEPTEMBER

It did not take Sam long to find a favourite place in her new school. There was a carrel desk at the end of a magazine shelf. It was invisible from everywhere in the library except the whiteboard chart where the librarian filled out bookings for the computer lab. There was a big window beside the carrel that looked out from the front of the school, across the salt marsh and the dyke on the river, and out into the green of the trees that rose into the sky on the eastern horizon. She had one free period a day, plus lunch. And she almost always spent all that time here, tucked out of sight. She'd settle in, spread out her books, do her homework, listen to her brother's nineties hits playlist on her iPod, and stare out across the landscape.

Her cellphone plan was texting and calling only. And only her mother and Uncle Ray had the number. She'd written it on a slip of paper before she left the Valley and told her mother to give it to Morganne's mom. But so far she had not heard a thing from Morganne or Morganne's mom. And though she longed to hear her friend's voice, or even to see her name come up in her notifications after a text, she also knew that not hearing anything was sort of a good sign, considering what had come back to her about Becky.

Uncle Ray only checked in if she did not come directly home from school. That had only happened once or twice so far. She heard from her mother several times a day. Her mother's idea of settling into the new school was making friends. *RU making NE friends?* was a text her mom's phone was probably giving her as a one-push option any time she typed in an "r" by now. And Sam was not going to lie. She was not making friends. She was not making acquaintances. She was walking with her head down in the hallways and she had her eyes glued to her own desk in class, so she was not even making eye contact with anyone, let alone getting to know them.

Friends were not what she needed right now. What she needed was some time to herself. She felt as though she'd been dropped from a great height and shattered into many pieces. She was gluing herself back together now. Going to school, learning a few guitar chords, helping Uncle Ray around the house, staying in touch with her mother, this was everything she could handle while the glue was setting. But she felt stronger day by day. She did not need people to help her with that. People were what had broken her. Putting herself back together she could do on her own.

There were charges that had been laid. More to come, Maureen, the trauma worker, had said. Sam would be called upon to testify. As a minor, her name would be blocked from media coverage by a court-ordered publication ban. But there were other places than mainstream media where a search engine request might send a person. That was Sam's biggest fear about her old name. But so far, either no one at the new school had connected her with the *cyber slut* from another part of the province, or else no one cared.

It had been Uncle Ray's idea for her to transfer to this school. The school his own kids had attended. He said the academic program was strong, there were lots of extra-curricular activities, and although the town itself was relatively small, kids were bussed in a long way from multiple directions. The school was big enough that people could remain anonymous in it if they wanted.

The idea of going to a school that was almost ten times the size of the school that broke her seemed completely wrong to Sam at first. All she could imagine was ten times as much unwanted attention. Ten times the bullying. Ten times the humiliation. Ten times the threats.

But Uncle Ray had been correct so far. If she kept her head down, almost no one took note of her. Aside from raising her hand for attendance, she'd managed to avoid communicating with teachers, or with anyone else. A few kids had turned to her in class and spoken to her. Twice she'd spoken back. To girls only, and both times, she'd spoken so quietly that the girls did not hear her. The boy named Robert had tuned her guitar once. All she'd done there was hand the guitar over.

Before she'd found the hidden carrel in the library, she would sit at the far end of a long table in the reference nook. The tables and chairs there were darker, fancier wood, and the area was surrounded protectively by waist-high shelves of atlases, encyclopedias, foreign-language dictionaries, massive hardcover books, items that the internet had transformed into furniture. On top of one of the shelves was a huge globe on a fancy wooden stand. The colours and wood grains in the reference nook reminded Sam of the Harry Potter movies, and the globe was the sort of antiquey item that would seem right at home in Dumbledore's office.

On the wall across from the reference nook, there were several posters of old-school celebrities: Alanis Morissette, Justin Timberlake, Britney Spears, each with a book open in front of them. The posters featured pro-reading propaganda slogans: *Reading feeds your brain. Reading makes you look cool. Get caught reading.* Sam liked to sit in the reference nook and imagine the posters like the portraits in the Harry Potter movies: containing images that could move and speak. Images that lived in an alternate world, a world where answers to seemingly impossible questions could sometimes be found.

Then one day in the first uncertain weeks of school, she was snapped out of a reference nook daydream by a harsh voice.

"Hey! Hey! Can you talk? Hey! Can you talk? Somebody said you can't talk. Can you? Can you talk?"

On the other side of the table, backed up against a shelf of boxed *National Geographic* magazines, were two girls Sam had seen several times around the school. One girl was moon-faced and solid-looking with straight brown hair that hung to her shoulders. She had big boobs under a loose-fitting green T-shirt and she had a big rear-end that at the moment Sam could only see the sides of: wide, broad hips. She carried herself in a languid, dreamy manner. Her expression tended to be somewhat distant, but she always had a smile on her face. Her mouth was wide. Her lips were full. Sam could imagine her in a movie, but not as the star. She'd be the plainer-looking best friend.

The other girl was thin as a finger. Her cheeks bony and sharp. Her face was wide under her eyes, but angled sharply off at a pointy chin below a narrow little mouth.

Her hair was streaked several colours. Her mouth was so small, her lips so thin, that when she brought them together they looked tight and drawn, as though she were deliberately stifling herself.

"Can you talk?" It was the girl with the small mouth who spoke. Her friend smiled a blank sort of open-mouthed smile.

Sam looked at the two girls without moving. She was careful not to change the expression on her own face or to even shift her weight in her chair. Her heart set up beating hard in her chest. Her vision began to cloud with panic.

"We heard you can't talk," the slight girl said. The bigger girl nodded, her smile still wide. The slight girl pointed accusingly at the yellow notebook that rested on top of the school books in front of Sam.

"We heard you write stuff down in that notebook. Instead of talking like."

Jesus. When had she done that? She was sure she'd not done it once since school started.

She pressed all expression from her face, a blankness she wanted them to read as hatred. That's what she wanted them to see. And then, because they did not seem to recognize the sight of hatred, she decided to let them hear some.

"Fuck around!" Sam growled at the girls. She'd flinched in their direction as she said it.

Both girls jumped. The skinny girl put her hand protectively over her heart.

"She can talk!" the skinny girl said. "Oh, she can talk all right!" They saw the librarian coming in their direction, so they were already moving toward the exit. But they laughed and pointed back at Sam. "She can talk! See that girl right there! She can talk all right!"

After that, Sam no longer felt comfortably invisible in the library.

What she should have done was to ignore them and to keep ignoring them. They'd have got bored and wandered on to torment someone else. And that would have been the end of it. Instead, they came back for her regularly, almost daily, it seemed. And they no longer stood to confront her. They sat down. They settled in. They made themselves comfortable.

"Do you give blow jobs?" the skinny girl said one day. "Don't be ashamed if you do. This girl here," she indicated her friend, across the table and slightly behind her, "she gives blow jobs." She turned to the other girl. "You give blow jobs, don't you?" The girl responded with one hand in front of her mouth, her tongue inside a cheek, the whole time smiling her slightly dopey smile. "It's nothing to be ashamed of. Anyway. We heard you give blow jobs is all. Just checking to confirm that. If you stay quiet, that means *yes*."

Another time, the skinny girl dropped a notebook-sized piece of lined paper onto the table in front of Sam. *We found out your seceret*, was scrawled across the page in blue pen.

Sam had math work in front of her. She looked from the math to the note, then up at the two girls who had been tormenting her. The bigger girl had bright red lipstick smeared in alarming jags all around her mouth. It was a complete, clown-like mess and the bloody shock of seeing it flushed Sam's system with danger chemicals.

"Hey! How do you like her lipstick?" the skinny girl asked. "You can probably tell what she's been doing. You should see her boyfriend's—"

"No!" Sam said. She stood up and both girls straightened to face her. Every aspect of the bigger girl's expression was affected by her crazy lipstick, and her surprise-widened eyes took on a sort of insane lolling aspect.

"*I* found out *your* secret," Sam said. She held up the note and shook it at both girls.

"What are you talking about?" the skinny girl said. She looked at lipstick girl with fear in her eyes.

"For one thing. You're dumb. You can't even spell *secret*, that's how dumb you are. But *that's* no secret. Everyone knows you're dumb." The skinny girl's face had gone from satisfied smirk to unconcealable hurt. "Your secret," Sam said. She paused for a bit of suspense. "Is that you feel worthless." Her own eyes were filling with tears of hurt as she said it. And the skinny girl was tearing up, too. "You feel worthless and shitty. And you're pretty sure nobody likes you. You don't even really like each other. Who would treat a friend the way you treat her?" She pointed at the girl with the smear of lipstick around her mouth. "And you come here to fuck with me over my silence, but you never let her speak." The bigger girl was looking at her friend as though a reasonable question had been asked and she wanted to know the answer.

"And you never shut up. And you never shut up because you can't stand to be alone with your thoughts. Because all you ever think about is how totally worthless you feel. Nobody cares about you." She looked the girl in the eye and asked: "What's your name?"

"What?" the girl said, surprised.

"What...is...your...name?"

The girl looked around the library. Some people were looking at and listening in on the confrontation, but most people had grown bored and drifted away.

"Helen," the girl said.

"Why doesn't anybody care about you, Helen?" Sam said. The girl's eyes filled up with tears. Her lips trembled. "I don't." She shrugged. "I don't know."

"Well, that seems like an important unanswered question," Sam said. "Maybe you should focus on answering that and just leave me the hell alone."

It was after that incident that Sam retreated to the carrel by the window. She was no longer frightened or intimidated by the two girls, but she didn't want to take any chances.

She left the bigger, smiley girl alone when she saw her. That girl was just a harmless sidekick, anyway. But when she saw Helen, she'd steer directly at her in the hallway. She was always prepared to say something crazy-sounding and aggressive, like, *This girl can talk*, or *I know your secret*, but so far, that had not been necessary. Helen had kept her gaze averted. Sam had stung the girl and she could feel the sting herself. But she'd only done what was necessary.

Today she'd had free after lunch and she'd spent all of her lunch and all of her free period hidden away in the library carrel. She had her math book open, but she'd barely looked at it. Her mind had drifted out into the ridge of hills on the other side of the river. The bell rang at the end of the period. Sam gathered her books and dropped them into her shoulder bag. The strained quiet of the library erupted into a sudden rush of voices, chair legs on the floor, and bookbags being zippered and clipped shut.

Sam waited until the bulk of the commotion had passed before she stood to make her way to her last class of the day: music.

There was a five minute break between classes, and the shortest way from the library to the music class involved crossing the front foyer. Between classes the foyer filled with friends meeting up. In the first couple of minutes, most of the people there had their faces in their phones, texting *I'm in the foyer* to their people. Then the hallways near the foyer filled with people texting back: *I'm on my way.*

At first, the packed hallways before and between classes had terrified Sam. It was not so much the crush of bodies that threw her back in time to where she did not want to be. It was the presence of so many eyes. So much potential for scrutiny.

The first time she saw the video, someone had texted it to her without a warning or an explanation and she'd watched almost a minute of it with a strange, detached repulsion. That's how long it took for her to realize that the girl in the video, the girl being yelled at and abused, that girl was her.

She'd been lying in bed, days after the events in the video had taken place. Half asleep. It was three in the morning when the text had come through and woken her. She'd cried out in shock, slammed the phone over on its face on her bedside table. But she could still hear the awful sound it made.

This is what she'd flashed back to in the first few days in the crowded halls of her new school. She'd freeze up in the hallway. Her eyes clamped tight while the terrible video loop played in her mind. Her own slight body in a shaky, dark-drenched video. The terrible, tinny sound of her face-down phone at 3:00 A.M. She'd been able to unfreeze quickly every time so far. And if anyone had noticed, no one had said a thing. She took a cleansing breath. Made a forceful push with her left foot to move her body forward, an outward explosion of mental energy, and she had always managed to wipe away the mental pictures, drown out the sounds.

She was learning to navigate the halls in new ways. She was learning that the more crowded the hallway, the less you got noticed walking down it. Leading with her right shoulder, but with her face turned floorward, she could cut slowly through the centre of a large crowd. Find a spot for your foot on the floor, then move your shoulder through. Read the current in a crowd-blocked hallway and maneuver around the outskirts almost as quickly as you could walk through the same space empty.

The music room was at the centre of the building, so at this time of day the route there was hallway after hallway, dark with bodies.

She turned the final corner and the sound of a bouncy rhythm came down the final hallway in her direction. Live music. Most of the students people called the "Jazz Kids" were in the Music 12 class the period before Instrumental Strings. They loved music class so much they did not like stopping when it was over. How cool was that, Sam thought. The Jazz Kids were a half-dozen or so students who got together before and after school, sometimes at lunch. Today they were jamming on what sounded to Sam like something difficult. But she was new to playing music and almost all the music she heard in the music room sounded hard to her.

She loved it when she got to the music room and these guys were still playing. The tall, long-faced bass player, a boy with spiky red hair and slightly crooked front teeth, he always smiled at her, no matter where she saw him in the building. The drummer was a girl with wide shoulders and big arms who wore an expensive-looking black porkpie hat, like the old man in *Breaking Bad*. She liked boys' jeans with low-cut cowboy boots. She wore T-shirts that she probably printed up herself from nerdy stuff on the internet. *Give Them a Blank Czech*, today's said. A stylized cartoon face, an outline devoid of features beneath the words, doubtlessly belonged to the Czech in question.

The sax player was the kid they all called *No*. Sam did not know if that was his real name or just what his silly jazz friends called him. "Can everyone jam tomorrow before period one?" she'd heard them saying. "No? Are you a yes?" No was quiet with a wry, ironic grin. He'd nod and someone would say, "Yes! No is a yes!" No always wore stylish, casual clothes that you could tell his mom bought him. A&F T-shirts. Jeans from American Eagle.

The piano player was a shorter girl with raven black dyed hair to her shoulders and bangs that jagged crookedly over her straight eyebrows. The trumpet player was a thin-faced, narrow-hipped boy with acne scars and hair that was long, but grew out from his head instead of hanging down from it. He wore black Dickies work-weight pants and had about a hundred T-shirts that all said *Shut Up* across the front. Some commercially screen-printed, some hand-painted, some scrawled with bleach on black cotton.

There was something real about the Jazz Kids that put Sam at ease. They would pick a chord progression, get a beat going, and play for thirty solid minutes, trading solos, laughing without making fun of each other. Shouting out with joy at something someone had just played. It was impossible to come into the room when the Jazz Kids were playing and not feel jealous, not wish you were one of the Jazz Kids.

One day after lunch as Sam was entering the room, she'd seen the trumpet player writing on one of the panels of the chalkboard at the front of the room. After he'd gone she looked up to see what he'd written.

If it sounds good, it is good. –Duke Ellington

This quotation summed up what she liked about the Jazz Kids. What they respected was how you sounded when you played. If you sounded good, you were good. That seemed fair.

Just above the Ellington quote were the words that had really taken root in Sam's mind: *Singing is a way of escaping. It's another world. I'm no longer on earth. –Édith Piaf.* It was in yellow chalk, in writing that did not match what Trumpet Boy had written. There was a drawing beside the quotation that looked startlingly like the Girly Girls from Morganne's sketchbook. A small ball of Earth, swirling with cloud shapes and encircled by spiralling spin lines. A woman in a dress, her mouth open with song, lunging away from the planet, triumphantly facing outward, her swirly, stylized face a mask of strength, of joy.

Sam was stunned at the resemblance to the girls from Morganne's notebook. But a quick glimpse at the tattoo on her hand revealed the obvious differences. The drawings were, at best, a bit alike in style. It was the attitude more than anything that was similar. Boldness. Confidence. Self-possession. Sam copied down the quotation and later that day, back on Uncle Ray's Wi-Fi, she'd googled the name Édith Piaf. And that was how she got connected to the song called "La Vie en rose."

She was in her bedroom with the door closed and her earbuds in. The opening of the song was some cheesy-sounding horn music. And the song had a loose and casual first verse. Sam did not really understand French at all. She thought "La vie" meant *life*. And she knew "rose" was a colour. Probably some shade of red. But as soon as the main melody came in, strong and bold and soaring, something inside her leapt beyond itself. Something physical, at the level of the abdomen, reached out in the direction of the song. She'd never heard a song like this. A woman's voice as tough as iron, but gentle, too. And genuine. Even without the meanings of the words, she could hear a human soul, stating its case to the world.

THERE WAS A GIRL IN SAM'S STRINGS CLASS. EMILY SOMETHING. Sam had heard kids say she had just come out as trans. She was big-shouldered and over six feet tall. She was in grade eleven this year and had played varsity football in her grade ten year, before she'd transitioned.

Most of the kids at school seemed pretty chill about her gender. A couple of times Sam had heard some asshole yell *Logan* at her, which was her deadname. She'd never seen Emily react to that. But Emily looked awkward and uncomfortable a lot of the time. Her facial features were not very feminine, and it must have been hard to get girls clothes that fit. She wore loose dresses a lot. Her hair was chin length. She wore a little bit of eye makeup. She kept to herself in music class. If the teacher asked her a question, she answered in a barely audible whisper. Emily was the only person in class who seemed even more socially awkward than Sam did. And playing guitar looked hard for Emily. Her hands were big, meaty football player hands that she did not seem to like calling attention to, and it seemed impossible for her to even hold the instrument in what looked like a comfortable manner.

Today, the teacher had got the class to work in pairs, choosing a simple, three-chord song, and taking turns singing the melody and listening to how the melody moved over the chords.

As usual, Sam had recused herself from any work with a partner. She slipped away into a corner and hid behind a big instrument she thought was probably a vibraphone. The music teacher was supposed to allow her this sort of leeway due to her multiple diagnoses, but she could tell by the pointed way he had of ignoring her at times like this, that he did not approve of her not having to do the exercise.

She held the guitar in her lap and put the chord practice sheet on top of the vibraphone where, if she stretched her neck up just a little, she could see the rudimentary notation. Chords diagrammed above a five-line staff. Slashes that represented downward strums. D, G, and A7. She had not even moved beyond practice sheets yet, was not looking at an actual song with lyrics and a beating heart inside it.

She flipped to the back of her music binder and pulled out the chord chart for "La Vie en rose" she'd downloaded. Six pages of impossible squiggles. The chord changes, with no diagrams for how to finger them, hovered above the staff. The first four bars had six chords: G(add 9), Em9, Cmaj7, Am9, D13, and D7.

She laughed at herself. The guitar class practice sheet was a challenge, and it was not even a real song. D, A7, and G. D and A7 were pretty easy for her by now. But getting from D to G involved such a major repositioning of fingers that she doubted she'd ever be able to do it smoothly.

She made the little D triangle and slowly sounded each note, wiggled her fingers if the note buzzed or was partially deadened or muted, then tried all the notes again. She dug out the diagram for the G chord, balanced that on her knee, dropped her elbow down, and angled the forearm out and tried to sound the notes in that chord.

Her fingertips burned against the steel strings. The teacher told them this was normal. It would not take long to build calluses.

The room around her filled with sound. Discussions among partners about what song to try turned to the hesitant testing out of chord progressions. Self-consciously at first, her classmates began to sing. People struggled to find starting notes and consistent melodies. But as the class went on, songs took shape in the air, a note at a time until the room was awash in a clash of sounds.

Emily ended up paired with the only person in the class people were less comfortable with than with her: the guy who everyone else called Robot, but who the teacher called Robert when he took attendance.

—

IT SEEMED ROBERT HAD WORKED OUT HIS CONFLICTS WITH THE teacher over the ukulele. Mr. Foley could not get over his distaste for the instrument, but he saw that Robert was easily the best student in Instrumental Strings 11. So he brought in his own personal acoustic guitar. "My second-best acoustic," he said loud enough for the room to hear. The teacher's second-best acoustic was a Gibson that most people made a big deal about, but that Sam felt left out of the conversation on. People called it *The Vintage Gibson*, and she was not sure if *vintage* was part of the guitar's actual name (it only said *Gibson* at the top, the part of the guitar that the diagram on the wall called the headstock) or whether that just meant it was old. The guitar looked like any other acoustic guitar, really. And it was beyond her to hear anything different when it was played. But everyone understood that the teacher had brought in this guitar not just to keep Robert happy, but to keep him from playing ukulele. Robert still brought his ukulele every day. Sam saw him playing the instrument in the halls. Even when she did not see him, she'd pass by the end of a hallway or a locker section or an empty classroom, and she'd hear the instrument's plucky little sound, as recognizable as the voice of a child.

But in music class, Robert played the teacher's vintage Gibson. And that was a right no one else challenged or complained about.

As the classroom filled with the sound of partners playing and singing, it did not take long for the sound of Robert's playing to ring clear beneath the clash and din. It was consistent, solid, and even, like a professional recording. But soon another sound arose. Emily, slumped sideways in a plastic chair that seemed as though it might collapse beneath her weight, was singing in a more and more audible, more and more confident voice. The songbook the class used was relatively new. The classroom copies showed light wear, but the content was mostly dated, its authors under the impression that all the good acoustic folk songs came from the sixties. Both Robert and Emily seemed less sure of themselves at first. Their eyes were glued to their songbooks and, though the pleasure on their faces was obvious, they both appeared strained as they struggled to work with unfamiliar material.

"Do you know that old Deathcab song?" Emily asked Robert when they'd finished the second song from the book. Robert seemed to know exactly which song she was talking about. He launched into the intro of "I Will Follow You Into the Dark." By the time they got to the second or third line of the song, the whole class had come to a standstill to listen. Emily looked self-conscious when she realized what was happening. Her voice, already quiet, lowered in volume so as to become almost inaudible. Self-conscious or no, there was a raw, clean power to her voice that made Sam want to cry at the sound of it.

As Emily's voice grew quieter, Robert's playing became more subdued and muted. He was getting out of her way, working to spotlight her voice in the song.

When "I Will Follow You Into The Dark" ended, the whole class applauded. The teacher came out from his office with a smile on his face.

"Play that again," someone said.

"Play some Ed Sheeran," said someone else.

"Taylor Swift."

"Adele."

There was a generous, knowing smile on Robert's face. "What else do you know?" he asked Emily.

They decided on "Rolling in the Deep" by Adele. But as soon as Emily began to sing, people interrupted the song: "Louder, Emily. Sing louder."

"The guitar is there to support the voice," Mr. Foley said. He seemed completely oblivious to the fact that his entire class had come to a halt and that no one was doing what he'd asked them to do except for these two who now had everyone's attention.

"Wait a minute," Robert said. He leaned the vintage Gibson against a nearby instrument rack and dug his ukulele case out from beneath his seat.

Sam looked at the teacher for a response, but his expression was like that of everyone else in the room. He was impatient for the song to recommence.

It only took Robert a few seconds to tune the ukulele. He looked at Emily, and Sam noticed the way Emily's singing transformed the way Robert looked at her. Before he'd heard the amazing instrument of her voice, Robert had looked at her the way a lot of people did: he'd half-ignored her, half looked through her. Sam scanned the other faces in the room and saw that everyone had been transformed in the same way. They were not staring at Emily as though she were a freak. They were not looking through her, as though she were not there. They were not looking around her or away. And Emily's demeanour changed along with the way people were looking at her. She'd moved from the precarious plastic chair and was now sitting up straight on a high wooden stool. Her face was alive with an endearing mix of bashfulness and pride.

This was the other world from the Piaf quote. Emily was no longer on Earth. She was gazing at them all from far away and beyond.

Robert gave a few warm-up strums on the ukulele. Its sound was subtle and hesitant in comparison to the rich bass the guitar had provided. He began tapping his right foot, looked at Emily, and said: "How's this tempo?"

Emily closed her eyes and swayed gently to the beat. She opened her eyes again and nodded at Robert, slow and trance-like. Robert played the opening chords. Emily's eyes rolled upward dreamily, then: There it was, the voice again! Sam felt a surge of...something...shoot through her like a drug. She leaned her guitar against the wall and slowly came out from behind the vibraphone she'd been hiding behind.

The teacher dug a tambourine out of a box of percussion gear in a corner. He had a plastic-tipped drumstick and was playing what Sam had recently learned were called the two and the four. At the start of the first chorus, Robert sang a second vocal part wordlessly, like a hornline: "babba da-DA da!" and the teacher switched to playing every beat of the bar.

Halfway through the song, the bell rang to end the school day, but not only did no one leave the room, people started coming in from the hallway. At the start of the second chorus, several people had figured out simple harmonies to add to Robert's vocal horn line. They were singing and laughing: "Babba da-DA da! Babba da-DA da!"

Robert and Emily stood up for the last verse; Robert had all the strings of his ukulele muted with his left hand and the *chunk-chunk-chunk* rhythm rang out across the room. When the song ended, the room erupted in applause. Sam's eyes were closed, but when she opened them, she could see that the kids from the jazz combo were now in the room.

"Guitar class represent!" the trumpet player yelled over the hubbub. He high-fived the drummer, and even though you could see their reaction was tinged with irony, it was only a tinge. They were legitimately excited.

"That was *amazing*, you guys!" It was Sam's own voice she heard. People passed looks around the room. It was the first time she'd used her voice in this class, and who knew what stories they had heard or made up to explain the weird new girl's silence? The words had come from her mouth unbidden and she felt a chill of fear in the brief rush of attention.

But the applause for the performers continued and she relaxed as the spotlight drifted away from her again.

"Here's the singer we've been looking for," the trumpet kid said. His *Shut Up* T-shirt was one Sam had not seen before. Orange letters on a black shirt. He nudged his way to the front of the group that had gathered before Emily and spoke as though no one else were in the room.

"Have you ever sung jazz standards? Can you stay after school today for like thirty minutes?"

Sam backed away, toward the edge of the room. She dug her guitar case out from under a keyboard on a stand, and as she was fitting the guitar into place inside it, she noticed Robert at the other side of the thinning crowd. It had been his idea to accompany Emily on ukulele, to get the music out of the way of her vocals. But that had gotten him ignored.

Emily had told the jazz guys she could stay a few minutes into their rehearsal and already they were setting up for that. They all had a copy of a thick, coil-bound volume called *The Real Book*.

"I gotta warm this thing up," the trumpet player said. He went through the door into the adjoining practice room. The sound of him running through repetitive trumpet exercises was moderately muffled by cinder block walls. The bass player was using the big walnut-coloured upright that stood in a rack against the back wall of the music room. Emily was looking over the shoulder of the girl who played piano.

"Let's find something you know," the piano player said as she leafed quickly through *The Real Book.*

Robert slung his ukulele case over one shoulder and his bookbag over the other. "I'll see you in class tomorrow, Emily," he said.

Emily raised a hand absently in Robert's direction without looking up from the piano player's *Real Book.* "Thanks, uh..." She shook her head to pull her thoughts together. "Thanks, Robert." But Robert had already gone out into the hall.

"Here's the main part of the melody," the piano player said to Emily. She pointed at the staff with her left hand as her right hand played a few notes. "Ring a bell at all?"

Sam watched Robert leave the room and felt an urge she could not resist. She had to talk to him. She could tell he was disappointed. She'd been watching him in silence since the first day of school, and she knew that, more than anything, Robert wanted the attention and approval of the Jazz Kids. He was always hanging at the edge of the room or just outside the band room door when they were playing. She saw the way his body moved when he listened to the jazz combo. His movements so obviously those of someone who longed to play the music he was listening to.

In the few moments of commotion, as the Instrumental Strings class filed out through the narrow door and the Jazz Kids gathered their instruments and stands for their after-school jam, Sam watched as No followed Robert out of the room. He had his saxophone case in one hand and he gave a quick look over his shoulder as he entered the hallway, as though he knew someone behind him might not approve of what he was doing if they saw.

Sam's school books were lying loose on the floor at the foot of her music stand. She scooped them up under her arm and slung the guitar case over the other shoulder. Her left hip caught the corner of a table just before she got to the door. The collision swung her sideways into the door frame, where the big hollow-sounding box of the guitar case clopped against the metal.

The hallway outside the music room seemed considerably brighter as you stepped into it from the music room.

"Robert!" Sam called as she stepped up and out the door. She felt her anxiety building. Words were coming out of her mouth.

"Robert!"

"What?" He had not got very far down the hall at all. He stood waiting.

No was behind Robert, just over his shoulder, where Robert had turned away from him.

"Robot? Robot?" No was saying. He was speaking very quietly, barely audible, though Sam was sure Robert could hear him. How could he not?

Sam looked at No, then at Robert.

"Robot?" No said one last time. But it was humiliating to be ignored and he quickly made his way past Sam and back into the music room.

"Do you just ignore people like that?" Sam said to Robert.

"Like what?"

"That kid obviously wanted to talk to you."

Robert made a face that Sam could not read. "No he did not."

"Well, he..." but she did not know what else to say.

The hallways were full of people fidgeting with combination locks, slamming their lockers shut. And Sam stood rooted to the floor, still half-blocking the music room door. Her voice had unexpectedly switched on a moment ago, and now it seemed to have switched off again. She looked Robert in the face. Her mouth slowly opened, soundless and seemingly without connection to her brain, which had come to a halt as well.

"I thought you couldn't talk," Robert said. Then, as her mouth continued to move, her jaw hinging open and shut without words, he said: "That's more like it. Way to play into your own stereotype." He had kind, uncertain eyes that made her think his words were not meant harshly.

The blue of his eyes was intense. He had a wide, square jawline and the hair of his stubbly beard was a couple of shades darker than the stuff on his head.

"That was really nice of you," Sam said.

He nodded uncertainly. His gaze shifted to the floor, then came back up to meet hers.

"You made it so Emily could sing," she said. "You made it so her voice could be heard."

"Yeah. Well. Emily can sing."

"Did you know she could sing like that? Did anybody?"

Robert frowned briefly and shrugged. "They know now," he said, turning away from the music room and throwing a thumb dismissively over his shoulder in the direction of the door. "The jazz assholes are interested in her now." He began walking down the hallway. Sam followed him.

"Jazz assholes?"

"Jazz assholes."

"They're not so bad."

"They're interested in her now until she disappoints them."

"What do you mean? How could she disappoint them?"

"She won't live up to their standards. They're just a bunch of snobs."

"I kind of like the Jazz Kids. They're...I don't know. They're funny. That guy with the *Shut Up* shirts." She tried smiling.

"He's the worst! He's the worst one! Music for Dummies. That's what he calls our class. He's calling us dummies. Right to our faces."

"I don't think he means that. He's just..."

"Trumpet is a loudmouth instrument. It can't say anything without shouting."

Sam found herself frowning and shaking her head.

"I used to be all about noise. Volume. But..." Robert's voice trailed off. "That's why I'm loving the ukulele right now." He swung the gig bag up level with his face and let it fall again. "Hey. Listen. Let's go... Let me show you something." His voice brightened. He stepped down the hallway.

Sam had not intended to have a conversation or even much of an interaction with this large boy she hardly knew. She'd already said way more to him than she'd imagined saying. But she was half hypnotized by what had happened to Emily, the way the music had moved her to another realm. She stuffed her loose books into her floral bag and threw it onto her shoulders. She picked up the guitar case by the carry handle and followed Robert.

When they got to the T-intersection, Robert headed toward the back of the school. It was an unusual direction to be headed in at the end of the day. Unless you were going to the gym. There were exits at that end of the building. But the only street that could take you away from the school was outside the front exit. If you went out the back, you'd have to double back to leave school property, through the side parking lots.

"Come on," Robert said from down the hallway. His excitement was slightly dampened by the sight of her hesitating back at the T.

In her imagination, she'd already closed up half the distance between them. But her body was slower to trust. Robert came back toward her.

"I want to show you something cool," he said. "It's about music. It's about sound. But if you're not cool to do that, it's fine." He waited for her to respond.

"No. I'm...good. I'll come," she said.

She followed him past classrooms and labs, through a hallway lined with glass-fronted cabinets containing sports trophies, past the gym and the wood shops, past locker rooms and storage closets, through a narrow corridor with windows on the left side that showed the backs of the football bleachers.

"Are you sure we're allowed to be here?" she said.

Robert placed a hand on the handle of a steel fire door. He looked over his shoulder at her and shrugged. "There are no *Keep Out* signs," he said.

With the door open enough for Robert to go through it, Sam had a short flash of memory that took her breath away. She paused at the threshold and backed up until she felt the steel door frame between her shoulder blades. She closed her eyes and breathed in deep as the images flitted through her mind's eye: The back of Morganne's head as she passed through the doorway of an unfamiliar house.

Reading Morganne's lips through the glass of a closed door: *Where's Becky?*

Rhythmic pounding rose in Sam's ears and she breathed through it. A long breath in through her nose. Hold it in a moment. Then slow release.

What Robert stepped into was a stairwell that obviously hardly ever got used. All the light was artificial and came from metre-long fluorescent bars on the ceiling and on the walls at each landing.

Sam stood in the doorway with her arm propping the door open.

"You good?" Robert asked.

"I'm good," she said, through audibly shallow breath. "Sometimes I get a thing with doors. I might just need to stay here. With this open."

Robert climbed the first flight of stairs and turned at the landing. Sam looked up at him. She shifted her weight forward as though to step in his direction, but her body would not move. The air was stale and smelled faintly of dust. Every step Robert took was amplified by the space around them. Echoes made the stark walls seem strangely alive.

"You know what?" Sam said. "I'm not okay with closing this door." She felt hollowed out and trembly. She used her guitar case to prop the door open. "This is not about you," she said to Robert. "This is...I had a..."

Robert stopped at the second landing, farther up than where she could see him. There was at least one more flight of stairs. She could see the handrails leading up, Robert's hand closed around the metal tube where he'd stopped.

"I know it's probably...like, maybe this is weird," Sam called up to him, but he was not far enough away to warrant the extra volume she'd given her voice. She put a hand to her chest and felt her heart hammering away in there.

Robert descended to the first landing and sat down, his feet two steps below him. Sam leaned back against the metal fire door casing. She shouldered her way out of the strap of her floral bookbag and set it on the floor at her feet.

"You stay where you're comfortable," Robert said. "I just thought you might want to hear something."

His voice sounded deep and rich in the echoey stairwell. He unzipped the gig bag on his ukulele, and the sound was a deep authoritative ripping. "I come here for this reverb." He took the ukulele from the bag and held it against the upper part of his chest.

He closed his eyes and began to strum. He played in quick-changing chords, sweeping the strings with his extended index finger. His foot began to move, hinging up and down at the ankle to keep time. After a minute, the strumming settled into something that sounded familiar to Sam. Robert's eyes were closed and Sam could tell he was getting ready to sing. Then suddenly he stopped playing, sat upright where he'd been slouched slightly over his instrument, opened his eyes, and said: "Isn't it amazing? The reverb in this space? It's actually better closer to the top. But...whatever. It's still pretty deadly right here.

"Here," he held the ukulele out to Sam.

"I can't play that," she said. She shifted her feet nervously in the doorway.

"You can play *that* thing," Robert pointed at the guitar case.

"I know, like, three chords."

"There's a fourth chord?" Robert smiled, nudging the ukulele toward her. When she did not move, he took careful steps down the staircase toward her, leaning out until she could reach the instrument. When she grasped it near the top of the neck, he let go and went back up to the landing.

Sam turned the ukulele over in her hands.

"This thing is cute," she said. She took in a slow, deep breath.

"It looks like a toy," Robert said. "It looks like a toy guitar or something. But it's a real musical instrument."

"How do I play it?"

"It's tuned like a guitar," Robert said. "Do you know about intervals?"

She frowned and shook her head.

"Doesn't matter. It's tuned higher than a guitar. But you can use the guitar chord shapes. Go ahead and make a D chord."

Sam made the little "D" triangle and played all four strings. "Hey. That sounds okay," she said. The nylon ukulele strings felt thick and smooth beneath her fingertips and she thought they would hurt more than the thin steel strings of her guitar, but they didn't. They hurt less.

"It's so easy on the fingers," she said. "I just press down and the note sounds!"

She strummed away on the D chord for a moment. On the guitar, you had to strum only the high four strings when you made a D chord, and she found that almost impossible to do. She always ended up sounding the two other strings by accident, ruining the work she'd done to get the strings of the actual chord to sound.

"Try strumming with your index finger," Robert said. "You'd never do that on guitar. You'd rip all the skin off your finger, and maybe even the nail. Not too stiff. Let it flop a bit." He put his finger out and rotated his wrist to demonstrate.

How could one chord be so much fun?

"You're going to get your richest strumming sound by choking your strum up the neck a bit." He motioned, but she did not understand. "Strum closer to the headstock. Not that far. I like the sound I get right where the neck meets the body."

"Why does this sound so good, but when I play guitar, it sounds so shitty?"

Robert laughed quietly. Then after a moment: "That's actually a legit question. I think I've been asking myself that question, in a way. Ukulele is just so forgiving. It's got very little sustain. Which means you can't strum rich, complex, chords and let them ring out all dramatically or whatever. But the short sustain means that as long as you've hit the right note, it doesn't matter as much how well you've hit it. You hear the note, it's gone. Same with mistakes. If you've got a bad note in your chord on guitar, that note might be around for a while, making your life miserable! Hit a bad note on uke: zap! It's gone."

Sam was strumming now, and bouncing in place, a smile on her face. "What's another chord I can play? I've got D. I'm all about D. I need another chord."

"Okay. Remember. You're playing the guitar chord D shape. On ukulele, that's not a D chord. This ukulele is in what's called D6 tuning. That's actually an A chord."

"Don't care! Don't care!" Sam was deliberately trying to be childish and annoying. "Another chord! Another chord!"

"Best next chord for you right now is the guitar G shape."

Sam put her fingers on the strings. "Too many fingers, not enough strings." She strummed what she'd fingered. It sounded like hell.

"Picture the guitar G chord in your mind."

"Okay."

"You're not picturing it."

"Okay."

"Close your eyes."

She looked at him carefully. His face was kind and he was beginning to smile. She looked over her shoulder, through the doorway to the empty hallway behind her. She took a breath. Then another. She closed her eyes.

"Picture a G chord."

"There it is." She opened her eyes and noticed that Robert had closed his. She closed her eyes again.

"Now. Get rid of the bass strings," Robert said. "Forget the E and A strings."

"I've only got one finger pressed down."

"Where?"

"First string third fret."

"Now you're ready to make that chord on your ukulele."

"Oh my god. This is dead easy!" She made the chord and was practicing changing back and forth between the two chords she now knew.

"Okay. If the guitar D shape is A on ukulele... What's the G-shaped chord?"

Sam opened her eyes and shrugged. Robert looked at her, waiting for the reply.

"I'm not letting you off the hook. You can figure it out. D is A. So what is G? It goes in a circle, right? The musical alphabet doesn't stop at G. It goes back to A."

She was shaking her head, but she was thinking. She began to chew on her lower lip.

"Think of where that D chord is on guitar. Now picture an A. You want a chord that is to G what A is to..."

"D. It's a D chord! Oh my god! That was like a math problem."

"BOOM! It wasn't *like* a math problem. It *was* a math problem. Look at you! You're transposing! You are now officially too smart for guitar class. Welcome to the world of social isolation." Robert's demeanour was getting a bit too teachery. But she was willing to put up with it for now. She was learning something she actually felt like learning.

"Once you're back and forth between these two chords, that's almost everything you need to play and sing songs."

"What songs?"

"All of them."

Sam was still standing, but she allowed herself to relax enough to rest comfortably back against the door frame. She looked up at the underside of the staircase above her and began to alternate: two beats each out of the only ukulele chords she knew. A and D that felt like they should have been D and G. The stairwell filled up with the music she made and she felt at ease in a way she had not done in a long time.

She closed her eyes and pictured the vibrations from the strings of the ukulele like a rush of water, a full bucket thrown into the air above her, spreading out in slow motion, a cone of liquid sound.

"Oh my god," she said.

Robert was quiet a long time. Then he said, "What?"

She was still playing. Two beats per chord. "This is like a drug."

"I know, right?"

She opened her eyes long enough to see Robert fold his hands behind his head and lean back on the landing.

"That's *my* ukulele, remember?" he said, and laughed.

"Fuck that!" Sam said. "I can't let this thing go now. It's part of me."

She felt like singing. She thought about taking the chart for the Piaf song out of her bag and letting Robert look at it. She was sure he could play it. But it was too much of a leap. And she'd have to let him play for that and she did not want to let the ukulele go.

"*Take this hammer,*" Robert began to sing. "Stretch it out a bit. Two more beats per chord. You know this song?"

Sam shook her head and kept playing.

"*Take this hammer.* Chord change here. Good. *Take it to the captain. Take this hammer.* Change. *Take it to the captain.* Don't rush, now. Don't get excited and speed up. This is a three-chord song that you only need two chords for.

"*Take this hammer. Take it to the captain.*

Tell him I'm gone. Tell him I'm gone."

Sam kept playing even after Robert stopped singing. "Don't stop," she said.

"I'm not stopping. This is a lesson."

"I hate lessons."

"I don't care. *Take this hammer. Take it to the captain.* That's the melody. Those notes I sang?"

"Jesus," Sam said, still playing. "I know what a melody is."

"Shut up. Every note has other notes built right into it. They are component notes in a way. They're, like, associated with each other. Some of those notes are the best harmony notes. Harmonies are just relationships. They're relationships between notes. If you could figure out that the chord that's played as G on guitar is really D on ukulele, you can work out harmonies. It's the same thing. It's about relationships."

"Just give me a note. I'll try to sing it."

"Better if you can find your own note. Play the chords again."

"You said this would be easy."

"No I did not."

She played the chords again.

"Strum once a bar. One strum, then hold for three more beats. And listen for every note in the chord."

She had never really thought of chords that way: of being constructed of individual notes. Notes you could isolate, pull apart, and relate to other notes. She'd never really thought at all about what they were.

It was a lot easier to listen for individual notes in a ukulele chord than in a guitar chord. Not only were there fewer notes, but the lack of sustain actually made each note snappier, clearer, easier to pick out on its own.

"Listen to the notes I'm singing now."

"Take this hammer..." He went through the whole verse.

"Strum your chord. Listen for the individual notes. Find a note in the chord that I'm not singing. And you sing that note. Just that note. You only need to sing one."

She listened while he sang the verse again slowly. It was mentally taxing, listening for a single note, listening to all four notes of the chord, picking only one of those notes to sing, singing it, paying attention to the lyrics and singing the note she wanted without being drawn to his note.

"That's good," Robert said. "Find your note and stay on it. Let's just keep playing that until you can nail it every time."

The song was a perfect choice for practicing harmony. You didn't have to think too hard about the lyrics. It did not have the subtle complexities of the Piaf song, but it was a real song with emotion you could feel as you sang it.

"You're getting pulled over to my part. Sing all the words. One note," Robert said encouragingly.

A few times through was all it took until Sam was doing it without hesitation or error.

"I don't even know what note I'm singing," she said as the chords turned over and repeated.

"The names are not the notes. If you're singing the note, you know what note it is. The only thing you don't know is its name. Names are just made up by people," Robert said when he should have been singing.

Sam played the chords and sang her harmony part, a single note she sang all the words on. Robert sang his melody. The sounds of their voices mixed with the sound of the ukulele and reverberated throughout the stairwell. She felt it humming in her chest and tingling in her sinuses.

Their voices met in the air between them. They sang the same words on different notes and she felt the stairwell pulsing, alive. Singing harmonies was like bringing the air to life. When two notes came together in harmony, a whole new something was born.

If he asks you was I running
If he asks you was I running
If he asks you was I running
Tell him I'm flying.

9

OCTOBER

L ate summer stretched unseasonably into fall and Robot left his bedroom window open at night right into October. On the weekends, the few blocks at the bottom of Lemon Street could be an auditory trauma centre. Drunk people who'd forgot their keys yelling in through windows at their brother, their mother, their roommate, to come and unlock the door. Drug-ravaged people, purposely locked out by the folks in their lives who'd had enough of them, pounding, swearing. Fed-up girlfriends screaming "fuck off" or "go away" at boyfriends they'd deadbolted from their lives for the night. Occasionally he himself was the target of the yelling. The first time he'd been woken up by some drink-emboldened asshole on the street outside the house, calling out for him, he'd lain awake, heart thumping in his chest, waiting for what seemed like the inevitable escalation: the pounding at the door of the flat. The sound of stumbling at the side of the building, by his bedroom window.

"Murderer!" He heard the drunken voice again.

"Shut up, just shut up!" came the voices of the screamer's concerned friends, trying to keep him out of trouble.

"He killed Gink! Get out here, murderer! I'll kick your ass!"

"Shut up. You're not kicking anyone's ass."

"Come on!"

Robot had his cellphone in hand, ready to dial 911 if needed. But one of his neighbours beat him to it. He saw the strobing red and blue against the window pane, heard the quick, single *whoop!* of the siren as the cops announced their arrival. It had happened that way several times since. Robot never left the house on any of those occasions. He'd never even gone to the window to see who the police were talking to.

But the chill of night eventually settled in. The windows in the apartment were closed up. If anyone was yelling in the street, he could not hear it.

His mother's condition had fluctuated slightly over the past few weeks, from near death to not-quite-near-death as far as he could see, and then back again. She had been to the walk-in clinic a few times. He had no idea what for. It was hard for an addict to go to the hospital. The only thing that was keeping you alive was also the thing killing you. And in the hospital they would not give you that thing.

He tried to stay out of the house as much as he could during daylight hours. He lingered at school, hiding by himself in the back stairwell, playing his ukulele and singing into the reverb. Reverb had a spooky power, and if he could land on the right song in the right key, he could play and sing back into the sound of himself until a deep calm came over him. He remembered the dreamy, sort of stoned look on Sam's face when he'd stood up from the landing where they'd been harmonizing. He'd had that pleasantly mixed-up feeling that playing and singing could leave you with, that feeling you'd disappeared into something bigger than yourself. Something more important. Something meaningful.

One day, after having put off coming home from school for as long as possible, he saw his mother at the front door, taking a liquor store sack from a young man he had never seen before. In profile, his nose was long, his lower jaw large and forward of his upper lip. In a quick ruffle of bills, Robot saw his mother hand over four twenties. Eighty dollars was more than double what a forty of vodka—his mother's usual order—was worth.

His mother had caught sight of him over the shoulder of the bootlegger and quickly shut the door and disappeared back into the house.

"You should be ashamed of yourself," Robot said. The man wore a brown, heavy denim Carhartt jacket with matching double layer pants, clothing designed for hard physical labour. But there were no signs he'd ever done anything in it but sell grossly overpriced booze to desperate people. His boots alone, steel toe monster lace-ups, probably cost more than all the clothing Robot's mother owned.

The man squared his shoulders, made himself taller. He looked down at the wad of twenties in his hand. His hand twitched toward the front pocket of his Carhartts, but then he stopped himself, brought the bills up closer to his face, and counted carefully before folding them double and tucking them casually into the inside of his jacket.

"*You* should be ashamed of *your*self," the man said. He began to walk toward the street. "Murderer." His movements were stiff and determined. Robot could tell the man was afraid of him, but that mostly he was afraid of looking afraid. The man did not break eye contact as he sidled past and reached the sidewalk.

"Don't let me catch you back here," Robot said.

The man opened his mouth as though to reply, but when Robot took a half-step in his direction, the man turned and hurried away down the sidewalk.

Two nights later, Robot was dragged from his bed in the middle of the night. There was no shouting from outside this time. No name-calling. No accusations. He was asleep. He became aware of noises. There was a confused moment when the banging in his apartment and the hard voices of intruders got mixed into a dream he'd been having. Loud footsteps. And then he was completely awake; someone had him under each arm and yanked him up out of his bed, up off the mattress on his bedroom floor.

"Hey! Hey!" he shouted and when he tried to shake off the two people who had him under the arms, a third person, a dark silhouette against the night-lit backdrop of his squalid bedroom, punched him hard in the stomach. That took all the fight out of him.

His knees and lower legs dragged against the floor, out the front door, down the hard, pebbly concrete walkway, and into the street. When they dropped him on his face, he rolled onto his side and was partway to his feet when they began to kick him.

Except for the sound their boots made against his arms and ribs, the night was quiet. They kicked him until they began to get tired. The sound of their grunting got louder than the muted smacks of steel-toed boots against his flesh.

The initial adrenaline rush of being dragged out of his bed had all been worn out of him. Getting assaulted was hard, hard work. And he felt tired now, felt like putting his head onto the cold surface of the street and drifting off to sleep. But as the blows subsided, he looked up at his attackers. There were three or four men in the groggy dark. Like idiots who thought they were on a TV show, they had ski masks pulled over their faces. Balaclavas with eye holes. But he recognized the clothing of one guy right away. The Carhartt pants and jacket. The rubber-tipped steel-toed boots.

"You fucking bootleggers!" Robot managed to say. But all he had in him was a slurry, drunken-sounding whisper. He was face down on the street. His hands were not far from his head, so he mustered the strength to gather his forearms beneath his cheek, softening the feel of tarmac and providing a little warm reprieve for his face, which was beginning to feel the cold of the surface it rested against.

"Tag him," he heard one of the guys say. Away in the distance, as though it might have been coming for him from an oncoming dream, he heard a siren building up, swelling in his direction.

A hissing sound and the sharp, toxic smell of spray paint. He could feel it wet on his hands and arms, and feel his head swim with the nauseating fumes. *What the hell are you doing?* he wanted to say. But he was so hoping for an ambulance, so waiting to be picked up and placed in a warm vehicle and driven to a safe room. He was tired out from being beaten, and could only think the words. The siren came closer. His attackers seemed to have gone. And then he was vaguely aware of voices, the flashing lights of emergency vehicles, his pulse being taken by a firm finger at the top of his neck.

"Well. He's alive," said a male voice matter-of-factly.

"Jesus! He's covered in wet paint!" said another voice. And then nothing.

10

FIVE MONTHS EARLIER: MAY

When Trisha wakes up, the light in Morganne's bedroom has shifted. It's early evening. She can smell the cinnamon from her own skin, from the skin of her face, and from her hands, which she used to both apply and remove the facemask Becky had made. She rubs her face with her hands and groggily becomes aware that some movement in the room has woken her up. It's Becky, noisily clomping on the floor and rattling the doorknob of Morganne's room.

"Becky. Where you going?" Trisha calls after her. There is an abruptness in Becky's movements that Trisha has learned to find alarming. This is how Becky moves when she gets into her wild mode, when she does something rash.

Trisha gets up on an elbow on Morganne's bed. "Becky?" she calls out the door. At some point since she drifted off to sleep, Morganne has gotten up from the floor and lain down on the bed beside her. It's a single bed and Morganne's body now takes up most of it, so that, if Trisha moves at all, she'll tip over the edge of the mattress.

"What? What?" Morganne begins to stir.

There is a bumping sound from the room beside Morganne's: Becky's room. Drawers are opening and slamming shut.

"It's Becky," Trisha says. "She's on the move."

"Fuck around, Becky!" Morganne yells at the walls. She sits up and inchworms to the end of the bed with her heels and her butt. "Becky? Where you going? Hey! Make us another face mask!"

Becky has left the door open and she rushes past the doorway, in her high-waisted jeans and her seashell print shirt she got at Louis last month when the three of them had split on a garbage bag full of pre-owned clothing on Fill A Garbage Bag for Five Dollars Day.

Morganne gets to her feet. "Becky, I don't like the look of you right now."

There is no response from Becky. They can hear her clomping around the house. Trisha and Morganne are just entering the kitchen when they see the back door slam and Becky and the seashell shirt blur past the window in the direction of the street.

"Oh, fuck!" Morganne looks at Trisha. Trisha shrugs. They put their shoes on at the back of the house, then run through the downstairs to the front door, to gain a little distance on Becky.

Becky's a block and a half ahead, walking in quick, firm steps, looking down at the phone in her right hand, then up at the house numbers and street signs. Trisha and Morganne make no attempt to close the gap on the lead she has on them.

"Becky!" Morganne only calls after her once or twice. Becky never turns around. "Oh my fuck I'm tired of this girl's shit," Morganne says at one point. But she says it in a quiet voice and Trisha can tell she feels sort of bad about saying it, so she does not respond.

It's an early evening in May. The lawns of Morganne's neighbourhood have all greened up. Bicycles propped against the sides of garages. It seemed like daytime when they left Morganne's house, but the sun has left the sky, and darkness is creeping up fast. They've only come a few blocks, but the streets are unfamiliar to Trisha, and as she looks around she sees that the light in the sky has become dim enough that it's hard to tell west from east. There's no glowing edge of horizon visible where there must just have been a few minutes ago.

Trisha and Morganne are only about a half a block behind Becky when Becky looks down at her phone a final time, its screen a luminous rectangle in her palm. She looks up at the civic number of a house and juts off the street and up the driveway, down a front walk, and disappears through the front door.

The house is not far from Morganne's, less than a fifteen-minute walk. It's a smaller house than Morganne's, no garage, just a paved driveway along the side. The siding looks brand new: aubergine with white trim. There's a fenced yard at the back. A garden shed. All of the curtains are closed.

Morganne stops and looks at Trisha. Then she looks across the short distance to the house. "Oh my fuck. Becky. Jesus." She looks at Trisha.

"Fuck it," Morganne continues down the street. Trisha keeps up with her.

When they get to the front door of the house, they can hear music booming from inside. The glass panel in the door is rattling with the sound.

This is not the first time Becky has brought them to an unfamiliar house. One time last summer there had been a pool party a boy in one of Becky's classes had texted her about. She'd dragged Trisha and Morganne there, the two of them complaining to Becky the whole way in the wavering heat, but when they got there it was actually fun. There was a slide and there were other girls there, and nobody was wearing some ridiculous bikini that was just meant to make everything awkward, which is what Trisha had feared. And the parents of the boy whose house it was were home, but they stayed indoors the whole time until they ordered pizza for everyone and came out the back door to the deck by the pool with the pizza boxes stacked up with paper plates and napkins on top.

And just a few months back, in the middle of winter, Becky had convinced Trisha and Morganne to sneak out of Morganne's house at like 2:00 A.M. on a Saturday night when Trisha was sleeping over. There was some boy waiting for them in a beat-ass car just one block over from Morganne's house. They were not dressed for the cold, but the boy had the heater blasting and he took them to a party at the house of a girl they all knew from school. Her parents were in Cape Breton for the weekend.

Trisha had a vodka cooler at that party. She got it from a girl at the top of the basement stairs just handing bottled coolers to random people going by.

Morganne drank two beers called stout that had tasted like molasses mixed with ginger ale when Trisha had tried a sip.

There were four or five guys there from some hockey team or other and it seemed like Morganne sort of knew them and they were trying to prove how tough they were by drinking stout. "This is a *man's* drink," this big guy with square shoulders and a square head was saying as he snapped the metal cap off the glass mouth of the bottle. Morganne took the open one from his hand and started drinking it like he'd offered it to her. And when he reached around to the counter behind him and took another bottle with the cap still on it, Morganne said, "Thanks. I'll take that for later," and she walked off with that one, too.

Trisha and Morganne had lost sight of Becky for a while. She went down a hallway with the guy who had driven them there, and it was almost an hour before they met up with her again.

But the boy who'd taken them there had driven them back to Morganne's house when they asked him to, after Morganne made him swear he had not been drinking. And they got back into their beds and slept until after twelve noon, as they might have done anyway.

So Trisha does not feel alarmed or afraid as she and Morganne stand on the doorstep of the house that Becky has led them to this early May evening as the sky darkens into night. She is pissed off at not being consulted or told where Becky might be headed. She is a little embarrassed because of the way she and Morganne are dressed, in shorts and T-shirts that are starting to be not warm enough for how fast the air is cooling down.

"For fuck sakes." Morganne hugs herself against the cold. The light over the door is on, and as the sky darkens, Trisha and Morganne are getting reflections of themselves in the glass of the door. Morganne puts a hand up to the glass to shadow herself from her own reflection and peers inside.

Trisha can see down a hallway, to where it seems some people are gathered in a kitchen. She can't see Becky, but there are people moving about and it's hard to make out any individual faces.

"Morganne." Trisha grasps her friend by the upper arm. Morganne turns toward her with an angry look frozen on her face. "Let's go back," Trisha says. "I'm tired. Whatever this is, I don't have it in me."

"Becky is in there," Morganne says.

The sound of whooping comes through the walls of the closed-up house.

"Do you have any idea whose house this is?" Trisha says.

Morganne shakes her head and shrugs. She presses her face to the door again. "I can't really see." She rings the bell a bunch of times before there is a lull in the pounding music inside and the sound of the doorbell finally cuts through it. When someone comes to the door, it is a kid they both know from school. He's older than them, and Trisha can't think of his name. It seems like he's the older brother of someone in their grade, but she can't quite think who.

"Hey, girls!" he shouts in a too-loud voice.

His eyes blink slowly, drunkenly. He has an arm across the door frame, and in the sudden charge of pounding, featureless beats that pour out the door, Trisha smells cannabis, alcohol, Axe body spray, and vomit.

There is a commotion just over the guy's shoulder. "Fuck all you guys! You fucking assholes!" A very angry girl—young woman, Trisha corrects herself—comes careening out the door. She wears a tank top with a university name on it Trisha does not recognize. She is very drunk and her words are slurred as she yells.

"You fucking pricks! I fucking hate you!" Her voice is up into a pitch that Trisha can hear is tearing at the young woman's throat.

The drunk boy in the doorway pays her no mind. "Come on in, girls," he says to Morganne and Trisha.

Trisha turns her head to watch the young woman in the tank top walk in angry, unsteady steps down the driveway, away from the light over the door and into the dark.

"Where's Becky!" Morganne demands. Trisha remains on the landing as Morganne goes through the door. The guy who answered the door staggers back a step into the wall behind him and regains his balance. The door clicks shut in Trisha's face and the volume of the music again pushes against it. Morganne is a head taller than the drunk guy she is talking to. *Where's Becky?!* Trisha can read Morganne's lips through the closed door.

The glass door rattles against its frame with the pounding of the music. Trisha wants to leave, but she does not want to leave without her friends. She opens the door and steps inside so she can get Morganne to hear her, to listen.

The music is almost deafening. When the door seals over behind her, the music is so loud she feels the pressure of it against her chest.

Moments before, when she was looking in through the front door, Trisha had seen people moving. Now suddenly she can't see a soul. "Morganne!" she yells. But the music swallows the sound. She begins walking slowly through the house.

There is a massive TV in the front room on her right. It's tuned to the aquarium channel, which offers a jarringly peaceful visual counterpoint to the blasting electronic beat of the dance music that is pounding out of the same room. The room is empty of people and the sound of the music recedes somewhat as she nears the kitchen.

There are stylish new cupboards in the kitchen. And an expensive looking countertop that could have been from some home reno show. On the right, the table is wooden. A honey-coloured grain. There are empty beer and vodka cooler bottles and half-empty tumblers with mixed drinks on the table's surface.

The cupboard and sink area open out on the right as Trisha reaches the kitchen and stands on the tile floor. There are five or six people wedged in there, lit by the rectangular fixture overhead and by the light of the open fridge door. Morganne is talking to a guy who looks too old to be at a high school party. He has a high forehead and black hair that is cropped close at the back and sides but stands up a bit from the top of his head and flops out front in a tuft that reaches halfway to his eyebrows.

Morganne has a smile on her face that looks like she is fighting against it, like she wants to not like this guy she is talking to, but can't help thinking he is cute and being flattered by his attention. She has a drink in her hand. It is gold in colour, like ginger ale. And the black-haired guy, who is a little taller than Morganne, is backing away from her every few seconds so he can look down and check out her body.

There's a boy Trisha recognizes behind Morganne. Carl? Kyle? is drunkenly slumped against the electric range. His eyes are locked onto Morganne's rear end in her Lulu shorts.

"Trisha!" Morganne shouts over the music. She's only been out of Trisha's sight for like a minute, but she sounds sort of drunk. Or maybe it is just the pitch and volume of voice she has to use to be heard above the noise that makes her sound that way.

"This is Henry!" Morganne shouts. She puts out her arm in the direction of the guy with the black hair. Henry takes a microsecond to scan Trisha's body before he says *hi*. He places a hand familiarly on Morganne's shoulder and rests his gaze back on her.

"Morganne! Morganne!" Trisha shouts to get her friend's attention, which is locked in a dumb grin on black-haired Henry's face.

"Morganne. Where's Becky?"

"What?" Morganne shouts back.

"Oh my fuck. Just"—Trisha puts a hand up in Henry's face—"just a minute." She grabs Morganne by the shoulders and turns her around, pulls her all the way to the far end of the kitchen, past Carl/Kyle at the stove, and gets right up in Morganne's attention.

"Where the fuck is Becky, Morganne? And who is that guy you're talking to? He's old."

"Becky's here. You saw her come in here. We'll find her. Let's just have one drink."

She holds up the tumbler with the gold liquid. "Let's just have one drink. We can talk to Henry. Henry seems nice. One drink. Talk to Henry. Then we find Becky and go."

"We don't even know these people."

Morganne points at Carl/Kyle. "We know him."

Trisha shakes her head and rolls her eyes.

"Are you drunk, Morganne? How can you be drunk already?"

"What are you, a fucking cop? No, officer. Let me at that Breathalyzer."

"This is fucked up, Morganne. How old is that Henry guy, even?"

"He's like...seventeen...eighteen."

"Are you fucking kidding me right now? That guy is like twenty."

"I neglected to ask for his ID, officer."

"COME ON, MORGANNE!" Trisha shouts. She is so close she can feel the heat of Morganne's body.

Suddenly Morganne's demeanour changes. She appears serious and sober and she speaks in a reasonable tone, though she still has to compete with the volume of the music coming from the living room.

"Look. This is all good. I've got a drink. I'll finish the drink. We'll get Becky. We'll go. We're like six blocks from my house. What can happen? We're fine."

Trisha can tell when Morganne is drunk and faking sober, and this is what she sounds like when she does it. But how can she be drunk already? They've just got here.

"I want to talk to Henry. My drink is half gone." She holds up the glass. "When it's gone, we'll go."

Trisha closes her eyes and shakes her head in frustration. "I don't know who I'm more pissed off at right now, you or Becky." She takes a big breath. "Finish your drink and then let's go."

"Wicked," Morganne says.

Henry is waiting for them when they get back to the other end of the kitchen. He has moved over to a chair at the table, where he has a gold-coloured drink in a glass for himself and another one poured for Trisha. He stands up as Trisha and Morganne approach.

"What's your name, again?" he shouts at Trisha and holds out the drink for her to take.

"I never said my name," Trisha says.

"What?" he leans in close.

Trisha closes her eyes and breathes. "Trisha," she says.

"Here," he says. "Have one of these."

She takes the drink and rests it on the table top. There is a chair in the farthest corner of the kitchen, and a window that looks out at the backyard. Trisha sits in the chair and looks out the window. She thinks she sees the outline of a fence out there, diminishing against the darkness as it moves away from the house.

Morganne is at the other end of the table, her back against the same wall as Trisha's. Henry's chair is pulled in close to Morganne. Their drinks are beside them on the table, the golden liquid trembling slightly with the pounding beats. Morganne throws her head back in laughter and Henry moves in closer on her. His hands are down below the level of the table top, where Trisha can't see them. But she thinks he might have both hands at the sides of Morganne's legs now.

Morganne picks up her drink. She looks over to Trisha and motions with her glass for Trisha to pick up hers.

"Twenty minutes!" Morganne shouts. Trisha can barely hear the words, but she can read Morganne's lips.

Trisha holds up her drink in Morganne's direction and she and Morganne both put the drinks to their lips at the same time.

Trisha turns to the window, but this time all she can see is her own face in the lit kitchen reflected against the darkness outside. The drink has a strange peppery burn to it and she smacks her lips and feels her teeth with the end of her tongue.

Behind her own reflection, she can see Morganne again, raising her glass for them both to drink. Trisha turns and raises her glass and she and Morganne drink again.

"Twenty minutes!" Morganne says. But that does not make sense, because she's already said twenty minutes.

"Wait a minute!" Trisha tries to say. But her mouth has gone weird and it sounds more like she's said *watermelon*. She thinks that is funny and she rests her head on the table so she can laugh without tiring herself out.

—

SHE'S NOT SURE HOW LONG SHE SPENT IN THE HOSPITAL. It cannot have been more than a few days. She spent a lot of that time asleep. Or half asleep. They'd probably had her drugged out with pain meds.

She has no memory of how she got there. Ambulance? Police car? Morganne's mom? At the point where her memory picks up, her mother is already in the room with her. And like a dream, Trisha is just letting things happen to her. Doctors and nurses examine her, treat her abrasions with disinfectants. She says yes to everything and passively goes through it all. Her mother sits on a chair in a corner of the room, her face in her hands, sobbing, it seems, non-stop. But it's not long before Trisha reaches her limit.

"I can't stay here," she remembers telling her mother. A nurse had just left the room. "I need to be home right now."

For days after she gets released back to her mother's house, Trisha lies in bed, the curtains pulled across the window. She cannot bear for the light to be turned on. When her mother opens the door to her bedroom, she must first shut off the light in the hallway. If her mother forgets and that light enters the room, the pain behind Trisha's eyes is like a bomb going off in slow motion.

She is unable to get out of bed for anything but a wobbly trip to the bathroom with her mom under one arm. She has

bruises on her face and neck that her mom can see. But
when she is alone in the bathroom, only she can see the
fist-sized circles on the insides of her thighs. Her hips ache
from deep inside the joints. She has marks on her lower
ribs that are whole handprints. When she twists her neck
around, she can see parallel finger marks. High up on her
ribs, where Trisha herself cannot see, there are tender
spots that make it hard to find any comfortable position
to lie down in.

She feels so many painful feelings at once. Anger.
Terror. Hurt. Frustration with herself. She should have
grabbed Morganne's arm while they were still standing
outside that front door and marched right back to the
street with her. She should have told Morganne to call her
mom. She should have dialled 911 as soon as Morganne
went through that damn front door.

She feels broken down. Crushed shut. She feels unable
to speak to her mother, to the police when they come
stomping into her bedroom. People ask questions and
they are like ghosts before her, wavering like heat mirages
in a movie. Their lips move, but their microphones are
turned off. She can hear the sounds of the room, but not
the voices of the people in it.

She knows what they want her to say. They want to
hear names. They want her to say the details. Identifying
features. They know it all, anyway. They just want one more
person to say it. For corroboration. Like corroboration is
going to make any difference now.

A couple of times she opens her mouth, thinking: Now
I can do it. Now I can tell it all. But everything swirls
inside her like a poisonous infection. A flash of Becky's

body naked before she even realizes it's Becky. The sound of Morganne screaming that rises through a lull in the pounding music. The blur of pain, repulsive smells, blows, and hateful words.

She knows the address. She knows a name she heard inside the house. There was at least one kid from her school. But as the thought of speaking about it tips toward action, as the cop by the bed leans forward, as her mother's eyebrows rise expectantly, all the physical pains in her body tighten like a vise. The prospect of speaking becomes cataclysmic, as though it will cause anything that has not broken in her already to burst. Get the boys, the men. The man. Get those bastards to tell. Torture them the way she is being tortured now. That will get them talking. Fuck the guy who said his name was Henry. Literally fuck him. Tear him up inside. Tear them all up inside. Grab *their* throats and choke them. Leave marks on *their* skin. The boys who used a house as a rape trap. Punch their faces to make them comply. Call *them* hateful names. Pull *their* hair. Make *them* drink a poisoned drink that will turn *their* lives into a nightmare, a death spiral, a ghastly spasm. Share *their* pictures on social media. Make raping *them* a joke. Turn *them* into a local viral sensation.

No. She will not open her mouth to speak of this. If she is going to die from what they did to her, she will not help by doubling the pain, by making herself go through again what they'd already made her go through. This is a trick. It's a trick to hurt her. It's a trick to kill her. She'll open her mouth and everything she has left, everything she has that is alive, everything she has that links her to a continuing place among the living: all of that will come bursting out of her. The poison will break her on the way out.

The only person she actually speaks to at first, for days, is Morganne. And they are only in touch through their phones. Becky has gone silent. She's ghosting the shit out of them.

The first contact she has with Morganne after the assault is a pic Morganne sends through Snapchat. It shows Morganne's swollen, bruised face. Her mouth is open in a deliberate snarl that shows her teeth. It is hard to tell through the blurry pic, but at least one of Morganne's upper teeth and one lower one are missing.

Those fuckers broke my teeth! is written in the text band across the photo.

Morganne sends her screenshots of text messages she is getting. More than ten screenshots. First Trisha stops counting. Then she stops looking. They are all so awful.

You dirty thot.

Why don't you kill yourself. Whore.

You disgust me, you slut.

You are fucking worthless.

You are shit. You are dirt.

Why don't you let me fuck your drunk ass you dirty whore.

Trisha is broken down, made heavy and unmoving by the pain. She is getting the same kinds of messages, but she finds it easier not to look at them. Morganne is broken open. The pain is just spilling out of her.

Trisha gets text after text from her.

Those bastards.

I want to go back there with a gun and make those fuckers pay.

I can't talk. My teeth are broken. My mouth is swollen. I think I have a broken rib.

In Snapchat video selfies, the camera is close up on

Morganne's swollen mouth. The dark, jagged squares where some of her teeth are gone. Her voice does not even sound like her. Her words are slurred. She is using a high, loud register that gives her anger a demonic edge. Her voice seems channelled in some frightening way, as though it originates from somewhere outside of her altogether. Or somewhere so deep within that what comes out is next to unrecognizable.

The Snapchat videos all begin with Morganne speaking. So loudly. So much monstrous pain in the voice. "Oh! Trisha! We got raped! They fucking raped us!"

"My life is over! My life is over now!"

"Oh, what they did to me! They violated me! They fucking violated me!"

"I did not consent! We did not consent! Oh, Trisha! This is not okay."

"I am not okay right now. I don't think I'll ever be okay."

"Where are these fucking haters getting my number!"

She always manages a few words. Clear but so emotionally fraught that they scare the hell out of Trisha. Then, every time, in every brief video, Morganne breaks down with such passion that Trisha's own stomach muscles tighten and ache in sympathy.

She convinces Morganne to shut down her texting account. It's just giving evil a way in. They open a two-person Messenger conversation. They try to get Becky in the group, but there is no word from her.

Fuck. Morganne. Where is Becky? Trisha manages.

My mom won't tell me, Morganne writes back. *She's not here. She's not at my house. Our lives are over, Trisha. My life is over.*

Stop saying your life is over.

It is. It feels like it is.

Please. Please. Please. Please stop saying that. Your life is not over.

Watching Morganne is like watching someone on fire. She is beyond her own control. Shouting, screaming. Morganne is incapable of asking how Trisha is. She cannot see past the sheet of flames that engulf her.

"My fucking parents are not fucking helping me right now," Morganne says over video chat one day. "My dad. Fuck. My dad. My dad thinks this is a fucking legal case."

"It is, isn't it?"

"It's not a legal case when your fucking life is over. It's a funeral. Fuck! He just thinks it's a legal case because he's a lawyer. If he was a carpenter, he'd be building me cabinets."

It is funny. Even through all the pain. The thing about the cabinets is funny. Trisha laughs in a single burst of breath. That one breath is all she can afford to give the funny part. Morganne is not joking. Morganne video chats her for no other reason than to cry. She says what few words she has to say and then crying is all she has left. She cries loudly. Strongly. She cries like a person in tremendous physical condition. Her core is strong. The muscles there hard as steel. She's tightened up many times and had Trisha put her hand there, high on her stomach, just below the ribs. She cries in long syllables that begin as though they will lead to further words: *Oh! Ah!* This experience has opened her like a full-body wound. And for a few days after the assault, Trisha gets to see all that raw pain come out of her friend. She gets to hear it, hear the pain.

"Look at this!" Morganne says in one of her Snapchat

videos. She holds up her hand to show the knuckles swollen and barked, scabbing over. "That fucker Henry? I know it's not even his real name. He got this bad boy in the face." She opens and closes the fist slowly and turns it in the light. "Oh, yeah. I felt that connect. And so did he."

Then Morganne's mom takes away her phone. First she shuts down the data package. Morganne switches over to Wi-Fi and it takes her mother a day to catch up to that.

And then Trisha is on her own. Becky remains completely silent. Morganne is out of reach, but she manages to get one last message through on Messenger: *Mom taking phone.* And that is the end.

Trisha still has hundreds of hateful messages coming every day. She's shut down her Snapchat. She's shut down her Facebook. Her memories of what happened are fragmentary, almost non-existent. The photos people send her are meant as weapons. And they do wound her. At first she feels she has to look at them. She cannot help herself. She wants to know. She needs to know. She has a right. For all she knows, hundreds, thousands of people are looking at pictures of her naked body, sharing them through texts and group chats and direct messages. She needs to know what is out there. She needs to know what the world is looking at. She needs to know what it is based on, all the hatred now directed at her.

With Morganne out of reach, and with, it seems, the whole rest of the world turned against her, she decides to give away her cellphone. She lets it run down to 3 percent, and is about to password lock it and give it to her mother when her mother flips.

She comes into Trisha's room, sees that Trisha's got the

phone going and that she's been crying. Without speaking, she snatches Trisha's phone and throws it hard against the laminate floor. The phone was the only light in there, and when it blacks out, Trisha's mom goes fumbling for the light switch.

"Mom!" Trisha says. She does not care about the phone. She was relieved to hear the crack it made against the flooring, a blow she is sure was fatal. But her mother's face looks crazy when the light comes on. And she makes a terrible grunting noise as she jumps and stomps on the phone. A wild, animal sort of sound that is so full of anger and sadness and desperation. And when she stops jumping, Trisha can see the blood-smeared floor and the wound that has opened up on her mom's foot. And her mother is face down on the floor in a shapeless heap, sobbing as though the world has come apart.

Without a phone, Trisha's life contracts to the room she is in. Her bedroom. The hallway to the bathroom. The bathroom, the hallway, the bedroom. The bed. She can't eat. She is afraid of putting anything solid in her mouth. After seeing Morganne's broken teeth, her own mouth aches as though her teeth, too, are broken. She has long, uneventful dreams that involve probing her own mouth with the handle end of a dessert spoon, looking for secret broken teeth, but breaking teeth, one after the other, by accident, with the spoon.

She is *treated and released* from hospital, a phrase she hears on the radio and finds herself thinking about before she even realizes it refers to her. She is a news story. What happened to the three of them is all over the media, though there is a publication ban on their names. "Three sixteen-year-old females," they are being called. She hates being called a female. It makes her feel like an animal. Why can't they say *girls*. Why can't they say *young women*. Why can't they say involuntary porn stars. Why can't they say three sixteen-year-old owners of highly sexualized body parts? Why can't they shut the fuck up?

"Charges are being laid," they say. But they don't say against who. The only people mentioned in the report are the girls who got attacked. So it makes it sound like the girls are being charged for their own assault.

She sleeps briefly, then wakes up and lies in bed for hours, in a drowsy state of brain fog, uncertain whether she has any teeth in her mouth. She is thirsty a lot. She drinks water at first. A homemade smoothie through a straw. Her mother leaves solid food on a folding tray at her bedside. She cannot stand the thought of having it go into her mouth. She is sure it will snap her teeth off like pieces of chalk. She feels woozy even looking at it. She drinks Dairy Queen milkshakes. Herbal tea after it cools. A clear soup in a broad-lipped cup. Tomato soup from a bowl, no spoon. Beef broth with tiny chunks of vegetable in it: pieces of carrot and celery a quarter the size of a sugar cube.

She curls into a tight ball, pulls the covers over her head, and sleeps through darkness and light. Sounds come to her from other parts of the house. Her mother on the phone. Male voices in the kitchen, probably police. The television. One day her mother comes into the room with the cordless phone from the living room.

"Trisha," she whispers. Trisha is already having a terrible response to her own name. It puts a knot in her gut just to hear it. It goes through her skull like a nail. It is going to have to go, she knows it, though she has yet to put those thoughts into words.

"Trisha, it's your brother. It's Simon. He's on the phone from Alberta. Won't you talk to him?"

She pulls the blankets back from across her face. She looks up at her mother. She shakes her head slowly and pulls up the blankets again, covering her whole head.

Sometimes she hears the voice of her Uncle Ray down the hallway from the kitchen. There is a slow sureness to Ray's voice. She cannot make out any words. But he says a short something. Then he pauses a long time and says another short thing. He's come there to reassure her mother. Trisha can hear that in his tone. But he does not come into her room. And she does not want Uncle Ray to see her in the condition she is now in. So when she hears his voice, she does what she does in response to any voice: she pulls the covers over her head and waits for the voice to go away.

One day comes a commotion. It starts in the kitchen. Someone has come to the door. She hears her mother's voice. Her mother sounds alarmed. More alarmed than she has in days. There is a disagreement. After a long back and forth between her mother and whoever it is who's come with something extraordinary to say, her mother's footsteps come down the hallway. Her bedroom door swings quickly back on the hinges. Her mother comes in, sits on the edge of her bed. Trisha wants the door closed. She is raising a finger to point at it when her mother takes a deep, dramatic breath and says, "Oh, Pattycakes. I've got terrible news." *Pattycakes.* Trisha sits up in bed. She knows what it is. What else can it be?

Her mother says the name: "Becky." Trisha tries to stop listening after the single word. But her mother keeps going.

She hears the word *gone*. Then her mother gets the nerve together to speak clearly. "Dead." And finally: "Suicide."

She sees the puzzled look on her mother's face as her own hand goes up to her mouth. She runs the tips of her fingers against the crescent of her upper teeth and pushes firmly to check they are all present and firmly rooted. She does the same thing to the bottom teeth. Then she puts her head on the pillow and pulls the covers up over her head. She sticks her right hand into her mouth sideways, feels the meat at the root of the thumb against her lips. She clamps the flesh there in her teeth and bites as hard as she can. She bites until the pain runs up her arm to the shoulder and her whole right side feels a twitching, numb paralysis. She bites hard until her jaw begins to ache and until she tastes the metallic taste of her own blood come trickling back across her tongue. *Becky!* She knows her mouth wants to scream the name. But she will not allow it. The harder she feels the urge to scream, the harder she bites her hand.

She wants Becky back. She wants to see Morganne. She wants her phone so she can try to get through. She wants the last week back. She wants to go to Morganne's bedroom on the afternoon before the so-called party, the rape party, the rapety. She wants to stand up from the bed and smash the fuck out of Becky's phone and whatever that creepy guy was telling her on Tinder. She wants to hold Morganne. To tell her: *Let's not follow behind Becky. Let's run ahead and stop her. Let's drag her back to your house. We can lock her in the bathroom. It'll be funny as hell. Let's watch* Sharknado *on Netflix. Let's look at Khloé Kardashian's Instagram and laugh. Let's make another honey and cinnamon face mask. Let's go swimming. Let's go running. Let's call your fucking volleyball team and break into the gym and get arrested for having an illegal volleyball game! Let's not die! Morganne! Let's not kill ourselves! Let's not let those bastards win!*

II

OCTOBER

Ray had his head in the oven, checking on the bacon. He closed the oven door and turned to where Lynne Redmond sat at his kitchen table. The first light of morning was coming through the window over the sink and it brightened her face on one side, leaving the other in shadow. She'd brushed her hair and pulled it back so that the streaks of white ran back from her hairline against steel grey and black. She lowered her face into the steam from her coffee and inhaled the smell of it in a slow, deep breath, like a meditation.

"Ray, I think you'd be making a mistake to bring this up with her," she said.

Ray had not touched his own coffee yet, but he was jittery and unsettled, opening and closing cupboard doors, wiping the spotless counter with a rag.

For one thing, he was awkward about having Lynne there first thing in the morning. It was the first time she'd come to Hubtown and spent the night. She'd tacked a couple of vacation days onto the weekend and taken the Maritime Bus from Sydney. Ray had gasped when she told him the price of the round-trip ticket, but she'd waved a dismissive hand at his offer to pay half. It was wonderful that she'd come. He felt wanted in a way he had not felt in a long time. And looking at her unadorned beauty now, there was a certain giddy feeling he remembered having in his early twenties, those first few magic times he'd been lucky enough to have shared a bed with a woman and to still be with her in the morning.

But it was a school day, and it was embarrassing knowing that Patricia was about to come into the kitchen with him and Lynne in it. It was hard enough to figure out, after all this time, how to have a sex life. Even harder was going to be the gaze of a needy teenager, to whom he'd only shown the outermost shell of himself.

Ray had picked up Sam at school recently, and when she'd come out the front door, she'd been talking to someone Ray would rather have not seen her with. It was the kid who lived at the bad end of Lemon Street with a mother people said was at the far end of alcoholic decline. Ray knew the kid had just spent a year in youth prison. For manslaughter. Everyone in town knew it.

And Patricia was not simply talking to the kid. She was smiling in a way that Ray was not used to seeing. She was carrying an instrument case that she handed to the kid from Lemon Street, and she waved a cute little wave as she walked toward Ray's car.

Part of Ray felt happy for the girl. After all she'd been through, she'd obviously trusted someone enough to befriend them. But mostly he felt concerned. And he'd been holding in his misgivings for days. He'd not said a word to the girl, but he'd been having trouble sleeping. His stomach was hooked up in knots.

When Lynne had landed last night, he'd let it all spill out to her. He'd even choked back tears, he felt so upset, so afraid of the weight of his responsibility to the girl and her mother.

And he'd told Lynne he planned to talk to the girl about it today. She needed to know about the boy she'd befriended.

Ray could still hear the shower going, so he knew there was some time before the girl would be coming into the kitchen.

"Come here, Ray," Lynne said gently. She stretched out a hand and motioned with a nudge of her head for him to sit across the table.

"Sit down. Here." She wiggled her fingers and when he did sit down across the table from her, she insisted he put his hand in hers. When she saw him look over his shoulder at the doorway to the hall, she laughed and said, "Don't worry. When I hear her coming, I'll give you your hand back."

He put his hand in hers, and it did feel better that way. He felt bolstered, confident. A little calmer.

"What is it, exactly, that you want to say to her?"

"What I told you last night." Ray felt angry suddenly. Why was she making him say this when she knew?

"What? About the boy you saw her with?"

"Oh nothing really. Just that he killed someone. Pleaded guilty and got sent away for it."

"I just think you'd be taking an awful chance, Ray. Telling her."

"It feels like an awful chance not telling her."

Lynn squeezed his hand and brought his fingers to her lips, kissed them. "I understand that. But look at you, Ray. You're so wound up over this. If you do this wrong, it could damage the most important relationship in the girl's life right now. Her relationship with you."

Ray felt his eyes well up. He'd never thought of things in those terms. That what he'd done by taking in Eleanor's girl was to start a relationship with her. And that the relationship was the most important one the girl currently had.

The smell of bacon suddenly became overpowering and Ray stood up from the table and switched on the fan in the stove hood. When he opened the oven door, Lynne said, "Good lord, Ray. What have you got in there?"

"It's a bacon weave." He gripped one of three squares of woven bacon strips in a set of tongs and held it up proudly as he turned it over on the cast iron sheet. "In fact, it's three bacon weaves."

Lynne's eyebrows went up and she appeared to recoil slightly. She inhaled a short breath as though to speak, but there was a long pause before she said, "Seems like a lot of bacon."

Ray had worked on perfecting his bacon weave, figuring out which brand and cut of bacon to use, how tight to weave it raw, what the optimum oven temperature was. He'd made one for Lynne before. At her place in Sydney. He'd brought his own bacon for that. She'd said she'd liked it, and it irked him now that Lynne seemed put off by it.

"For one thing, there's no way she does not already know," Lynne said.

Ray nodded. They'd gone through this last night.

"It's a big school. And who knows what kids are saying about this boy. But they're saying something. And Sam has heard them say it. She's been there over a month."

Lynne, of course, had no trouble with the girl's new name. It was the only one she'd ever known.

"Do you think this boy is a danger to her?"

Ray found himself shaking his head before he even had a chance to think about the question. From what he'd heard, the death of the other boy...Mancomb, he thought the name was, was more of an accident than anything else. It was a teenaged fist fight gone bad.

"Not really. I just...I'm responsible for her well-being while she's here. She's been to hell and back."

"If you really want to make sure she knows, get some-one else to tell her. Someone she can afford to damage her relationship with. I'd do it, but she'd see me telling her as just another way of you telling her. Is there a social worker who can do this? A teacher? A school counsellor?"

The sound of the shower had long let up, and they both got quiet as footsteps approached the kitchen.

"Lynne! I didn't know you were here!" The girl opened her arms and Lynne stood up into them. The two of them hugged and their embrace became like a secret handshake that transformed Ray's kitchen into Woman World, a space where he suddenly barely belonged.

"My bus got in late. You were already in bed. Sam, that top looks so pretty on you," Lynne said. Even calling the shirt a top felt like a way of locking him out. He looked at the shirt and tried to see what was pretty about it, but it just looked like a shirt to him.

Lynne was wrapped in a housecoat she'd brought with her, and that's what he'd imagined would be the biggest source of awkwardness, the way the housecoat was linked to the bedroom, the way the bedroom was linked to sex. But there was a conspiratorial look in both Lynne's and the girl's eyes that, though it irritated him because he did not understand what it was about, was also a great relief because it was not about Lynne and Ray having sex.

"Ray, what are you doing with all these eggs?" Lynne

looked into the mixing bowl where Ray had beaten a dozen eggs into a froth. The bacon weaves were finished, and he'd stacked them on a paper-towel-covered plate beside the stove.

"Bacon weave omelette," Patricia said. She had a smirk on her face that she was unsuccessfully fighting off. "A good day begins with a proper breakfast." She was no longer fighting the smirk. And the line was simply something he himself was fond of saying. So this part of the mockery he understood.

"You two are making fun of me," Ray said in a voice he hoped expressed some anger, but not too much.

"No we're n—" the girl began to say, but Lynne cut her off with, "Yes, we are," and the two of them laughed.

12

SEVENTEEN MONTHS EARLIER: MAY

Fifty minutes carrying a Les Paul in a hardshell case. The walking is not a challenge. He can walk for fifty minutes, although he is not in particularly good physical shape. But he knows that carrying the guitar for that long will tire his hands. It is only fifteen minutes from Lemon Street to school, and there have been days when he's lugged the Les Paul that distance in the morning and his hands were stiff and shaking when he started to play. That stiffness and muscle fatigue will work itself out in a few minutes, but he wants to get off to a strong start. When he begins playing, he wants the Jazz Kids to think: *all right. This guy can play.* He does not want to have to play through a bunch of shakiness first.

So he sets out with the case in his right hand. As much as possible, he is going to carry it in his strumming hand. He thinks that is the better hand to be weak.

When he finally arrives at 6 Wren Crescent, there is a new-looking Hyundai on the pad of tarmac outside the garage door. The front yard has some flower beds with ever-green shrubs. A waist-high fence runs down one side of the driveway.

He has been hearing music since halfway down the block. The occasional thump of a bass drum. The low thrum of an amplified upright bass.

He stands a moment at the side door of the garage. He looks over his shoulder at the house to make sure no one from inside is watching him. He straightens himself up, stands to his full height, inhales a deep breath through his nose. He sets the guitar case down at his feet and lets both arms dangle at his sides. He gives them a couple of loosening shakes and holds up both hands, examining them for trembling.

He is standing with one hand on the door knob, the swing-beat pulse of the music detectable through his palm, when a gleaming black Mercedes turns into the driveway.

Holy fuck, a Mercedes, he cannot help thinking.

In the front seat is No, the saxophone player. His mom is driving. She looks right at Robot and smiles. She waves at Robot, says a quick something to her son. No reaches over the seat, pulls a saxophone case out of the back.

"Hey!" Robot says.

The car pulls out of the drive and No comes over to where Robot stands. They've seen each other plenty, but they've never been introduced. Robot puts out his hand, the way someone taught him once. No takes it and they shake.

"I'm—"

"You are fucking Robot," says No. "Everyone in that garage is thrilled you're jamming with us."

Robot hardens his face. Can this guy be shitting him right now? Is this the start of some sort of rich kid prank meant to hurt him?

"No way," Robot says. "Why would anyone want to jam with me?"

No smiles. "You're joking, right?"

"Uh. No."

"Is your real name Robot?"

"It's Robert."

"Oh. I get it!"

"Is your real name No?" There. He's said it. He's asked it. He was given the perfect opportunity and he took it. It might never have come up again.

No shrugged. "Sort of. It's my last name. Like. Family name? It's Korean. When you spell it in English, you're supposed to put an 'h' on the end."

"Is it, like, racist for people to make a thing out of your name like they do?"

Noh shrugs again. "I'm not sure," he says plainly. "You know what the Jazz Kids are like."

"Ha! You're one of the Jazz Kids!"

Noh's face droops with a frown of mild surprise. "I don't think so," he says. He raises his chin in the direction of the door. "Let's go in."

Robot is used to a dramatic *whoosh* when opening the door on people jamming. And there is a sudden rush of volume from the music. But the volume in the garage is not overpowering. The space is well-lit by rows of fluorescent tubes that hang from bare roof trusses. The ceiling and walls are bare, unfinished wood and plastic-covered pink fibreglass insulation. In a far corner, there is a red chest-high tool case on black rubber wheels. Beside it is a stack of winter tires, piled four high on the smooth concrete floor. There are two aluminum ladders hanging parallel, one above the other, on hooks against one long wall. Some paint cans on shelves.

Everything else in the spacious garage is a musical instrument or a piece of sound gear. The big-shouldered girl who plays drums is sitting at a kit. The setup is modest, but the drums appear to be miked. Cables snake out from mic mounts around her. She wears a black men's dress hat that looks like it is meant for winter. Her mid-length brown hair sticks out from under it, clumped with sweat. She is leaning over the snare and hi-hat at the moment, working her brushes, a dazed expression of musical absorption on her face.

To the left of the drummer, a tall ginger kid is playing a dark-wood upright bass. His gaze is locked on the drummer. He stares, not at her face, but at the triangle defined by her face at the top, the snare and hi-hat across the bottom. His bass is plugged into a Fender bass head with a homemade four-by-twelve cabinet under it.

The keyboard player is a girl named Jackie. She is the only one here who Robot sort of knows. He is a year older than the other Jazz Kids. He's pretty sure they're in grade ten. He and Jackie are in grade eleven. Their grade nine gym teacher thought his jokes were fucking hilarious and had a stupid name he called everyone in the class. He called Jackie *Jackie McClacky*, and that is the only version of her last name that Robot can remember now. Actually, the same teacher was the first one who called him *Robot*. It is hard to believe that was only two years ago. It seems like he's never had any other name.

Jackie has two keyboards on the go. There's a cheap-looking Casio side-by-side with a pro-level Roland. Jackie is plugged into a Roland keys amp that is raised up and tilted back in some sort of stand.

There are two mics on stands. Noh is putting his mouth-piece onto his sax in front of one. He's got a reed coming out of his mouth like a narrow, square-tipped tongue. At the other mic, Trumpet Boy has his eyes closed, his lips against the cup of his mouthpiece. He is not playing, but listening to the other players, waiting for his moment to come in. His *Shut Up* shirt, freed from the language restrictions of school, says *Shut the Fuck Up*.

The bass player smiles at Robot and points at a Roland CUBE-60 down beside him on his left. Robot digs his tuner pedal out of the guitar case. He plugs in, estimates a decent volume level, and dials it in on the amp. He straps the guitar over his shoulder and takes a minute to tune. Noh is on his left, and has just put a *Real Book* on a stand in front of him.

"Do you have a *Real Book*?" Noh asks.

Robot shakes his head.

Noh moves his music stand so they both can look at it. He leans over, takes a look at Trumpet Boy's copy, then pages quickly with an index finger to a tune whose name Robot does not have time to look at.

He is focused on the chords. His eyes scan the chord names on the page while his ears listen hard to the tune the players are in the middle of. He's trying to locate where they are in the changes. When he finishes scanning the page, he fills his lungs and empties them with great relief. He can do this. Jackie is on the other side of the room, and he cannot see her fingers well at all. But she is using some reedy organ voice that is cutting clearly through the mix. Robot can make out some of the important notes in the key. There's the one. There's the five. He looks at the names of the chords in the *Real Book*. It sounds like Jackie is playing them straight up, as they are named. Robot's arms are light now that the fifty minutes of guitar carrying are over. He stretches out both arms from the shoulders, yoga pose style. He lets his arms fall loose and relaxed at his sides. He wiggles all ten fingers, pulls a pick out of the guitar's headstock. He watches the chord progression on the page. When the hell will it circle back to the start? As though she's heard his thought, Jackie raises her head. She circles her eyes wide to let him know. *Here it comes.* She counts with nods of her head: one, two, three, and...

Boom. He digs in from bar one. Trumpet Boy points up for him to increase his volume.

Trumpet Boy and Noh are looking at each other now, playing a harmonized line, giving each other little twitching movements of their horns to help stay locked on the beat.

Robot listens to the rich, mellow sound his Les Paul makes through the CUBE-60. He adjusts the highs down and pulls the mids up a bit, thickening his tone further. He listens hard for the drums as he works his strumming pattern into the mix. He feels around for the bass. In a moment, he finds a little pocket he can drop into and suddenly he can stop trying so hard.

He has never played with horns before. Jesus! Listen to how clever those two parts are! The way they lean toward and away from each other.

He closes his eyes and sinks away into the harmonies. Before he knows it, he feels a tension building. They are getting ready for a stop. He opens his eyes and he can see that everyone has perked up, looking for who is going to direct. "Three beat stop!" Trumpet Boy shouts. "After the one," the bell of his trumpet goes up, and comes down, everyone stops playing. The drummer clicks her sticks together for the three beats. "To the bridge!" Trumpet Boy shouts, and...

whoosh! There they go. Back into the tune from the start of the changes at the bridge.

———

IT IS LATE WHEN HE GETS HOME. NOH'S MOM DRIVES HIM RIGHT to Lemon Street, even though it is out of her way.

In the dark, the houses at this end of the street look even dingier. The street lights are dim and have a weird tinge to them. All the cheery new green of coming summer has darkened into black.

"That was a great jam," Noh says from the front seat.

"Oh, man," Robot says. "You guys are all such awesome players."

Noh turns around and smiles.

"That was my first time playing with horns," Robot says.

Noh turns around again and with a disbelieving frown says, "No way."

"First time playing with a group off the written page. I've practiced off paper before."

"What do you normally play off? Like...tabs or something?" He says *tabs* like he has no idea what it means. He's heard guitar players use the word, so he's taking a wild guess with it.

Robot laughs. "I normally play metal. Or at least some kind of rock. Nobody reads that off paper."

"You play it by ear?"

Robot shrugs. "That's what they call it when you're not reading. But it's from memory, mostly. Anyway. That was pretty awesome."

Robot gets out of the Mercedes and stands on the

sidewalk as the vehicle corners right onto Elm Way at the end of the block.

His phone is still on his bed where he left it. He is feeling too good about things to check it. He knows it is only going to be full of awfulness. The asshole *Prank Fights* fans who want to see him and a kid he barely knows beating on each other. He picks it up and sets it on the floor.

He puts the guitar case against the wall, snaps off the light, and sits on the edge of the bed. Every cell in his body is popping. He feels electrified. Ecstatic. His mind goes back to the garage. The changes they played from the *Real Book* swirl past in his imagination. He hears the rattling, hissing interplay of the snare and hi-hat. He looks down at the dark form of his left hand in the shadows of his lightless bedroom. He tries to picture his hand in the shape of all the chords it played tonight. It seems impossible.

He lies back on his bed and pulls up the covers. How will he ever sleep? He goes through it all again in his mind. All the tunes, one after another from Noh's *Real Book*. He thinks of funny little moments when everyone got lost. There was an incredible four bars where the drums and bass and keys all dropped out and it was just him and the horns. And he'd cut the chords down to their essential triads on the high strings. And he was playing one beat per bar and he did not even know what beat he was hitting. It was like the *and* before the one, but the horn players were following him and they'd pared their parts down to an answering stab that echoed his chords. And that alone. That minute. That forty-five seconds of improvised fun was the high point of his musical life. Everything he'd ever practiced had brought him there, right to that moment in a garage on Wren Crescent. With players he'd never played with before.

He has an alarm set on his phone. When it rings, he awakes first to the dingy reality of his room. He is not in the clean, neatly ordered garage that was stocked with thousands of dollars' worth of musical instruments and sound gear. He is not going to be driven anywhere in a Mercedes. He does not have a sober, healthy mom who is going to look out for him, dote on him. His own mom is barely going to notice he is alive today. And she'll be lucky to live through the day herself. After the enormous high of last night, it seems a terrible injustice that he is back to his same old shitty world today. While they played music, he was full of so much joy. There was power and energy in what they did. Everything felt so right and full. Now he feels empty. Why? Why does his life have to be devoid of everything that feels right?

The room is dark except for the square of his phone on the floor by his bed, lighting up with the annoying beep of his alarm. As he nudges the phone to shut off the alarm, his notifications scroll across the screen. A hundred text messages. All of them angry, violent, hateful. He picks up the phone, pushes it back into sleep mode, and lies face up on his bed, the phone clutched to his chest. Now that his eyes are adjusting to the dark, he can see the square of light in the high window across from him.

What would have felt right and natural would have been to have a shower, grab something to eat, and go right back out to Wren Crescent. Spend the day in that garage. Play music. Have fun. Be positive. Use skills he's spent a long time practicing and developing. In a just world, a world that made sense and was set up correctly, that's what he'd get to do.

Instead, he is going to have to turn on the lights in this dirty apartment. He is going to have to check to see if his mother is alive. He is going to have to go to school, submit himself to the mob of idiots that the chief idiots, two guys with more YouTube subscribers than they have ideas in their heads, can just sic on him any time they want.

He pads across the floor and flips on the light. His own room is dingy, but it is not a chaotic horror, like the rest of the apartment. He has a bed with a box spring and mattress. He keeps the bed made. He keeps the bedding clean. He has a plastic milk crate for a night stand. There is a book on the crate. A simple lamp.

His guitar is in its case. The Peavey tube amp he started saving for right after he got the guitar. This much of his world makes sense. This much is in his power to order and control.

He opens his mother's bedroom door just a crack. He almost gags at the smell. The reek of alcohol and what it is doing to her body. But he hears her laboured breathing, the frightened dream sounds she makes in her drunken sleep. Slow-motion moans, half-muffled by sleep paralysis.

There is one frozen waffle left in a cardboard package in the fridge. But there is no syrup and no butter in the kitchen. Three of the four burner coils in the two-slot toaster do not work. So he puts the waffle in the one slot of the toaster that half works, and when he sees the waffle's side turning brown, he pops it out, turns it 180 degrees, and plunges it down for a second try.

The whole way from Lemon Street to school, he scans the roads and walkways with trepidation. The assholes with their video camera are going to be after him at some point in the day. And he would not have been shocked to find them right outside his door on Lemon Street as he left his house. The day is light. The sky partly clouded. There is free toast at school until five minutes before first period, and he walks quickly, on relatively quiet streets, his bookbag over one shoulder, his guitar in his opposite hand, thinking about what he would do if he got surrounded again, like he had that other day. Suitjon's camera in his face, Lucas Shortt narrating his response into a ridiculous microphone.

Will the Jazz Kids ask him to play again? Will it be today? Will he ever be one of the kids who does not even have to get invited to jam in the band room at school? One of the kids who can just assume they've been granted a place? One of the kids who comes into the room where everyone else is already playing, and just joins in?

He does not like going into the school through the front door. Too many people congregate there on the steps. Assholes can get tucked away behind one of the pillars and before you can prepare yourself or turn the other way, they're in your face. He prefers going through one of the entrances on the south side of the building, but sometimes they are not open first thing in the morning.

He steps across the teachers' parking lot.

There is a little gap in the hedge where he and his guitar case can just squeeze through. The principal's office is visible from this walkway. You can see right through the window. And there is the principal, in a charcoal suit, like an American president, his chin in his hand, staring at a computer screen on his desk.

The side door pulls open. Ahead of him there are people in the foyer, but he ducks left down the hallway in the direction of the cafeteria. As he gets closer to the band room, he can hear music coming through the open door. He can tell it is the same kids he jammed with last night. He recognizes all of their individual voices. It is a jam they played on, too. Jackie sounds like maybe she's playing the Yamaha upright acoustic piano, probably with a mic stuck in the back of it. It is a loopy little chord progression: ii, v, I with one tricky bar of 5/4 thrown into the middle of it. Last night, before they cottoned onto it, nobody could figure out how to get that five-beat bar right. They all fumbled their way through it, faking the counts and hoping it would work. Then they would all start laughing when it fell apart. They got so used to laughing on that bar that they laughed the first time Robot played through it correctly. They'd heard it wrong so many times that the right way sounded messed.

He walks down the hall toward the open door of the band room as though in a dream. What is going to happen? There is no way he is going to have enough nerve to just walk in there like he belongs. There is too much opportunity for high-visibility rejection there. He is going to walk past the door. Casually. But he is going to walk slowly, so that someone inside will have the chance to see him.

One, two, three, four, five: there goes the tricky bar again, but everyone plays through it correctly now. They've done it so many times, it no longer poses a challenge. And there is the open doorway. And there are the Jazz Kids. Jackie is standing up at the Yamaha upright, her back to Robot and to the open door. The drummer is playing the school's second-best kit, a beat-up wood-grained Pearl set. She has her face set sideways, staring at the bass player. Robot is past the door before he hears his name shouted. It is Trumpet Boy's voice. Shouting through the mic he's been playing into.

"Hello!" Robot shouts through the open door as he steps happily back to it. He pokes his head around the door post. Everyone keeps playing, but they all turn toward the doorway and smile at him. Trumpet Boy points at an old Peavey solid state stage amp. "Plug in, bro," he calls.

Robot holds up five fingers. "I'll be back in five minutes," he shouts over the music. He pauses a moment to consider whether or not to drop his bookbag and instrument case in the room before heading quickly to the cafeteria for some free toast. No. They invited him to play. But the room does not feel like his space. He does not leave his stuff there. He rushes down the hallway toward the cafeteria. As he climbs the stairs to the second floor, the aroma of buttered toast hits him square on the nose and his mouth begins to water. He is waiting for the bread to fall down the back of the conveyor when he catches sight of the first idiot.

Suitjon is outside the cafeteria. In the hallway with his camera rig. Robot gets a glimpse of him passing by, crossing the width of the double doors.

"Okay. Okay," Robot says aloud. He hears his two pieces of white bread toast hit the pan at the bottom of the toaster. "You knew this was coming," he says to himself. "Just. Handle it. Handle it." By the time he has the bread smeared with peanut butter and jam, there is a crowd gathering in the hallway outside the cafeteria. If they are staying there to ambush him on the way out, that will be better. At least he will be able to eat his toast in peace.

But, *fuck!* It just occurs to him. They are going to follow him. They will follow him down the hall, down the stairs. They'll follow him to the band room. That will be the worst. That will be humiliating. That will be it, the end of whatever fragile relationship he's just begun with the Jazz Kids. The Jazz Kids want to play music. The Jazz Kids want a guitar player, not some loser with an entourage from a YouTube fist fight channel. *Fuck!* He begins wolfing down the toast, folds one piece up and shoves it into his mouth, stuffing it in. Even as he stands there, the hallway outside the cafeteria is darkening with bodies. Their voices are growing in volume. In the kitchen at the far end, across from the toaster, two or three cafeteria workers are bustling about, already doing prep work for lunch. One of them, a stout lady in a white smock and white cotton kitchen cap, stops what she is doing to look suspiciously over at the increasingly noisy crowd in the hallway.

The idiots have spooked the room. The few people who were in the cafeteria with him, eating free toast, doing a bit of last minute homework, scrolling blankly through their social media, disperse now. They dump their paper plates and napkins into the trash bins. They fold their binders and books. They either go out the fire door in the back corner, or they squeeze out the cafeteria door and join the fight-hungry crowd in the hallway or they make their way through it to escape to some other part of the building.

Halfway to the office, in the school's central hallway, the Jazz Kids are jamming away happily. They'll stop after ten minutes, page their way through the *Real Book* until they find another number that interests them, and keep going until the first bell. Later, as they are packing up for class, they'll wonder where he went. But Robot cannot go to the band room now. There will be too much commotion. Too much humiliation. He's only just opened the door between himself and the Jazz Kids. He cannot risk closing it back up forever by trailing his fucked up life right to their literal front door.

Robot doesn't even have any of the Jazz Kids' numbers. He cannot text them with an excuse, an explanation, or even an apology for not coming back when he said he would. This might be the end, anyway, he realizes as he sits down in the cafeteria. If the Jazz Kids take his not showing up as a snub—and why wouldn't they?—he might never get a chance to play with them again. Not another hallway invite from Trumpet Boy. Not another call through the open band room door. If the assholes in the hallway outside are going to wait for him, he'll wait them out in here. He is not going to give them the pleasure of seeing him do what they want. He'll wait here for the bell, and when the hallway empties out, he'll make his way to science class. Late, if need be.

This time of day, the vice principals are outside, dressed in safety vests, monitoring the kids getting off buses. There are hall monitors, older ladies with icy, hardened stares they use to keep kids following school rules. And if the monitors happen by, they'll disperse the crowd that's hovering in the hallway waiting for him. But it's a big school, and there are really only a few minutes until first period begins.

Robot places his second piece of toast on the tabletop before him. Moisture and crumbs spread out from it into the napkin it rests on. He takes out his phone and places it on the table beside the toast. Out of curiosity and just to confirm what he knows will be true, he touches the *on* button and his notifications explode across the screen.

Come on out and play, Robert.

Come out in the hallway, you chicken piece of shit.

Do you think you can hide in there? We see you.

So many texts, though there cannot be more than a few dozen people in the hallway waiting for him.

First bell rings. He is not going to move.

"Get us both in the shot," he hears Lucas Shortt say. Then: "There he is. Across the cafeteria. He's refusing to come out into the hallway. As far as we know now, Gink is not even in the building yet today. But the crowd here is clearly expecting something to happen. Shoot the crowd. Get a shot of the crowd. Turn around. That's it. Now get up high and pan slowly past the faces. Stay tuned to the *Prank Fights* channel. More excitement soon."

13

OCTOBER

Sam had not seen Robert since they sang together in that back stairwell, Robert sitting high up on the landing, Sam standing by the fire door, her back against the wall. They'd had their eyes closed most of the time, in what felt to Sam like a dream state, and they'd sung for the better part of an hour. It had probably felt different to Robert, because he was used to playing music like that. He was used to singing, to opening up to a song. What had been a powerful and intimate moment for Sam, a moment when she had exposed a vulnerable part of herself to Robert with her voice, that might not have felt the same for him. She'd lost herself in that simple song about a hammer and about freedom and about self-proclamation and self-determination. A song she did not even really understand. *Tell him I'm gone*, she'd sung. And that's the way she'd felt, *gone*.

She'd felt gone in the way you felt the first time you got drunk and you thought that this was how drinking was going to make you feel. All happy and warm inside. And little did you know. But she'd felt in control of that amazing feeling while she and Robert had been singing. She had not given herself over to some drug. With her eyes closed in that stairwell and her head thrown back, she'd felt given over to herself. She felt as though that silly little song and that tiny, toy-like instrument she was playing, these things had helped her locate the best part of herself. The part that was willing to reach out to the best part of others. And not only had that part of her been well-hidden after the assault and all the terrible things that happened afterward, but the best part of her was something she'd never found before in her life. The closest she'd ever been was the peacefulness that used to come over her watching Morganne draw. And then, there it was, fluttering inside her like an awkward angel in her chest. And she'd opened her mouth to sing the next line and up it had gone into the air above her and that whole stairwell had echoed with what was best in her mixed with what was best in Robert.

And maybe that was something Robert was used to. But it had certainly never happened to her before.

So in the intervening weekend, she'd spent a lot of time looking forward to her next music class. She could not wait to see Robert again.

Maybe they'd pair up. Maybe the teacher would move them off to some private corner where they could sing again. Maybe they'd be doing some sort of book work all class and they'd only have enough opportunity to say hello. Or sit near each other. Maybe there was something, even some boring chart to fill out, that they could collaborate on and then when they'd finished, they could sneak out back to that stairwell again and sing till she felt better. Sing till she felt good.

She went looking for versions of "Take This Hammer," and there were many to choose from. But there was a version by a Canadian named Harry Manx that she thought must have been the model upon which Robert had based his version. It was slow and spare with a funky groove. And just hearing that version, listening to it three or four times in a row, she felt much more prepared to attempt the song again. She had ideas for the song. A fun place for a dramatic stop. Different ways of phrasing the lines.

When she switched from listening to Manx's "Take This Hammer" to Piaf's "La Vie en rose," the difficulties of the Piaf song were stark. The melody was all over the place. The chord changes were crazy. She could not keep track of them at all. And then there were the lyrics. She wanted to sing the song in French, even though she only really understood a word or two. There were English versions on YouTube she could have clicked on, but she did not want to waste her ears on them. The song. The singer. The language. These particular words. These specific things had gripped her and anything else seemed like fakery. Piaf's voice in that song seemed rooted to the earth like a hundred-year oak. Bullets would have bounced off her when she was singing it. That's what Sam wanted for herself. It was a goal so obviously ridiculous and unobtainable that there was no way she'd ever describe it to anyone else in those words.

Singing with Robert had connected her to some deep secret. The secret of inner power, inner strength. And the Piaf song seemed to have connected to the possibility of an even greater power, a power currently outside of her, but that she felt it might be possible to gather in and claim. Just listening to Piaf bend the whole universe with her voice brought Sam close to something important. But it was singing it herself she wanted. She wanted the power to bend the world. Singing so sweetly with Robert had brought her a step in that direction. She wanted to ask for his help to bring her the rest of the way.

—

MONDAY MORNING SAM SAT IN MUSIC CLASS ANXIOUSLY awaiting Robert's arrival. The chart for "La Vie en rose" was carefully folded up and stuffed into the front pocket of her jeans, like something she might need in an emergency. She'd tried singing a few bars of the melody. She knew enough about chords now to fumble her way through playing just the root notes that accompanied the few phrases that felt within her reach. She had her head down and did not want to make it too obvious she was looking for anyone. But she'd scanned the room furtively on arriving and did not see Robert, so she sat where she could see the classroom door if she shifted her eyes a little.

The Piaf quotation and the drawing had been erased from the blackboard, but she looked down at her hand and saw the little tattoo in a new light. The girl on her hand was Piaf now, somehow, and somehow Becky, too. *La Vie en rose. I want to smell La Vie en rose.*

When the teacher called Robert's name for attendance, someone behind Sam spoke.

"Did you hear what happened to that guy? Robert? Robot?"

In her anxious state, the room felt formless around her. She turned around and looked at the boy who'd spoken: a skinny metal guy with black hair dyed blacker, blue-black. He had an Illuminati tattoo on his forearm, an eye over a pyramid with rays of light spiking outward.

"He got the shit beat out of him. Yeah. He's in the hospital... Dragged him out of his house in the middle of the night...I heard he's *bad*. Like. Broken up. I don't know. I heard it was a bootlegger or something. I would not mess with Robot. He fuckin killed that guy? Gink? One punch. Did you see that video? I've got that on my phone."

"Everybody's got that on their phone."

"And they spray-painted him. Kicked the shit out of him, then tagged him with spray paint. My friend who lives over there told me it was the word *shame*. They left a mark. A smear of paint right out on the pavement on Lemon Street. Right out in front of his house."

"What's wrong with that girl?"

Sam's heart was pounding in her chest. She closed her eyes and tried to slow her breathing. She lowered her head until it rested, sideways, left ear on her thigh, down in her own lap. Hearing of Robert being assaulted had made her want to cover her own body, to fold up and protect herself from the blows that flashed through her mind, that came pummelling in at her from all directions.

"Sam? Sam? You okay?" It was the music teacher's voice. He'd come to her side. His voice was right up against her ear.

She had to get out of this room.

"Sam?"

A lightning storm in her head. All sounds mashed together into a sweeping roar. Faces had flipped through her mind at first, movements, gestures, threatening grunts. But now there were no distinguishable shapes, just a rapidly blossoming brightness followed by a collapse into black.

"I'll be okay." She hoped that's what she was saying. She could not hear her own voice above the thundering of her mind. But she was fairly sure her lips had moved. She'd felt the buzzing of her voice down in her throat.

"I need to get out of this room."

She opened her eyes and it was like a video shot from a camera swinging at the end of a rope. A swath of floor, the material of the leg of her jeans, every thread and dent in the fabric like a landscape of craters. Chrome of chair legs, the beige of painted cement blocks. She stood and the path to the doorway was a blur of dark objects, lighted background, toothy grins as assholes enjoyed her distress. Someone was probably posting about this right now. Using her panic attack for clout.

When she reached the hallway, she felt the extra air. Her lungs opened up. Her head was down, her eyes were open. The teacher was at her side, but he was nothing more than a blur of motion in her periphery. "I know what to do," she said dismissively, waving him away like a nuisance fly. "Yes. Yes. I'm going to student services." She felt him drop away, jettisoned like the used-up stage of a rocket in a launch. She took a few staggering steps down the hallway, one hand against the high-gloss paint of the cement block wall. By the time she got to the front of the building, she felt her legs strong beneath her. But she did not go to student services. She walked right past its glass doors and continued out the front door of the school and onto the street. The chill of the autumn day was invigorating.

While she was still in range of the school Wi-Fi, she got out her phone and looked up Lemon Street. It looked kind of far away but easy to find. Up the street. A left, a right, another left.

She walked through the town in a decreasingly delirious state. The walking was good. The breathing she had to do. The sense of going somewhere.

By the time she got to Lemon Street her emotions had

calmed. The internal noise and ruckus had quieted. There was an ambulance on the street, and for a moment she felt confused. The lights of the ambulance flashed in red and blue against the daylight. Most of her brain understood that Robert had already been taken away in an ambulance. If what the boy in music class had said was true, it would have been hours ago. The middle of the night she was sure he'd said. She stood at the bottom of the street as paramedics came out of the front door of a house on the left. They had a wheeled stretcher that they rolled and lifted, professionally, calmly, out the door and down a walkway to the ambulance. There was a woman on the stretcher. A bony face and a tuft of grey hair above where the thin ambulance coverings were folded back. The woman's eyes appeared to be closed. The body was still and helpless-looking. When the ambulance pulled away, there was a single blast from the siren and the vehicle came rushing down the street, lights flashing.

Sam walked up the sidewalk with some hesitation. At the house the ambulance had just left, there was a cloud of fresh white spray paint on the street. She made out part of a handprint. There was a rounded, angular outline that could have been a knee, drawn up. If something had been written with the paint, as the boy she'd heard in class had said, it could not be deciphered from this mess.

A woman stood in a doorway in the house beside the one the ambulance had attended to. The woman in the doorway was standing with her arms folded in a self-protective way. Her face was on the young side. Her expression betrayed no emotion, but she looked haggard, tired to the point where she might be ready to cry. Her hair was dyed a brown that did not suit her skin tone. She had a child on one hip. An older child stood by her side and her free hand rested lightly on the top of this child's head.

"Bad luck day," the woman said to Sam. "First the son, then the mother."

Sam took a few steps closer so she would not have to shout in response.

"Oh my god," she said. "Was that Robert's mother?"

The woman nodded slightly, as though that's all she had the energy for. "I called 911 for him. Not sure who called for her. Landlord maybe."

14

OCTOBER

"I don't know any names."

There were two cops. The older one had one funny eye: half closed all the time, giving him a permanently sceptical look. He had his cop hat in his hands and his short, grey and black hair was dented and slopped around from the hat. The younger cop was a lot taller than the old one. You could tell, even under his police uniform, that he had a big, powerful torso and his upper arms were jacked. He looked at Robot, then at the other cop.

"I'm not bullshitting you. There were three guys. At least three. They were wearing masks like in a dumb movie. Two of them I have no idea. The third guy is a bootlegger I chased off my doorstep a few days ago. Dressed in all brown Carhartts like that? Work clothes that he's never done any work in. And the steel-toe boots. Spotless. Like the day they were bought. I guess I know what he needs those for now." He had an urge to pat the injured parts of himself, his ribs especially, where the pain pulsed and throbbed a half-beat behind his heart, but he'd done that several times already, and touching the bruises only made the hurt worse.

The cops stood directly at the side of the bed, practically right up against it. Robot had been dozing when they'd come in and when he'd opened his eyes, it was the police officers he'd focused on. Now that he was waking up, he noticed some movement right beside the cops. In an armchair against the wall was the girl from his music class, Sam.

Her eyes were locked onto his. The look on her face said a lot of things. It said she was frightened. It also said she was concerned. There was a layer of warmth in it somewhere, a degree of caring beyond just fear.

Robot was reclined on the bed and looking at her sideways. He moved to lift his head and straighten out his view of her, but pain shot through him in so many places that he could not identify them all. He let his head fall back onto the pillow.

"What about the spray painting?" the older cop said. His face showed no empathy. No emotion at all. Robot looked down at his own arms. There were still small dabs and flakes of white paint where someone, some underpaid nursing assistant, probably, had tried to wash the paint off him. Up until that moment, he'd actually forgotten about the paint. It had happened at the end, after the beating was over. A sharp memory of the smell came back to him, the fumes.

"Is spray-painting people a thing now?" Robot asked.

"That's what we want to know," the older cop said.

"Shame," the younger cop said.

"What?"

"That's what they painted. The word *shame*. It covered your entire body. The EMTs reported that. By the time they got you here, the doctors..."

"Shame," Robot said. He took in a breath and exhaled, let his head sink back into the pillow. He liked the antiseptic gleam of the hospital, its comforting lack of squalor.

"As if I need to have that word spray-painted on me. As if I need some poison-selling bootlegger to tag me with that word." He looked over at Sam, whose look of concern for him had not changed.

He was in a ward room with several other beds in it. Some of them seemed occupied to him, but he did not have the energy to even look around and take note. There was a window in the wall opposite. Most of the light in the room seemed to be coming through that. There was the clean, chemical, hospital smell. It was a smell he associated with the Springtown Youth Centre, and therefore with incarceration and consequences, and also with not worrying about the possibility of rats or whether or not there would be enough food for breakfast when he woke up.

A short interview with the police wore him out. And though they were still talking to him, he found his eyelids heavy. He blinked slowly at the police and then drifted off.

When he woke up again, the police were gone, but Sam was still there.

"Isn't this a school day?" he said. "What time is it, anyway?" He swivelled his head around as much as he could do comfortably, but there was no sign of a clock. Sam did not answer.

"Seems like you might have a thing about not talking," he said. "Sometimes you talk. But...I don't know. Sometimes you just don't seem to talk. Is that right?" He rested his head sideways on the pillow. Felt the stiffness of hospital laundry on his cheek. Sam's expression had not changed. It seemed an impossible position to hold a face in, frozen in a mix of emotions.

"I probably look pretty scary right now, do I?" He put his hands carefully up in the direction of his face. There were bandages and other medical appliances that he was afraid to probe too vigorously. Something was bound to become dislodged. His finger was bound to touch something that might hurt.

"You're not from around here, are you?" he said. "Where are you from?" Sam's expression darkened and she hinged her head forward, lowered her gaze. "There's something about me I don't think you know," Robot said. "I'm famous around here. Infamous. I looked that word up. It does not mean the opposite of famous. It means famous for a bad reason. Did you know that?" He was speaking gently to the girl, but he could feel a well of emotion filling up inside him. A pain ripped through the muscles around his ribs every time he shifted his weight, and he groaned as he turned to get a better look at her, just the top of her head as she gazed silently down into her hands. Into the little stick-and-poke tattoo he'd noticed before, at the base of her thumb.

"I killed a guy. Did you know that?" Now she looked up. "His name was Travis Cody Mancomb. I barely even knew him. I didn't mean to kill him, but it wasn't really an accident. It should have been a story we could both tell when we got older. A story about how tough we were when we were young. A story about how dumb we were. But only one guy lived to tell the story. There's a video of it. They took it off YouTube, but it's everywhere else. If you haven't seen it yet, you're the only one in town. The worst moment of my life. For anyone to watch whenever they want. The worst thing a person can do. Kill another person. And I did it. And I don't need some lowlife bootlegger's reminder."

His eyes filled up and then spilled over. Tears ran down his face and he began to sob. Once he started crying it was like some crazy spirit had overtaken his body and he just cried and could not stop. Hot, shameful tears. The way the crying convulsed his body was the worst thing for someone who'd been beaten up as he'd been. Every place he'd been hurt lit up with pain as he cried. And now Sam was crying, too. She'd pulled her chair next to the bed and put her face down into the mattress. Their crying was loud. Robot could hear it fill up the room and echo down the long hospital corridor. A nurse came into the room to check on them. There were other beds in the room, but a privacy curtain had been drawn most of the way around. The nurse pulled the curtain the rest of the way, closing off the bed and the little place beside it where Sam sat in a chair. There was an IV tube in Robot's arm, taped in place just above his wrist. The nurse gently lifted the arm and examined the needle and tube. In a whisper barely audible over the unbroken crying she said: "Just let's be careful of that IV," and she backed out the door to the hallway again, the sound of two teenagers' crying unrelenting in the room.

15

FIVE MONTHS EARLIER: MAY

The girl who used to be Trisha sits on a folding chair in a large, well-lit room. *Community Room,* she heard someone call it as she and her mother came through the front door of the Town of Westervale Fire Hall.

"We're gathering in the Community Room," the voice said. It was the voice of an older woman. Soft, friendly, but also matter of fact. The tone was of someone who had work to do, someone who was trying to stay detached during a time of emotions.

It rained hard during the funeral mass. There were large windows on both sides of the church, and the girl who used to be Trisha could hear the hard pelting of the drops against the glass. But by the time they'd got to the Fire Hall, the clouds had broken and the sun was out.

The windows are small in the Community Room, high above the heads of the people in the room. You cannot see out the windows except for the white blue of the sky. But the light of day comes through in abundance.

The girl has her head down. Her mother has tried to talk her out of coming here. To her mother, Becky's suicide is like an infection the girl who used to be Trisha is in danger of contracting. Also, although her mother would never say so, and although she has never shown anything but respect and affection for Morganne, the girl knows her mother is afraid to be around Mi'kmaw people.

Becky was white, and her immediate family is white. And the town of Westervale is a town mostly full of white people. But it is a small town. And the Mi'kmaw community of Running Brook is only a few kilometres away and has almost twice as many people as Westervale. Becky lived with a mixed family that the girl can tell her mom thinks of as Mi'kmaq. Becky had Mi'kmaw cousins and friends. A big part of the congregation of the Westervale Catholic Church is Mi'kmaq. There were Mi'kmaw language banners on the wall. Maybe half of the people who attended the funeral were Mi'kmaw people.

The girl who used to be Trisha has no reason to think her mom does not like Mi'kmaw people. It's simple fear of the unknown. And her fear is generational, as the girl sees it. She grew up in a time when Mi'kmaw people and white people did not mix. She has never been well acquainted with anyone but white people her whole life. She isn't really racist or prejudiced, but she still calls Running Brook *The Reserve*, which is actually what most Mi'kmaw people call it. But you are not supposed to call it that anymore if you are white. And she doesn't call Mi'kmaw people *Mi'kmaq* or *Indigenous*, like you are supposed to now. She says *Natives*, which is the old right thing to say instead of the *I* word.

The girl has not left the house since being released from the hospital. Except to go to the bathroom, she's barely left her room. She knows this for all the concern her mother has for her, about her physical state. About the possibility of suicide. For all the protectiveness her mother feels. For all the danger her mother thinks she might be inviting by leaving the house—physical assault from the people who are attacking her online, physical or emotional collapse—her mother will also feel a certain hopefulness in having her leave the house. She cannot stay inside forever, and going to her friend's funeral seems in some way a sign that she might be recovering.

The girl has her hand wrapped in white gauze that is held in place by white surgical tape. The self-inflicted bite mark has turned her whole hand dark purple, and the brown and purple edge of the bruise has blossomed past the crease of her wrist. She cleaned the wound herself. Disinfected it with hydrogen peroxide in the bathroom. Her mother was outside the locked bathroom door attempting to convince her to see a doctor over the injury.

"Trisha. Trisha," her mother called through the door. And by the third or fourth call, the girl inside the bathroom knew she was through with that name. The internet was full of shitty people using that name to hate on her. "That's not my name!" she yelled at the door. She knew even as she was yelling how crazy it must have sounded. So crazy it actually slowed her mother down. Stopped her in her tracks for a time. For minutes there was silence as the girl inverted the bottle of peroxide onto a cotton makeup pad, then dabbed the pad over the deep, blood-seeping holes she'd bitten into her own flesh.

"What?" her mother shouted at last, in confusion and disbelief.

"Leave me alone!" the girl shouted. "I'm not going to the hospital! I'm looking after this myself!"

"Please, Tri—" her mother stopped herself. She was a fast learner. "If you won't go to the hospital, please. At least... Open the door! I'm worried sick out here."

The girl who used to be Trisha paused. The sour smell of peroxide filled the inside of her sinuses. She looked up at herself in the bathroom mirror: bruises, abrasions. The sunken, expressionless look of her face did not seem the face of a sixteen-year-old. It was the haggard face of someone twice her age. Shit. Her mother wanted the door open because she was afraid that the girl was in here killing herself.

She set down the peroxide bottle, threw the pad she'd been smearing over the bloody teeth marks into the toilet, where it oozed oily peroxide and pink diluted blood into the toilet water.

She paused another instant at the ragged sight of herself in the mirror, then leaned over and clicked the bathroom door unlocked. The girl picked up a fresh makeup pad, soaked it with peroxide, and kept dabbing her bitten hand. Her mother rushed through the unlocked door with the urgency of a firefighter. She came to the girl's side and put an arm around her as she peered over her daughter's shoulder at the wounded hand. The mother pressed the side of her upper body against her daughter and squeezed with a force the daughter knew would not last long and therefore tolerated without complaint. The mother breathed in big breaths, big, slow, deep breaths through her nose. The daughter could feel the mother's tension relax a little with each exhalation. And every time she felt her mother's tension drop, the daughter felt a small improvement in herself. The daughter kept fussing with the brown plastic bottle of peroxide, kept dabbing a cotton makeup pad at her bite wound, but she closed her eyes in relief at her mother's touch. She let her body loosen and be drawn close.

—

IT WAS ONLY WITH HER MOTHER'S ACTUAL PHYSICAL SUPPORT that the girl who used to be Trisha was able to get through Becky's funeral. They entered the Westervale Catholic Church with their arms around each other. The girl knew she must have been an alarming sight. There were visible bruises from the assault. She knew that most people associated the way the bite mark on her hand was bandaged with cutting. And she could feel beneath her the wobbly weakness of her legs. Though a lot of the shakiness in her legs would be masked by her loose-fitting pants, her mom was practically carrying her.

The day before, the girl heard her mother on the phone, discussing with someone whose business it was not, the possibility of wheeling the girl to the funeral in a wheelchair.

"A wheelchair!" the girl called from her bedroom. "Fuck that! I'm not letting a single fucking hater see me in a fucking wheelchair."

But she was so fragile as she walked, hanging off her mother's side like a heavy parcel, that she'd probably have made less of a spectacle in a wheelchair.

"Bring it on, haters," the girl says now as she and her mother make their way into the Community Room.

"What?" her mother says.

Folding chairs make a loosely defined circle around the perimeter of the room. In the midst of the circle, people begin to gather, one by one and in clusters.

As she and her mother make their way across the floor to a pair of folding chairs against the outer wall, she catches sight of Morganne's mom across the room on the far side, near a counter that leads back to a kitchen area, where a lot of older-looking ladies are busy with food preparation.

She'd guessed that Morganne would probably not be at the funeral. She had not heard from her in days, since her mom had taken her phone. It is not hard to spot Morganne's mom. She is the tallest person in the room. As the towering, broad-shouldered woman moves in her direction, it takes the girl a moment to notice that Morganne's dad is at the mother's side. She rarely sees the two of them standing side by side like that, close enough to invite comparison. But it is remarkable how much bigger the mom is than the dad. She looms a whole head above him and her shoulders and hips are broader than her husband's. Morganne's mom wears a sleeveless black dress that goes straight down at the sides.

Even though it reaches to just above the knees, you can see her powerful thigh muscles working beneath the dress's material. The father wears what must be one of his lawyer suits. Dark charcoal. His thin body is lost in its outlines. His face looks drawn, as though he has not been eating. The mother moves ahead of the father when she reaches the girl. The girl has a sudden realization in the dark, determined eyes of the mother, in her strong, square jawline, in the grey-tinged fullness of the hair she's pulled back into a fist-sized bun. This is what Morganne will look like when she gets older. If she gets through this. If they all get through this. If what's left of them gets through this.

Before either of them can speak, they both reach out, lean into each other, and embrace. Both of them sob loudly and without pretence of self-control for what feels to the girl like a long time. Her sore cheek presses hard into Morganne's mother's hard rib cage, above her breasts at the centre of her chest. Her clothing smells like Morganne's clothing. Her skin smells like Morganne's skin.

She had so wanted to act mature in this moment, but the girl who used to be Trisha is crying like a baby. And like a small child, she says: "I want Morganne. I need to see Morganne."

"Morganne is going to be okay," Morganne's mom says. "Morganne is a strong person. And she is going to get through this."

"I need to see her," the girl who used to be Trisha says.

"Morganne cannot do this right now," the mother says. "Morganne needs to focus on her own healing."

"Please tell me Morganne is going to be okay," the girl says. She knows how stupid the request is. And Morganne's mother has already said. But she makes the request anyway. And then she makes it again. "Please tell me Morganne is going to be okay."

"Morganne is going to get through this," Morganne's mother says. "Morganne is going to be okay. You are both going to get through this."

When they end their embrace, the girl feels stronger than she has in days, as though seeing Morganne's mom has recharged her batteries. She stands up tall and feels her body balance itself over her legs.

Morganne's dad reaches out and puts a hand on her shoulder. His eyes fill with tears and he winces hard with emotion, keeping his hand in place where she can feel its strength.

"Morganne wants you to have this," Morganne's mom says. She reaches into her purse and takes out the little sketchbook. The girl knows without looking which sketchbook it is. It is the small one. The one with the hard, pebbly cover. The one in which she's seen Morganne sketching a hundred times. It is the one the girl loves most.

She cannot respond in words. But she looks deep into Morganne's mother's face. And it is so much like Morganne's face, and she is so happy to have the sketchbook. All she can do is nod at Morganne's parents and blink away her tears and lean back into the embrace of her own mother's arms as her mother guides her body weight backwards until she is settled onto a folding chair.

The Community Room is filling up with most of the same people from the church. Morganne's volleyball team is here. They probably thought they'd see Morganne. They wear their team jackets. Their coach, a tall young woman with a long face and big teeth in her friendly smile, is with the girls, directing and guiding them. Coaching even through a teammate's trauma. They sit in an uninterrupted line of blue, with yellow team logo on the left side of their chests. The girls all have long hair, and they all wear it today in the same style—a single braid down the back. The girl knows what the braids mean. They've been waiting together since before the funeral and to kill their nervousness, they started braiding each other's hair.

Morganne's cousin MacKenzie, a young woman of no more than twenty-five, and who the girl met before at Morganne's house, goes to a spot near a corner of the room. She beckons an older woman, who looks like she could be MacKenzie's mother, to stand at her side. The woman is holding a bowl-like shell, dark in colour and bigger than a curled fist. She leans forward, fanning a feather, and white-grey smoke drifts out into the room.

"What are they burning?" her own mother says, but she is speaking abstractly, as though she does not expect the girl to understand.

"They're doing a smudge," the girl says. "Cedar and sweetgrass and...I can't remember the rest. Smell it." She sees her mother look at her in confusion.

Morganne's cousin has taken the shell in her cupped palms. The older woman waves her hands, washing her own face with the smudge, then says to the room: "There's a smudge here for anyone who needs it." People come forward. Old and young. They lean over the smoke and use both hands to wash their faces in it. Some of them turn to have the smoke feathered against their backs.

"I need that," the girl says.

"What?" says her mother. The girl can hear fear in her mother's voice, but she herself is used to smudging. She's had Mi'kmaw kids in her class all through school, and she is used to having an elder come in, for various ceremonies and occasions. To burn a smudge and let whoever wants to bathe in the sweet smoke.

"I need that smudge." She struggles to stand. Her mother takes her elbow and helps her up, but the girl can feel the reluctance and hesitation in her mother's hands.

"Is that for..." the mother says. "Are you sure it's okay for...you?"

"She said it was for whoever needs it. I need it." Together they walk toward the smudge. When Morganne's cousin sees her coming, she begins walking in her direction. She puts a hand on the older woman's shoulder and they both step carefully in the direction of the girl who used to be Trisha. The older woman has the shell again, and a whitish grey cloud of smoke rises from the space between her palms. The girl closes her eyes, puts her face near the smoke, and repeats the actions she's seen other people do. She puts her open hands into the smoke and draws the smoke around her face and head.

When she opens her eyes, she notices a familiar shape on the inside of MacKenzie's wrist. She feels herself start, her gaze locking onto the inked outline. She looks up at MacKenzie through the white smoke, then back at the little tattoo on her arm.

It's the butterfly. The one from the painting in Morganne's bedroom. Asymmetrical wings. Whimsical, cartoonish antennae.

As her mother guides her back to their place near the wall, the room continues to fill with people and voices. The sounds rise to the cold ceiling of the Community Room and the girl feels them come down upon her.

The walls from the sides carry the reverberated voices back as well. She feels woozy, overpowered. She closes her eyes and imagines she hears singing, musical instruments, but when she opens her eyes again, she realizes it is just sorrowing people, talking, weeping.

The girl looks at her mother, whose face is flushed with emotion.

The sights in the room now begin to overwhelm her: Morganne's mom. Her dad. The cousin MacKenzie. And the priest is here now from the church, the man who'd said the mass. And kids' faces. Young people. People from her school. How many of them had seen the pictures of her and Becky and Morganne? How many of the people in this room had called her a hateful name on social media?

She squeezes her eyes shut and puts her head down between her knees. The echoing sound of voices has become deafening, nightmarish. She puts her hands over her ears to block the din.

Her mother is hovering over her. She can feel the grip of her mother's arm tightening across her shoulders. Her mother's mouth is near her ear. She can feel the lips moving against her hand, but all she can hear now is the clangorous reverberating of the room around her.

And then silence. The sounds of the room are switched off as though a mute button has been pushed.

And that's when she hears it.

Becky's voice.

A single syllable.

"Sam," Becky says.

Sam nods. She opens her eyes. She sits up straight in the crowded community room. The sounds of voices are slowly drifting back.

Her mother still has an arm around her shoulders and is speaking soothingly into her ear.

"Are you okay? Honey? Are you okay?"

"Sam," Sam says. Her mother looks at her with alarm and concern. "I'm Sam now," says Sam.

"I think we should leave," her mother says. "I think I should get you to a doctor."

"No," says Sam. "I'm good. I'm good now. I know who I am now. I know my name. I'm Sam."

16

TWELVE MONTHS EARLIER: MAY

Robot spends the whole day feeling angry, resentful, and doomed. He just wants those stupid assholes and their stupid YouTube channel to fuck off and go away. And the whole day, from math to bio to global geography, none of the actual classroom work gets through to him. He cannot listen. He is taking shitty notes, writing things down to keep the teacher from getting on his case. But his head is full of imagined scenes. In one scene, the bell rings at the end of the day, and he ignores the idiots mobbing him in the hallway and goes to the band room, gets followed there by the stupid *Prank Fights* crowd. Trumpet Boy meets him at the door: "Don't come here dragging this shit show with you. I knew it was a mistake to ever invite your sorry ass to play with us."

In another scene, he attacks Lucas Shortt and that fucking knob Suitjon. They are waiting for him outside the front foyer and he wades into the crowd, grabs Suitjon's camera, plows Suitjon in the face with it, then knocks Lucas Shortt over sideways, plugging him on one ear with the camera and then following through with it until Shortt is on the front step of the school, bleeding all over the concrete from the side of his fool head.

After lunch, his global geography teacher gets in his face about staring off into space. She is a bony old lady with grey roots at her scalp. In his mind, he is in the middle of a scene where he is trying to talk his way out of a fight with Gink. Suddenly he becomes aware of the teacher. Her lined face floating in the centre of his field of vision. There is that terrible bitter coffee smell that you get from old people's breath. She has obviously said something to him, because she is grinning expectantly, awaiting a reply. The kids around Robot laugh, but the laughter dies away quickly and Robot decides he can just wait this lady out. He has no idea what she said, but telling her that is only going to make things worse.

"Well..." she says.

He looks back up at her, at the mean, self-satisfied look on her face. Half the lights in the classroom are off. There is a screen at the front with an overhead image on it. A PowerPoint slide with a bar graph in three colours. He is completely lost. There are words on the bar graph: *production* is one. *Investment* is another. There are some country names. *China. The United States.* Whatever she said to him, whatever reply she is waiting for, it probably has nothing to do with the lesson, anyway. There is a growing tension around the moment that, the longer it goes on, the more determined Robot becomes not to engage with it. The teacher set out to humiliate him and she'd already succeeded. The whole class is gawking at him with their slack-jawed mouths open. Whatever he says now, whether it fits with what the teacher said to him or not, they will laugh at it.

The classroom has a single narrow window that stretches from thigh level almost all the way to the ceiling. Robot sits on the opposite end of the room, so that when he scans the room everyone is a glare-shot silhouette. All the kids in their rows of desks. Even the teacher, whose features were easy to make out when she was up close to him, has now taken a couple of steps back, to further make a specimen of him. Her face has become a darkened outline with only glimpses of contours as she moves her gaze from the classroom behind her back to Robot.

He raises a hand.

A few students giggle.

When she doesn't respond immediately, Robot says, "Excuse me."

More giggles in the room.

"Yes, Robert," the teacher says.

"May I please use the washroom?"

There is subdued laughter. The teacher makes an ironic face and shakes her head resignedly. "You might as well," she says.

Outside the geography room door, there is a landing at the top of a staircase. The boys' room is to the left.

"What happened to you this morning, man?" It is Noh, standing in front of the boys' washroom as though he's been waiting there since class started almost an hour before.

"Hey, Noh," Robot says. "Ah," he was not expecting this conversation, "I got delayed."

There is no way to explain to Noh what he's been going through today.

Noh's face is broad and square and handsome.

"We'll be there after school. Right after class. We usually jam for, like, a half hour before stage band rehearsal."

Robot takes a step back and looks into the geography classroom. The teacher stands in the projector light, her face partially coloured by a purplish stripe of bar graph.

There is literally nothing more important to him at this moment than playing with the Jazz Kids again. From their perspective, he's already blown them off once. How many times can he count on being re-invited? He is so angry with Lucas Shortt and Suitjon and even with Gink right now. They are all just idiots.

"Listen, Noh."

"Can I ask where you two are supposed to be right now?" There's a teacher coming down the hall.

Noh gets a slightly scared look on his face. It is the look of a kid who has never been in any real trouble. He looks at the teacher and opens his mouth as if to speak. Robot can tell by the even pace of the teacher's walk that he has no intention of following up his question. He is just playing a role.

"Good afternoon, sir," Robot says, just as the man disappears past the corner of the hallway.

"I had so much fun last night," Robot says when he turns back to Noh.

Noh smiles. "It was a good jam, right?"

Robot thinks. "It's...it's the most fun possible. It's fun that's so far beyond fun that you need a whole new word for it."

"'Euphoria'?" Noh says. He shrugs. "I don't know. I looked it up one time." Everything Noh says seems to be the most honest, genuine thing he can think of saying. But at the same time, he always seems on the edge of laughter. Nobody else Robot knows seems so close to laughter all the time unless it is bitter, ironic, hateful laughter. But Noh is not like that at all. He's like a little kid on the verge of the giggles.

"Euphoria," Robot says. "That's it."

Noh nods.

They both laugh.

"Anyway. You can tell everyone I'm sorry about this morning. And I have to deal with something today right after school. But starting tomorrow, I'll be able to jam as much as anyone."

"That'll be awesome, man. We're going to, like. There's a slot in the talent show we're already booked for," Noh says. "And there's this other gig we might have. Like, a corporate thing over at the Holiday Inn. Just playing in the corner while all these business people get drunk and eat snacks. We played one in the fall. It was a smaller one. This one is bigger, I think. Paid."

Paid! "Yeah, man. I'm all about that. Just. Today is no good. I got that thing to take care of after school. After that, I'll be free..."

What is he even talking about? A thing after school? All he knows is that the bullshit with Lucas Shortt needs to end. Now.

———

AFTER GEOGRAPHY CLASS, ROBOT HAS A SEVENTY-MINUTE MATH class in which to prepare himself for what is coming. He opens his math book and his binder, grips the edges of his desk, and stares blankly down at the pages while the class drones on around him. The math teacher is less concerned than the geography teacher with making sure every single person is completely focused on the lesson at all times.

There is an old-fashioned analog clock above the whiteboard at the front of the room. When he looks up and notices that there are only five minutes left until the bell rings at three, he unlocks his hands from where they grip his desk. He feels the stiffness come out of his fingers, and he loosens up his elbows. He looks around the room. The teacher has written an assignment on the whiteboard. It is a page number and an exercise number. He jots that down on a sheet of loose-leaf in his binder. Most of the kids look like they are furiously working through the homework exercise in class, hoping to get it done before the bell rings.

When the bell does ring, he slings his bookbag over one shoulder and picks up his guitar case from the aisle beside his desk.

By the time he finds himself walking toward the front entrance of the school, he has a woozy sense of detachment.

Inside the door at the front entrance, a girl he knows from Lemon Street is speaking loudly and self-consciously to a boy in a One Team school athletics T-shirt. The sun is shining through the newly-leafed-out maple trees on the school's front lawn. There is a line of cars on the half-circle drive that leads up to the landing in front of the main door. One at a time, the cars pull forward, kids step off the landing, get into passenger seats.

It is not until Robot gets to the sidewalk and starts heading toward the main street of town that he notices the crowd gathering at the edge of the school grounds. They spike across the emptying parking lot and wander partway onto the street.

Suitjon has his camera going. Robot hears Lucas Shortt's ridiculous voice. His heart is now racing in his chest. He feels pressure in his bladder and thinks how bad it will be if he pees his pants on camera.

He barely knows Gink. He tries to conjure a picture of him in his mind as he scans the crowd. He looks for a broad torso and a shock of spiky red hair. Mostly what he looks for, based on the *Prank Fight* videos he's seen, is a scared- or angry-looking person in front of a mob pushing him forward.

But Gink does not appear to be there.

The crowd floods over from the parking lot, across the sidewalk, and out into the street. Horns are going. Traffic leaving the school begins backing up.

Robot hears Lucas Shortt yelling at the crowd: "Get off the street, you assholes. If someone calls the cops..." Robot sticks to the sidewalk and plows straight ahead. The crowd, almost all boys, clears away the space in front of him.

"Fuck," he hears Lucas Shortt somewhere on his right and behind him now. "Where the fuck is Gink?"

Robot walks farther, careful not to speed up, slow down, or react to the crowd in any way. People get in his face and yell: "Fight! Fight!" But he is careful not to acknowledge anyone.

Traffic from the end of the school day continues to spool past him on the left as he makes his way to Prince Street, the main drag at the centre of town. The pedestrian light turns red, and when he stops, he realizes he has broken from the pack and most of the crowd is almost a full block behind him, coming up the sidewalk in a bunched knot, trampling grass with overflow.

Some in the crowd are just coming even with him again when the light goes green and he continues across the street. He gets two blocks up Young Street, across the tracks, and has turned in the direction of Lemon Street when a ripple of emotion goes through the crowd at his back. He guesses they've found Gink, or Gink has found them, and a quick look over his shoulder confirms it. The crowd's speed has doubled now, and the entire dark mass of bodies is catching up to him up quickly. He stops a moment and turns full around to see what's coming. A path has opened in the middle of the noisy group and he can see Gink in there, broad-shouldered in a tight red T-shirt and black jeans, his fists pumping away at his sides as he comes.

There is a white house on the corner and he goes down the uneven gravel and dirt driveway and bursts through a little opening in the wild scrub maple at the end of it. He is in a small grassy clearing at the end of a municipal park. There are two or three wooden benches and an ancient, indestructible see-saw away at the far end where the park squeezes between several backyards and driveways and comes out in a footworn track of hard-packed earth in the centre of the grass. Beyond that lies another street whose name he cannot recall at the moment. Still a few blocks from Lemon Street. The entire crush of boys comes squeezing through the opening in the scrub brush at the end of the driveway and into the clearing. There is yelling and jostling now. Guys are shoving each other out of the way to get to the front.

Near the front of the pack comes Lucas Shortt, who Robot can now see is wearing a green T-shirt with the *Prank Fights* logo in white across the chest. "Keep up! Keep up!" Shortt is yelling at Suitjon, who is running, red-faced and huffing, across the front of the crowd, which is still spilling into the clearing but is pushing outwards along the periphery of the grassy centre of the park, along the edges of trees and backyard fences on both sides, leaving the middle of the clearing open. No one needs to direct this action. It's just what crowds who want to see a fight do. Robot has seen this happen a dozen times. But this is the biggest crowd he's ever seen open up this way. And it has always been for someone else, not him.

"Let's get this done," someone says. Maybe he said it himself.

"Wait! Wait!" Lucas Shortt wants to hold off until he can better direct the camerawork. Well, fuck him.

Robot shucks his backpack to the ground and leans the Les Paul case against it. He takes several steps away from the guitar, so as to make sure it does not get damaged.

Gink is in the clearing now, stepping in his direction. Robot looks over his shoulder at his guitar. The crowd is nowhere near it.

"Fight! Fight!" the crowd is shouting, trying to get a rhythm together.

Gink steps ahead. Should I say something? Robot thinks. What is there to say? He can see Suitjon out the corner of his eye, circling the centre of the fight ring. "Here they go!" says Lucas Shortt.

For a brief second, an image of the band room at school flashes in Robot's mind. The Jazz Kids are in there right now, their hearts pounding with euphoria. He steps in Gink's direction, cocks his fist, and lets go with it. A split second before he makes his move, someone in the crowd yells, "Gink!" Gink's attention breaks, his gaze turns slightly in the direction of the voice.

Robot's fist makes a terrible sound against the side of Gink's face, striking just at the intersection of cheekbone and eye socket.

Robot springs back from the punch. Before Gink even hits the grassy earth beneath him, Robot knows a terrible thing has happened.

"Fuck!" someone says. Somewhere a kid is throwing up. Robot hears the retching.

Lucas Shortt has an ecstatic expression. He stands over Gink's slouched body. "Yas!" he shouts. Suitjon has lowered his camera, bewildered a moment before recalling his role. He films Gink, limp on the ground, a stream of blood coming out of his left eye.

"Oh, fuck," Robot says. He backs toward his guitar case and looks at his hand before bending to pick up the guitar. His knuckles are barked and swelling. There's blood across the front end of his fist.

"Run!" somebody shouts at him. A face darkens his field of vision, but he cannot make out features. "You killed Gink. Run!"

"Gink is dead!" he hears someone else say.

Then comes Lucas Shortt's voice: "Gink's not dead! Are you, Gink? Gink! Get up, buddy. Stop fucking with us!"

Robot expects to be followed home. He's forgotten his backpack in the clearing, but he has his guitar. He runs to the far end of the park and continues in the direction of Lemon Street. But when he gets to the first corner, he looks back over his shoulder. No one has come in behind him. He can hear sirens now. The first to arrive is an ambulance. Then a police car. They drive over the curb and right into the little clearing.

He sits on the grass at the far end and watches the paramedics work on Gink.

He lies back and looks up at the rapidly changing clouds in the sky. For what seems like a long time he lies there, expecting the police to cross the field and take him into custody. When that does not happen, he gets back up, picks up his guitar, and walks the few blocks to Lemon Street.

When he gets home, there is no sign of his mother. He does not think about or care where she might be. He goes straight to his bedroom and sits on the bed. He places the guitar case against the wall and sits looking at his swelling hand. He pulls out his phone and checks the time: 3:18 P.M. The Jazz Kids are jamming on their second or third tune. Stage band rehearsal is at 3:30. People are coming through the band room door with their instruments, grooving to the music, getting ready for rehearsal to start.

17

OCTOBER

Sam fell asleep crying, face down on Robert's hospital bed. When she woke up it could not have been more than a few minutes later. Creases in the hospital bedding pressed into her face. She'd slumped sideways and the arm of the chair she was sitting in jammed into her ribs. Robert was still asleep. She sat back in her chair and dared not move in case she woke him. The white privacy curtain cocooned them. The clear plastic of his IV bag magnified the black and red letters printed on the side that faced away from her. Robert's breathing was deep and restful except for an occasional twinge where, even in his sleep, the pain of his injuries cut through him.

She knew Robert's mother was probably in here somewhere. The woman had looked all but dead coming out the front door on the ambulance stretcher, a motionless loaf of human body beneath a white sheet. Had anyone made the connection? Had anyone told Robert his mother had been admitted to hospital? Maybe he already knew. Maybe there were things he would not want to know.

She stood up carefully, pushed the chair back just enough to allow her to straighten her legs, and edged away from the bed. Robert did not stir as she pushed the privacy curtain aside.

There was a nurse's station halfway down the hall. A serious-looking woman in her late twenties was scrolling through some information on a flat-screen monitor. There was a counter between them, and behind the woman there was a narrow doorway with two video monitors mounted near the ceiling. One showed the hallway outside the nearby elevator, the other was tuned to what looked like a news channel. A reporter in an overcoat, a dark city behind him. A sideways scroll of text at the bottom.

The nurse did not look at her.

"Excuse me," Sam said. The nurse did not budge. "Excuse me."

When the nurse looked up, Sam hesitated slightly over what to say.

"I'm a friend of Robert's?" Her mouth felt dry and rubbery. And she had a shaky, anxious feeling. She licked her lips and swallowed a dry swallow. "From down in room..." She pointed back over her shoulder with her thumb.

The nurse had raised her eyebrows to indicate she was listening. "He was... ah. He is asleep right now..." There was now some sort of movement around the nurse. A doctor or another nurse going past. Sam was trying hard to not let that distract her.

The nurse wanted to give up and look away, Sam could tell. Sam's eyes were wide now. She knew it and could not help it. And they were filling with tears that threatened to roll down her cheeks. It must have been hard for the nurse. Most people she dealt with in the run of a day were probably either in tears, on the verge of tears. How much sympathy could she be expected to have?

"Can someone update him on his mother's condition when he wakes up? I'm not even sure he knows she's been hospitalized."

"His mother?" The nurse looked down at her computer screen. She clicked the mouse and did some typing. "There's nothing in here about his mother's condition." The nurse widened her eyes for a half-second, inviting more information.

"Well, I don't know much myself," Sam said. "I'm not a family member or anything. They have the same address. Lemon Street? I was told." *I was told.* "She was hospitalized this morning? After Robert was hospitalized? I was told by ambulance?"

The nurse put her head down to the screen. "I'm going to look into this," she said.

"He's got enough trouble already," Sam said. "But he'll probably want to know when he wakes up." The nurse did not look up again. She was busy clacking away at the keyboard. "Thanks for bringing this to our attention," she said, still looking at the screen.

Robert was still asleep when Sam got back to his room.

He lay flat on his back with his arms straight down at his sides. The pillow was bunched under his neck and his head crooked back. He was snoring quietly and intermittently, and Sam found the sound reassuring, healthy, normal.

The privacy curtain had been pulled all the way back, and when she settled into the chair by Robert's bed she could see every occupant in the four-bed ward.

Robert was by far the youngest patient in the room. The two beds against the far wall contained old men. The one on the right had a little hospital TV on a mechanical arm pushed right up beside his head. His head was at a 45-degree angle. His eyes were closed, but the TV was on, though it was mostly turned away from Sam, so all she could really see of it was the flickering light on the old man's face. His cheeks were lined and sunken. Both of his bony hands were up at one side of his face, and the grey-white wires of the TV earbuds were tangled like a rosary in his fingers.

Beside him, in the bed on Sam's left, was a grey-faced old man with a high forehead and a bald crown fringed by short white-grey hair. He had his bed up too. He was awake and had just put a newspaper down on his lap and was taking a hard sip from a straw in a sweating wax cup. Sam could hear the ice in the cup as the old man brought it to his mouth, then placed it back on his bedside tray. He was looking straight at her but made no indication he could actually see or was in any way aware of her. He blinked slowly and walled himself again behind the newspaper.

In the bed right across from Robert was the only other person whose ailments were visible. This guy was in his late twenties or early thirties. He had a beard that appeared to have once been neatly trimmed, but around it grew a kind of shaggy outer beard, no doubt the result of his time in hospital. Both arms were strapped into splints that left them immobile from the shoulders down. His hands were free. In one hand he held the controls for his bed, in the other he had his phone: a black screen like polished stone in a white case. He did not appear to be in pain, but the splints on his arms looked awkward and uncomfortable and he fidgeted non-stop, rearranging himself in the bed and readjusting the bed with the remote. At an arm's length distance, he was forced to crook his head uncomfortably to look at his phone. He swept his thumb across the screen impatiently and texted slowly with one thumb. Once, he brought both hands together to try to text normally, but the splints crowded out his chest and he looked like he was struggling to breathe.

"I'm like a caveman with a stone tool over here," the man said. It took Sam a moment to realize he was talking to her. "I was in the hospital once when I was a kid. Some white blood cell thing. I never understood it and then it went away. But I read books for two weeks. How cultured is that! Two weeks I did nothing but read books. That's what everybody did in the hospital back then, I guess. What do I do now? This thing!" He indicated the cellphone by holding it up as high as he could and pointing at it with his chin. "Cat videos, celebrity gossip, and illiterate text messages from my friends. I'll bet my brain has shrunk by like...I don't know. Some significant percentage. I'll bet if they scanned my brain fifteen years ago, before I had a cellphone, and now. I'll bet a scientist could see where my brain has shrunk. I'll bet it's measurable."

"There are books down in the gift shop," Sam said. Why was it that sometimes she could not make her mouth move, could not will her voice to work at all, and then suddenly words were just popping out of her mouth as though it was the easiest and most natural thing in the world?

The man tilted his head and looked at her. "What?" he said. He'd been talking away, but Sam realized that he was expecting to be ignored.

"I'm pretty sure there's a rack of books downstairs. In the canteen. The gift shop. If you give me the money, I'll go get you one. What do you want?"

The man's face lit up. "Are you serious?" He turned toward his bedside table. He flapped his arms at it, like a penguin in a cartoon. "Can you look in that top drawer for my wallet?"

When the elevator doors opened onto the ground floor of the hospital, Sam noticed that the windows that looked out onto the parking lot and the on-ramp to the highway were dark. As if waking from a dream, she remembered Uncle Ray. She'd left school in the middle of the day. He would have gotten a robocall about her attendance. She dug her phone out of a side pocket of her bookbag, and a string of notifications, all from Uncle Ray, scrolled down the screen. When he picked up before the end of the first ring, she knew he'd been waiting with his phone out.

"Uncle Ray."

She heard him breathing, checking himself. "The school called. They said you skipped. Absence without excuse."

"I did not really skip, Uncle Ray."

"You're here with me for school. That's the reason you're here."

She thought she remembered leaving Music at the start of class. Right after attendance. "I didn't miss the whole day. My friend..." She had never spoken to Ray about Robert. "My friend got hurt. He's in the hospital. I'm calling from the hospital."

"Your friend got hurt?"

"Yes."

"Is he going to be okay?"

"He got beaten up. Bad. But he'll probably be okay."

"Were you with him when he got hurt? You're not hurt, are you, Patricia? I'd feel better if I could see you right now. Just get a look at your face. If you've been hurt, your mother is going to box my ears for me."

"Uncle Ray. I'm fine. I was not hurt. I was not anywhere near Robert when he got hurt. I heard about it at school.

That's why I left. I got worried and I came to the hospital."

She could hear Uncle Ray exhale sharply into the phone as his mind switched gears. "Patricia. Your hospital visit needs to be over now. I'm that worked up. I just need you to be home here. I'll pick you up at the main entrance in a few minutes."

She knew better than to argue with Ray right now.

She had a copy of *The Shining* and a handful of change for the man in the bed across from Robert.

There was a nurse. Or a doctor. Someone in scrubs, beside Robert's bed. They had the privacy curtain pulled most of the way around. Sam only caught a glimpse of whoever it was from the doorway as she came in. Robert was awake. Blinking groggily. The nurse was explaining something, looking at a clipboard.

"What you get for me?" the man with the arm splints said. He extended a stiff arm in her direction.

"Ever read any Stephen King?" Sam asked.

"*Carrie*," the man said. "That was pretty darn good."

"I got you *The Shining*," she said.

"Great movie."

"The book is very different."

"I'm just going to devour this book, I can tell," the man said. He was shifting beneath the covers in anticipation of getting the book in his hand. When she handed it over, he got it in both hands and turned it over at arm's length a few times.

"Are you going to be able to read it like that?" Sam asked.

"I'm lucky my eyesight is good," he said and laughed.

By the time Sam put the change on his bedside table, he was already reading.

"Thanks a lot," the man said distractedly without looking up from the page. She could see him settling back onto his pillow. His body lost almost all its uncomfortable fidgeting as though he'd just been shot up with a pain med.

"Enjoy," Sam said. She put a hand on the edge of the privacy curtain and hesitated. She considered asking whether he wanted it pulled over, but he was already engrossed in *The Shining*, had it pinched between his arms as though in tweezers.

There was the metallic scraping sound of Robert's privacy curtain being drawn back, and the nurse pivoted on her heels and left the room with a purposeful gait.

"That was about my mother," Robert said when he saw her. "She's in a coma."

Sam felt her heart begin to race. "Was she...? Did the people who..."

Robert shook his head sadly. "Nobody beat her up. She was probably already in a coma when I was getting the shit kicked out of me. She's been in the hospital before. She has alcoholism. I kind of saw this coming." He closed his eyes as though thinking about all of this had tired him. "It's touch and go, I guess." He opened his eyes again. "She might not come out of it."

"Maybe I should go check on her," Sam offered. There was no way they were going to let Robert leave the bed he was in, and she thought if she were in his shoes, she'd want at the very least for someone she knew to just look in on her mother and report back.

Robert shook his head. "The nurse said they put a note in her file. Any change at all and they'll tell me."

"How are you feeling?" Sam asked. She sat in the padded

armchair next to the bed, but she settled on the edge of it. It was almost time to meet Uncle Ray at the main entrance.

"Honestly? I'm feeling pretty defeated. I'm even lower than an alcoholic's bootlegger. A man who will sell liquor to people at double the retail price right up until the liquor kills them, that man thinks I'm a low-life." Robert's voice was shaky and thin.

"I'm not exactly sure what you're talking about," Sam said.

"The people who beat me up were bootleggers. They sell overpriced alcohol to...to desperate people. I don't know what to do about my mother. I can't even think about her at the moment. Isn't that terrible? No sympathy for my own mother. For all I know she's breathing her last breath right now."

Sam burrowed her hand through the bedsheets until she had Robert's hand. She squeezed and held on firmly. Her heart set up racing inside her. She looked in Robert's face for some response, and when none came, she loosened her grip and began to pull her hand away. His hand immediately followed hers, found it again quickly, and held on.

"I'm going to have to go in a minute," she said. "My uncle's picking me up. He's pretty pissed off. I missed some school today. I'll come back tomorrow."

Robert nodded. His eyelids were drooping. Soon he'd be asleep again. "I need to ask you a favour," he said.

18
OCTOBER

At Patricia's request, Ray drove straight from the hospital to the address she gave him. He parked at the curb, and when he and Patricia left the vehicle, he pressed the button that locked the car doors. He scanned the street in all directions. No one in sight. Still. He had a vulnerable feeling, leaving his car parked unattended on that block of Lemon Street.

He'd been lit up with fear and anger all afternoon. Ever since he'd got the automated call from the school that said Patricia had missed pretty much the whole day.

She'll be fine, Ray, Lynne had texted him from Sydney. *Remember to be gentle with her when you see her. Be careful what you say and how you say it.*

A small part of him was ticked at Lynne for assuming he needed to be reminded not to lose his temper, but he was mostly grateful that she cared enough to say a difficult thing.

The concrete walkway was cracked and heaved, the grass on either side of it sparse. The apartment house it led into was rundown.

When they got to the apartment door, it was not even locked. All the fuss over where to find a hidden key or where to find the landlord, but not only was the door unlocked, it was not even closed the whole way.

"Someone's already in here. Treasure hunting," Ray said. Patricia pushed open the door.

"Hello?" she called into the dark flat. Ray found a switch and for some reason the smell of the place did not hit him until the lights came up.

"Oh, boy," he could not help saying in the sudden brightness. It was a dirty, lowdown sort of place. Which is what he knew it would be. Parts of the old plaster walls were papered over, but that had obviously been decades ago. The off-white baseboards were scuffed. The flooring was carpet and old vinyl, and bare wood with water stains and dirt. Strikingly empty. An echoey box of a place. The stale smell of sweated-out booze.

"You're too late," Ray said. "They've been robbed already."

Patricia walked across the main room, assessing the doors in the far wall as she went. She gestured at them one at a time, from left to right. "This must be Robert's room." She put a hand on the doorknob and opened the door. The room was just a black doorway from where Ray stood, but Patricia did not flip on a light.

"You okay?" he called after her. But before she had a chance to reply she was back out of the room with a little guitar-shaped instrument case in her hand.

"Got it," she said. "This is going to be a weight off of Robert's mind."

Patricia and Ray were both silent for most of the car ride back to the house. "What do you know about this Robert?" Ray asked her as they were about to pull into the drive.

She turned her head and stole a quick look at him before dropping her gaze to her lap, where she had the ukulele cradled.

"I know what you think I might not know," Patricia said after a pause. The car came to rest in the drive, but neither of them moved to get out.

"And what's that?" Ray wanted to hear her say the words. She slouched a bit deeper and sighed in frustration before speaking. "That he killed somebody." The motion sensor light over the driveway blinked off, leaving them with street lights, the greyed-out clapboard of the side of the house. The two of them were shadows in the hushed space of the darkened vehicle. "That was an accident."

"Well." Ray did not want to get judgemental. He was not her father and he was not responsible for her actions or opinions. But he was responsible for her well-being while she was in his care. "It wasn't exactly an accident."

"I know, Uncle Ray. I understand what Robert did. And he did time for it, too. But he's got no one. And I'm his friend. And all I'm doing is getting his ukulele for him."

"You were truant today."

"I don't know what that means."

"You skipped school."

The girl turned to Ray. Looked him in the eye. "I'm sorry about that, Uncle Ray. That must have worried you."

"That it did."

"I'm not going to do that again. I don't want to miss school. It's hard enough to keep up with schoolwork if you're there every day. I don't want to miss time and get behind. I'm here to get my credits. I know that."

Ray had been squeezing the steering wheel so hard that he chafed his hands against it. He let it go and let his hands fall loose into his lap, and the burning feeling in his palms began to dissipate.

"Here's what I want to say about this." Ray's mind seemed to have cleared suddenly and he felt he could just say what had to be said. "Everyone's life is complicated.

Multi-dimensional. Whatever. But you came to me wounded. And part of what you've got to do for yourself is just...you've got to do some healing of your own. And I worry that this guy, Robert. Maybe he's going to hurt you. Or maybe he's just too wounded himself to be a positive influence in the life of someone else. I feel like I'm on TV with Oprah, talking like this."

Ray had a big sandwich ready for her when she got inside. He knew she'd be hungry. The sandwich had cheese and tomato. And the greens she liked. And he did not butter the bread, even though making a sandwich without buttered bread made about as much sense to him as he did not know what. There had been this really good looking ham at Sobey's. Black forest. Thin sliced. That was piled up in there, too.

Patricia ate and Ray sat in the kitchen with her as she did so. The ukulele in its bag was propped up on its own chair as though it was waiting for its own sandwich.

"I'll clear this up," Ray said when Patricia finished eating. Not that there was much to clear up. A plate. Milk glass. Salt and pepper shakers. A few crumbs on the table. Patricia closed her eyes a moment and nodded. She looked exhausted, as though she'd aged ten years in a day. There were worry lines around her eyes and she shook her head very slightly and Ray thought she was chasing away tears.

Ray wiped up the table and the counter with a cloth and a spot of bleach solution and Patricia headed off to her room. He sat down and texted Lynne. *She's home. She's fine. And you'll be happy to know I did not lose my cool.*

Seconds later he got a notification that Lynne had ♥ed his text.

Later, as he was coming back from the bathroom after brushing his teeth, Ray heard what he thought at first was a radio. But he stopped outside Patricia's room and it was the ukulele, crisp and sweet and gentle. When he got into bed and clicked off the lamp, he could hear her singing. Long, sweet notes. He could not make out words, and he did not recognize the melody, though it seemed vaguely familiar. Was it French? Why did he think it might be French? In the dark of the house, that bit of music got inside his chest and fluttered around like a bird that had gotten in there. Something alive.

19

OCTOBER

When the nurse told Robot his mother had been rushed by ambulance to the same hospital where he was, he thought the nurse's next words would be that she was dead. Her condition had been so frail for so long. The whites of her eyes had been polluted and discoloured. Her fingernails weak and misshapen. Her skin gone hard yellow. He could remember a long-ago time when her drinking had only amplified certain parts of her personality. Made her quicker to anger, louder when shouting, more tearful, more prone to long evenings of what looked from the outside like quiet contemplation. Eventually, the effect of drinking had been to remove her for lengthy periods of time. She'd be at some other drunk's house, or even if she was home, she'd be in a silent stupor, slumped over the table, unable to do anything but sloppily pour herself another drink. Or she'd be passed out. Asleep. Sometimes the sleeps were fitful, restless bouts, a half-hour long, an hour long, interspersed with partially coherent stretches of wakefulness. Sometimes, after days of drunkenness, she'd sleep for twenty-four hours at a stretch.

When the nurse made clear that his mother was still alive, that she was in hospital, that someone else was looking after her, that the greedy bootleggers who'd been living off her illness and feeding her decline, the same people who'd put him in hospital when he'd threatened to get in their way, when the bootleggers could no longer reach her, his thought had turned to the empty apartment on Lemon Street and the only thing he cared about after his mother: his ukulele.

He pictured it where he'd last seen it, zipped into its nylon gig bag, leaning against the wall in a corner of his bedroom, where he once would have put his old Les Paul, within arm's reach of the mattress on the floor that he called his bed.

He didn't worry that someone would break in and steal it. That someone would break into his flat on Lemon Street now that the neighbourhood knew it was empty: that was a given. An empty apartment was like an unbroken pane of glass with a fist-sized rock sitting right on the ledge beside it. And anyone breaking into the apartment of a hospitalized drunk and her convicted killer son was not going to rob the place. They'd break what few dishes remained, whatever food containers they found in the fridge would be emptied over the floor, smeared against the wall. A ukulele was not small enough to be pocketed as a souvenir. It would have to be broken on site. Held by the headstock and swung against the wall until smashed, or simply dropped onto the floor and crushed with a single stomp.

When Sam had brought it in, he'd been asleep. It lay across his bedside tray when he woke up. It had not even occurred to him to play it at first. He'd picked it up and without even removing it from the gig bag, he held it against his side and let himself feel the relief, the relief that the only thing in his life that he both owned and cared about was safe.

"Is that a mandolin?" His eyes had been fluttering before he heard the voice. He'd been passing in and out of sleep for some time. So the familiar voice had not really awakened him. But it did bring him round. He opened his eyes to find a young nurse at his bedside. She'd been there the day before. He vaguely remembered talking to her as he'd dangled somewhere between sleep and wakefulness.

She had a shallow basin with gauze and tape and disinfectant that she placed on his bedside tray.

He realized he'd been holding the ukulele like a child would hold a teddy bear. He was not going to put the instrument away, but he loosened his hold on it a little. Moved it down his side so that it was level with his waist.

"Ukulele," he said.

"Oh." The nurse raised her eyebrows without looking directly at him. She was all business, arranging the materials in her basin. She pressed a button to bring his bed upright.

"I'm going to change the dressings on your face. I'll have to clean up a bit, too. Can you play?"

He had not spent enough time looking at himself in the mirror to have a clear idea of where his head was bandaged. She removed some adhesive at the back of his neck and just above one ear. Each momentary pull had hurt almost to the point that he wanted to cry out. She was slowly removing soiled gauze and pads, brown with dried blood, dropping them into an unseen pail at her feet.

"I can play. Yes."

Her cheeks were round and full. She was so close he could see the fine blond fuzz on them. Her eyes were large and dark. She wore makeup that made her lashes look angular and sharp at the outer corners of her eyes. She was only a few years older than him, he realized. Her gaze, so focused on what her hands were doing, communicated sharp intelligence and care. Her scrubs were two professional tones of green.

"Well," she peeled a sterile pad from its package, dropped the wrapper in the trash, and applied the pad to his forehead, just above the eye, "when I'm done here, why don't you play something for me?"

Robot felt his cheeks go hot with a rush of blood. She was just being friendly, he knew. But he was not used to being this close to adulthood. So close that a nurse in a hospital would be practically his own age.

"Too sore today," Robot said. "Too out of practice." He hugged the instrument closer again. "Maybe by this time tomorrow." He held both hands up and looked at them, palms out and away from his face. He stretched the fingers wide to test them, clenched both hands into fists, then let them loose again. He looked up at the nurse, who had finished her business with him and was gathering her materials back into the basin. She stole a moment away from her work to smile at him. "I look forward to that," she said. She picked up her things, placed them atop a stainless steel trolley, and wheeled out of the room with it.

"She took a shine to you!"

Robot looked across the room, and for the first time since he'd been in hospital, his self-preoccupation had subsided enough to let him be aware of someone else in the room. The guy in the bed across from him had both arms immobilized by identical splints. His bed was propped up at the back, leaving him in a sitting position. His arms rested uncomfortably on his upper body. In one hand he had a paperback book with a white cover. His hair was brown, medium length. Days of bed-bound restlessness and a dependence on nurses to brush it had left it a swirl, an unruly halo of stuck-out points around his head.

Robot smiled at him, not too encouragingly. The only thing he'd said so far was about the nurse, and Robot did not go in for the disrespectful way a lot of men talked about women.

"I'm reading *The Shining*," the guy said. He held up the book, awkwardly, at the end of a stiff arm. "Ever read it?"

Robot shook his head as slightly as he thought he could get away with. He did not want to encourage any further questions.

"I've seen that movie a lot of times. The book is very different. I'm only about...a little more than halfway through right now. I got sick of my cellphone." He pointed with his chin at the phone on the bedside table, then held up the book with both unbendable arms. "Lucky my eyes are good. I have to hold the book a half a mile from my face. Your girlfriend went down and got this for me." He must have noticed some look pass Robot's face at the use of the word *girlfriend*.

"Maybe she's not your girlfriend."

Robot unzipped the gig bag and pulled out the ukulele. It seemed the only alternative to sitting soundlessly while being talked at.

"Is that a ukulele?" the guy said, and although Robot was about ready to tell the guy to shut up, he was close enough to the moment when music would carry him away that he could just look the guy in the eye, smile a tolerant smile, and nod his head.

He muted the strings with his left hand and began with some percussive strumming. It only took a moment for whatever chemicals this released in his brain to take effect. He continued the strum, index finger of his right hand extended, pivoting back and forth with a twist of his wrist where the neck joined the body of the ukulele. Nothing he'd ever done on guitar had prepared him for this. Everything he'd learned about music dropped away, and the crisp, chunky beat he was getting out of the instrument felt more like a sophisticated hand drum than any melodic or harmonic instrument. He got a rhythm going with his index finger, two beats down, one on the upstroke. Once that beat felt solid, he tried working his thumb into the mix, first for double-time downstrokes, then flicking it up for a back-beat when he could fit it in.

"Sounds good," the guy across the room said. But as Robot closed his eyes and settled back into the mattress, the guy got bored of being ignored. When Robot cracked one eye open for a quick peek, he had settled back into his Stephen King book, turned uncomfortably onto one side, his arms stuck out over the side of the bed like a couple of two-by-fours.

Robot shut both eyes again and continued strumming against the muted strings. He moved his left hand up high on the neck, almost to where his strumming hand met the strings. His body was warning him not to move too much or too quickly. The places where he'd been struck flared momentarily with twinges of pain as he played. The percussive pitch went high and lost most of its resonance. He kept a steady pattern going with his right hand while sliding the muting fingers of the left hand slowly in the direction of the headstock, where the tone and resonance deepened.

20

FOUR MONTHS EARLIER: JUNE

Eleanor agreed to call the young woman named MacKenzie. She did not agree reluctantly. She did not need persuading or convincing. Her daughter Patricia, whom Eleanor herself had named Patricia and who had loved her when she gave her that name and had used that name lovingly the girl's entire life, had decided to reject the name, to eliminate it, to cross it out like a mistaken answer on a test. And she'd given herself (alarmingly she said it was her dead friend Becky who'd given it to her) the name Sam.

And Eleanor saw Sam's response when she caught sight of that little tattoo at the funeral. The strange little butterfly on the wrist of Morganne's cousin from the Running Brook reserve. The girl who'd seemed barely alive a minute before had surged suddenly to life at the sight of that tattoo. In a white and grey haze of smudge smoke, her face became reanimated. Her wide eyes looked from the butterfly to the face of the young woman whose arm it was on.

As she dialled the number, Eleanor looked around her at the kitchen of the mini home she'd been so pleased with just a few years earlier when she'd moved into it with her kids. It had been so new and well looked after compared to the apartments and shitty rental houses she'd been able to afford up until then. But now, after all that had happened, after what happened to Sam, the place just seemed shabby and inadequate, like everything else in their lives.

Eleanor had agreed to call MacKenzie, but because she did not fully understand what Sam wanted, she'd made a fool of herself on the phone. The kind of tattoo Sam wanted was called a stick-and-poke, but she called it a poke and stick. And MacKenzie was confused at first. Had no idea what Eleanor was talking about. And then when it dawned on her what this strange woman was saying to her on the phone, she'd laughed. Not a big, disrespectful laugh. Just a little snicker.

And she'd made a different kind of fool of herself when she asked about the price.

"The price of what?" MacKenzie said. "I'm sorry, ma'am. I don't want to seem rude. But I'm. I'm sort of disoriented by your call. I'm not a hundred percent certain who you are or even why you're calling me."

"I'm Patricia's mother."

"My name is Sam!" Sam yelled from her bedroom. Eleanor heard her loud and clear, but she was not certain whether MacKenzie had heard or not.

There was a long moment of quiet on the other end of the line. "I'm not sure I know a..."

"She was one of the... She's a friend of your cousin Morganne."

"Oh my god! Trisha! Oh my god! I'm sorry, ma'am. I feel so stupid right now."

"She's calling herself Sam now, my daughter."

"I'm not calling myself anything! That's my name!" Sam's voice came again.

"My daughter saw your tattoo the other day. At the. At the funeral."

"Oh my god! I saw her. I totally saw her looking at my tattoo. Oh, ma'am. Don't take this the wrong way. But...your daughter looked so...bad when I saw her. She just looked so... bad. I said to my mother when we got home, I said it hurt me to look at that girl. I felt like, when I was looking at her, I was feeling all the pain she was feeling. But bless her heart. She came for a smudge, didn't she? That's when I saw her eyes lock in on that stick-and-poke I put on my own wrist."

"I don't know much about this," Eleanor said. "I think she liked that tattoo because. I'm not sure. She felt some connection with it."

"That's an Alan Syliboy butterfly," MacKenzie said. "My own shaky version of it, really. Your daughter would know that from my cousin Morganne's bedroom. Morganne's got a print of that. The M'ikmaq Butterfly. Right over her bed. Her grandmother gave her that one year at Christmas. That'd be my grandmother, too." And MacKenzie said something that Eleanor did not understand, but she assumed it was the M'ikmaw word for *grandmother*.

"If she wants me to do a stick-and-poke, I can do one for her," MacKenzie said. "If I was a real tattoo artist, I'd need Alan Syliboy's permission to do a tattoo of his artwork. But I just do wobbly little doodles. I have time tomorrow afternoon. We can do it right here in my mom's kitchen. My mom won't mind."

Eleanor felt a big exhale of relief come out of her own lungs.

"Thank you so much," Eleanor said. "Thank you so much. Can you give me an idea of the cost?"

"The cost?"

"I don't care how much it is. I just want to make sure I come there with the right amount."

MacKenzie laughed. "Ma'am. I do not do this for money. Honest to God. I like that painting. I saw it first on

Morganne's wall. That's where I got the idea. But I mostly gave myself that tattoo because I was bored."

"Look. I don't mind paying."

"No. You look, ma'am. Not trying to be rude here. But I must insist. Morganne is my cousin and your girl is her friend."

So the next afternoon, Eleanor and Sam drove out to the Running Brook reserve.

Since being released from hospital, this was Sam's second time leaving the house. The first time was Becky's funeral. Now this. She was so frail and thin, so bruised and injured, Eleanor felt she might tip over sideways in the passenger seat and be unable to get up. She was wearing the baggiest clothes she could find, as tighter fitting items worked painfully against her wounds. Simon's old plaid work shirt, men's medium, draped over her shoulders like a smock on some painter from a hundred years ago.

MacKenzie lived on a little cul-de-sac of five or six identical bungalows. Each had a short, paved driveway and a little roofed carport that stuck out the side of the house. A round-faced lady with short, home-permed curls met them at the door. She introduced herself as MacKenzie's mother, Elizabeth. It took a moment, but Eleanor recognized her as the woman who had done the smudge at the Community Room after the funeral. Elizabeth asked them to wait in the kitchen while she went to get MacKenzie.

There was a TV on in the next room. Eleanor had not had her own TV on since Corporal Vernon had come to the house to give her the terrible news. The sound of a newscaster's voice on *CBC Newsworld* was a good reminder to her: there was a world outside her tight little circle of personal and family misery.

Eleanor and Sam sat at the kitchen table. The dining set had a honey-oak tinge to it. It looked brand new. Eleanor was almost certain she recognized the exact set from a flyer from The Brick. It had been on sale for a great price and it had taken her a long time to come to terms with the fact that, great price or no, she still could not afford it.

Sam had a little green writing pad with her. When she no longer felt like talking, she'd write a word or two in the pad. She put the pad on the table along with the thin-stemmed blue pen she sometimes used to write in it. Beside the pad, she placed a black, hardcovered book with a pebbly cover.

When MacKenzie came into the kitchen, she sat down at the table with Sam. Eleanor looked at the young woman's hands. They were empty. She'd expected to see tattooing supplies.

"I'm Eleanor," Eleanor said.

MacKenzie nodded at her. "Nice to meet you," she said. Her voice was hushed. Her manner was slow and subdued. She approached Sam as though Sam were a timid animal she were trying not to frighten away.

"Hi, Trisha," MacKenzie said.

"I'm Sam, now," Sam said.

MacKenzie looked at Eleanor and frowned at herself for her mistake. Eleanor shrugged.

"Sorry," MacKenzie said. "Your mom told me your new name. I should have remembered."

"That's okay," said Sam.

MacKenzie put a forearm on the table in front of Sam. She put the back of her hand on the tabletop so the inner part of her wrist showed. There was the jaggedy asymmetrical outline of an abstract butterfly. A couple of back-to-back crescents, bowing away from each other.

"I saw you looking at this before," MacKenzie said.

Sam's neck was bent. Her gaze down in her lap. She looked up, regarded MacKenzie's tattoo. "I recognized it from Morganne's room," Sam said.

"That's where I saw it first, too."

Sam nudged the black book in MacKenzie's direction. She used her left hand for the job, and for the first time, Eleanor noticed that Sam had her right hand down out of sight.

"What's this?" MacKenzie said.

"Open it," said Sam.

"Oh my," MacKenzie said when she opened the book. "Oh, my. These are just the sweetest things."

Eleanor stood up and took a half step in MacKenzie's direction, where she could see what MacKenzie was looking at. And MacKenzie was right. They were the sweetest things. Page after page of doodles. Swirly-eyed girls in dresses. Done in black pen.

"Morganne did these, didn't she?" said MacKenzie. "These are so Morganne."

Sam nodded. "Morganne calls these the Girly Girls. But...I always called them the Beckys."

MacKenzie brought her hands up to her face and began to cry in big loud sobs. Her mother came to the door between the kitchen and the living room, stood for a moment where she could see her daughter was overcome with emotion, but otherwise was all right. Then she backed away slowly into the living room again.

"Sorry," MacKenzie said. She waved her hands at the

sides of her face as though she were too warm. She looked up at the ceiling and made a futile attempt to blink back the tears that were rolling down her face in big drops.

"Ma!" MacKenzie called through the door to the living room.

"Yes?" her mother called back.

"Some emotional in here!"

"You okay?"

"I'm good."

MacKenzie began to laugh. "I find it helps if I just tell my mother." She laughed a bit louder, but the laughter only made her cry more.

Eleanor noticed a Kleenex box on top of the fridge. She took the liberty of plucking it from its place and setting it on the table in front of MacKenzie.

"I thought you wanted *this*," MacKenzie said as she wiped her face with a tissue. She put out her wrist to indicate the butterfly.

Sam shook her head. She tapped Morganne's sketchbook with the tip of an index finger. "Can you find one of these that would be a good stick-and-poke?"

MacKenzie balled up the wad of Kleenex she'd soiled, walked to the sink and dumped it into a little compost container there. She took a squirt of dish soap and washed her hands, dried them on a little hand towel that hung by a string from the fridge handle. She sat down again and paged through the stiff white pages of the sketch book.

"Ha ha!" MacKenzie said. She turned the book around so Sam and Eleanor could see. The girl in the image had her hands on her hips and was looking directly at the viewer. A voice bubble over her head said: *Fuck around.*

In spite of her determination to be supportive of her daughter, Eleanor had a moment of fear at the sight of the crude phrase.

"I know you don't want that one on your arm," MacKenzie said. "But still. Funny."

When MacKenzie returned to flipping through the book, Eleanor was sure her relieved exhale was audible in the room.

"How about this?" MacKenzie said after another minute. She spun the book round so it was right side up for Sam. Eleanor, who had backed away from the table, took a step closer in so she could see, too.

"Perfect," Sam said. The illustration MacKenzie chose was a cute little image of the swirly girl and a flower, half as big as the girl. The girl was leaning down to get a smell.

"It's got a bit of movement in it," MacKenzie said. She got up from the table and opened a cupboard. She took down a rectangular cookie tin. Eleanor heard what sounded like more than one hard-edged object, obviously not cookies, slide across the bottom of the tin. When MacKenzie opened the tin, the only thing that stood out was a straight steel needle, about the length of a finger. Eleanor flinched at the sight of it and experienced a moment of mildly rising panic that she breathed deeply through her nose to prevent from escalating. She had to look away from the tin. She stared dumbly at the white door of the fridge.

"Now. Where do you want this," MacKenzie said.

From the corner of her eye, Eleanor saw Sam take her right hand out from under the table. It was black and red and purple and swollen out of shape. Eleanor could not imagine anyone would mistake the markings on it for anything but a self-inflicted bite mark. The black dents that made a U at the base of the thumb were clearly nothing else but teeth marks.

"You can't be serious," MacKenzie said. A look of fear came over her. She looked at Sam, then quickly up to Eleanor.

"I'm serious," Sam said. She pointed at the skin at the centre of the horseshoe of teeth marks.

MacKenzie said: "Honey, I can't give you a tattoo in the middle of a wound like that." She looked again at Eleanor, who was slowly backing toward the doorway to the outside. She'd stay in the room with Sam as long as she could. But she felt close to fainting. Or throwing up.

"Please," Sam said. Her eyes filled with tears.

"Wait until that heals," MacKenzie said.

Sam squeezed her eyes shut. Hard. "I can't wait I can't wait I can't wait," she said. She was clearly on the verge of something.

The expression on MacKenzie's face turned desperate. Sam's eyes were still shut tight. MacKenzie turned to Eleanor. *Help me*, her expression said. Eleanor shook her head. Shrugged.

MacKenzie said, "Oh, girl. This is going to hurt so bad."

Sam opened her eyes and shook her head no.

"Oh yes it will," said MacKenzie.

Sam turned her head sideways and exhaled hard. She lowered her head until it rested briefly on the table top, left cheek against the woodgrain. Then she slowly sat back up straight.

"Nothing is going to hurt any more than I already do," Sam said.

"Ma!" MacKenzie called out.

"You good?" came the mother's voice.

MacKenzie put both hands on her stick-and-poke tin. She centred the box on the edge of the tabletop in front of her. Her expression turned solemn.

"I'm good!" she called though the door.

21

OCTOBER

Robot had been playing ukulele when Sam came back to his hospital room. He'd taught himself some movable chord shapes, and he was running circle of fifth patterns with the shapes, choking off the chords in shorter and shorter beats, throwing in four- and five-finger flourishes with his right hand, flourishes that would have sounded pointless and showy-offy on guitar, like someone who had no idea what flamenco music was trying to imitate the flamenco feel and sound. But these little tricks, cut short by the relatively low volume and short sustain, sounded amazing on ukulele.

He was also learning how to play music while wounded, sitting up straight so his ribs did not twinge. Holding the instrument lightly against the front of his chest.

"Sounding great, Robert," Sam said as she entered the room. She had her floral bookbag slung over one shoulder, and she slipped it off and put it on the floor against the wall. A half-step behind her was a stiff, scrubbed-looking older man. Robot set the ukulele out of the way, on the side of the bed closer to the wall. Sam approached the bed and put her hand palm up on the mattress where she'd held Robot's hand before. He put a hand on top of hers and felt the soft warmth as he pressed her hand briefly into the mattress, then released it. The man stood stiffly behind Sam, his eyes on his shoes until their little hand-holding ritual was over.

Then he stuck out his own hand for Robot to shake, and he introduced himself.

"I'm Ray," the man said. He eyed the bandages on Robot's head. "I'm this girl's uncle." He tilted his head in Sam's direction. "I'm sorry about your mother's condition," he continued. "And I hope you have a speedy recovery, too." He backed away from the bed in a formal manner, still looking Robot in the eye.

Robot nodded at him. "Nice to meet you, Ray," he said. The man was halfway out the door before Robot could say a further word.

"Patricia," Ray said. He looked at Sam and raised his eyebrows.

Sam nodded. "I know...I know when I'm expected home," Sam said.

Ray disappeared down the hallway.

When Ray called Sam *Patricia*, Sam shot Robot a look of alarm. When her uncle left the room, she said, "I guess you're wondering why he called me Patricia."

Robot shrugged. He raised his eyebrows for a split second. "You've got a story," he said. "You'll tell me when you're ready."

Sam looked suddenly irritated. "How do you know I have a story?"

"You're living with your uncle. In a town you're not from. You've got a secret name. You've got a bite scar on your hand. And it's got a stick-and-poke at the centre of it, framed like a portrait. These are all parts of a story. Aren't they?"

Sam stood up straight at the side of Robot's bed, her lips pursed tightly together as though she were restraining them. Her head was tilted toward the door, listening to the sound of her uncle's footsteps receding down the hallway. When they'd faded off, she unlocked her face and it slipped into a wry smirk.

"God bless that man," she said. "He volunteered to care for me. He puts three meals on the table and gives me a roof to sleep under. But..."

"But what?" Robot said. He'd seen only legitimate concern in Ray's face. He could not imagine what was funny.

"I don't know." Sam shrugged. "He just had to come in here and meet you."

"He was not here to meet me," Robot said.

"What?" Sam said.

"I'm not going to put you on the spot by asking you what he said about me. But if you told him the other day who you were visiting in the hospital... This is a small town. There was a publication ban on my name. But everybody knows what I did."

Sam folded her arms across her chest and looked at him with some scepticism on her face.

"He did not come in here to meet me," Robot continued. "He came here so that I could meet him. He wants me to know who you've got behind you. He wants me to know that you're good people. And that good people have your back. That man's handshake is like a cobra bite. It's like having a heavy stone lowered onto your chest."

Sam's expression brightened as she reconsidered what her uncle had just done.

"Anyway. Enough of this," Robot said. He turned toward the edge of his bed. He forced his legs over the side and pain shot from his hip bones up through his ribs to his armpits. The spasm of pain left him feeling weak, but he knew that if he just sat motionless for a moment, most of his strength would come back to him.

"What are you doing!" Sam came to his side, put her arm protectively around his shoulders. Robot winced, breathed slowly: in and out. He put his hands up in a gesture he hoped said *give me a second*.

"I have an idea."

"You're not getting out of bed!" Sam said.

"I am not trying to walk. Don't worry about that. The nurses down the hall have made that clear. I can barely sit up here. Let alone walk." He paused to get his strength back again, reached behind him and brought the ukulele around.

"Listen, now," he looked at her with a big smile he could not keep off his face. "If you can get a wheelchair, maybe we can find a nice singing spot."

Sam was only gone a minute and she came back pushing a wheelchair. Robot set the ukulele on the bed while he shifted his weight from the edge of the mattress and lowered himself onto the wheelchair's grey vinyl seat. He left the gig bag near his pillow, and pointed at the door: "Forward!" he said. A reluctant grin cracked across Sam's face as she fell into place behind the chair. She paused a moment by the door to pick up her bookbag and hoist it up on her shoulders.

Robot balanced the ukulele on his knees and put his hands in front of him as though he were holding a steering wheel. "Woo!" he said, but he said it at low volume, to avoid trouble. Sam was making a race car noise, roaring through the straight stretches of hallways "*err*ing" around corners at a volume that only Robot could hear.

"Look!" Robot said. "This could be our spot." Beside

the elevators, at a junction where several hallways met, the orange-red exit sign that marked a stairwell. Robot shushed himself and Sam with a finger to his lips as Sam pushed the fire door back on its hinges, propped it back with a foot, and maneuvered the wheelchair into the stairwell.

There was a fire extinguisher on a hook and a flight of metal stairs down to the next landing. The space was bright, well-lit, with white, high-gloss paint over concrete blocks. Over their heads: the black undersides of more stairs.

"This is..." Sam began. The fire door had a big window in it, and the stairwell was bigger and airier than the one at school. So Sam did not hesitate at all to let the door close behind her and put her bookbag on the floor near the wall.

"Sh!" Robot silenced her. His finger still over his lips. He picked up the ukulele from his lap and made a dramatic moment out of plucking a single fretted note on the first string. A D note. It reverberated satisfyingly against the walls.

"I bet it's even better down on that landing," he said. "We could sit down there and face back up this way."

Sam looked at him skeptically. "You're not serious," she said.

"I guess not," he said. But he had been serious when he suggested it. "Maybe next time. Maybe when I get some strength back."

The sound of his own voice saying the words had given him an idea, the rich resonance of the empty stairwell. "Okay," Robot said. He began fumbling through some chords, bouncing through some funky rhythms. "Listen," *doop-doop dah. Doop-doop dah!* Chord change: '*When I get my strength back.*'"

"What's that?" Sam said.

"A song."

"What song is it?"

"I'm not sure. No one has written it yet. It's called 'When I get my strength back.'"

"*I won't need this rolling chair.*

I won't breathe this indoor air.

You won't find me crying here.

When I get my strength back."

An uncertain-looking smile spread over Sam's face.

Robot sang the verse again, settled into it more confidently. He listened into the stairwell and rounded out his voice to take advantage of the reverb.

He stopped singing and kept playing ukulele. Barely conscious of what he was doing or how he was doing it, he adjusted his playing to fill up the resonant stairwell with the short, choppy *plunk* of the chords.

After a few minutes of humming and strumming, lost in his own inner world, he remembered Sam was with him.

"Do you have, like, a paper and pen, so I can write this down?" he gestured at her bookbag.

She gave him a notebook and pen. He wrote down the lyrics. Wrote down the names of the chords. That would be plenty for him to work from in the future.

"Thanks," he said. He handed her back the notebook and pen. "Maybe that'll come to something later. I think that's all I can do with it for now."

Sam's bag was in a corner of the landing. She closed the notebook, clipped the pen to its cover, set it on top of the bag. She leaned into the railing and looked down the stairwell. "*When I get my strength back,*" she sang down into the rich reverb.

"I have an idea," Sam said when she turned back around.

"What is it?" Robot said.

"Actually, it's more of a question."

"What question?"

"Actually. It's more of a favour."

Robot rolled his eyes. "Well?"

Sam reached into a pocket, took out some folded paper, and handed it to him. He felt himself frowning as he unfolded the sheets.

"I want to learn to sing this," Sam said.

Robot flattened the pages against the tops of his thighs. It was a six-page score, including French lyrics, for "La Vie en rose." In G.

"Where did you get this?" He looked up at Sam. He could tell there had been a change in the expression on his own face. Sam was beginning to smile in response.

"The internet. This isn't medieval Europe. People with questions don't need to visit a monastery."

"Ha ha." Robot supposed he must have been underestimating Sam's degree of interest in music. Singing a simple folk song had seemed a challenge to her and now she'd gone full-on Piaf. "Let's talk about this tune."

"I just feel a connection with it. With...her."

"With Piaf?"

Sam nodded.

"That's an interesting life, right there. Piaf."

"I don't know anything about her life, really. Maybe I'm picking that up somehow. Just from the song."

Robot shrugged. "If I'm honest, I don't know that much, either." He looked carefully through the score. "Okay. We have to face a hard truth." He paused dramatically, then said: "There's a fourth chord." He laughed and looked up at

Sam. Her face, he could tell, was mirroring his: lit up with excited expectation. "Have you listened to this song much?"

"Ha ha. A lot. I'm a bit obsessed right now."

"Have you tried singing it?"

"In parts. The main part of the melody. *Laa, de da dah, da dee dee...* Like that."

Her voice was wobbly, but he could hear a melody in there. "How's your French?"

22

OCTOBER

"**O**ui, non, cabane a sucre," Sam replied.

"Grade eight level. Noted," Robert chuckled.

"Literally true at my old school," Sam said. A spasm of dark emotion went through her at the thought of her old school.

Robert had the sheet music spread across his lap. He'd leaned over and carefully placed the ukulele on the floor beside him. Sam could see that she'd sparked something with that chart. He no longer appeared as sunken into himself and exhausted from his injuries. His face had brightened. There was excitement in his voice. He sat back in the wheelchair and looked up at her seriously. "There are English lyrics to this song."

Sam shook her head. "Honestly, I only have a vague sense of what these words mean. Something about seeing life through a positive lens. But the soul of this song is French. When this song goes to bed at night and dreams, it dreams in French."

Robert nodded as though what she'd said was a plain fact. "Not gonna lie," he said. "I can't play most of these chords on ukulele. Yet. You only get four notes per chord. This D13 here? I have no idea...I mean...technically, you cannot make a D13 chord out of four notes. I'm sure there are workarounds. But...this is a new instrument to me. So..."

"So we'll both be learning."

Robert nodded. "We'll both be learning. This is going to be a project, right? You know that, right? Like. We're not learning this song today. Or this week."

Sam nodded back. Of course she could see how big of a challenge this was.

"Here's what I'm going to do. I'm going to read through this score. It's gonna take me, like, ten, fifteen minutes."

"Do you want to listen to the recording?"

"Oh, I know this tune. And...I've got this, right?" He held up the papers.

"Right." She felt sort of dumb. She'd forgotten, really, about how much information was on those sheets, for people who knew how to decipher it.

"I'm going to look through this. Then I'll play through it, start to finish, a couple of times, and you sing whatever you can sing."

Sam sat on the landing, her feet down on the stairs, while Robert strummed and hummed, picked out individual notes, and fumbled his way through the chord changes. If anything, this stairwell was more resonant than the one at the back of the school, and she found that even the uncertain fragments of his first run through the song got amplified in a way that gave them a deep emotional significance.

Her phone buzzed. Two short *zerts* from the floral book-bag across the landing near the wall. She was unused to hearing that sound and associating it with her own phone. She was in the habit of shutting the phone off and only turning it on to get her texts at the end of the school day.

She chose to ignore the alert and stay in the resonant moment of the stairwell.

The music she was listening to now might be called "Robert Learns to Play 'La Vie en rose.'" It was, in a way, its own song.

"Okay," Robert said after a while. "This song is in G. And the first note of the melody is a G. Here it is." He plucked a note. "Can you sing that note, please? Just the note."

He plucked the note again and she sang it with a *la*.

"Exactly," he said. "Now here's the chord I'm going to be playing when you're singing that note." He played the chord. "Just...like...practice singing that note over this chord." He strummed the chord in a tempo that immediately brought the song to mind.

"*Quand...*" she sang. "*Quand... Quand... Quand...*" She knew the word meant *when*.

She had a separate sheet in her hand, one that only had the lyrics on it. "Bras" meant *arms*. So there was probably some kind of hug in the first line. But there was a meaning in the song that transcended words, that transcended meaning itself. There was a meaning, too, in the simple act of singing. Singing was meaningful, regardless of the words of the song.

Soon Robert was playing the intro. He said it was four bars long, and she was sure she could count them as they passed, but he said he'd nod when it was time to sing.

Trisha (Sam?):
It's Morganne. I got your number! Stalker extraordinaire!
DO NOT FUCKING REPLY TO THIS TEXT!!!!
This is my mom's phone. Do not even reveal that you know
this number. I'm sending this and deleting it.

It's skip the scale day at Frozu and mom was so excited to get
over there that she went out the door and left her phone on the
kitchen counter. I cannot believe it's taken her months to make
a mistake like this. I've been waiting to pounce.

Mom said you changed your name. Is that true? Smart move.
Fuck. I wish I could change mine. Maybe I will.

I'm okay, (Sam?). I mean. I'm not really okay. How okay
can I be? But I think I might be going to be okay. In the future.
Or at least better. I'm already a bit better than I was.

I still have not gone back to school. My dad is trying to get
me to go live with his cousin in Cape Breton. I want to get out
of here, but Cape Breton seems too far away. My mom talked
to the vball coach at Citadel in Halifax. I feel like I'll never be
well enough to play again. But I guess the coach wants me to try
middle, which I fucking hate. But maybe I'll end up in the city.

I hope you're okay. Did mom give you the Beckys? The book
with the Beckys in it? She said she did. You realized who those
girls were before I did. They belong to you.

Did my cousin do a stick and poke for you or something?
Word gets back to me. Stalker extraordinaire!

Anyway. I'm here. I'm probably going to be okay.

Let's get through this, Sam. Let's both get through this.

OMFG. *There's my mom back from Frozu already.*

I hope we can see each other soon.

DO NOT REPLY TO THIS!!!

Hey! Remember that fucker I punched? I hurt my hand on his face? #HenrynotHenry

He still can't eat! He's sucking on a straw. Needs jaw surgery. My hand is fine now. You can barely see a mark on it.

Fuck around!

ACKNOWLEDGEMENTS

First of all, when it takes pretty well a decade to write a book, it's inevitable that there are people who were important in that process, one way or another, whose contribution I am forgetting to include here. I apologize for that.

Whitney Moran of Vagrant Press responded enthusiastically when I sent her the manuscript. Without her, no book.

Stephanie Domet edited this book. I cannot overstate the importance of her contribution. I've worked with Ellen Seligman. Stephanie is on the same level.

Janis McKenzie provided detailed suggestions that were indispensable.

Dr. John Ross, hospitalist, author, and compassionate person, read a draft and gave encouraging feedback.

Paul MacDougall, King of All Cape Breton Media, provided important feedback as well.

Laura Hughes McKay read a draft and said: "That's a good book, bro."

For important conversations: Tricia Wilson-Grady, Evan Syliboy.

Google by proxy: Joel, Mairi, Laura.

Morganne's drawings in the book are based on work by Rhiannon Flemming.

The cover art is by Ben Brush. I consider him a friend and creative collaborator.

I recommend Ryan McLellan, of McLellan's Emergency Proofreading Services, for all your emergency proofreading needs.

Leo McKay Jr.'s best-known book is the novel *Twenty-six*, which Canada Reads named one of the forty most important Canadian books of the first decade of the century. It won the Dartmouth Book Award and was chosen for the One Book Nova Scotia event. His debut collection of stories, *Like This*, also won the Dartmouth Book Award, and was a finalist for the Giller Prize. He lives in Mi'kma'ki, the unceded, ancestral home of the Mi'kmaw people, where he has been a high school teacher for almost thirty years.